Praise for The Stall Keeper

National Award Winner ⸀

"A complex and ambitioι ⸍⸍⸍⸍ isto-
ry, poverty, politics, spo. ⸍⸍⸍⸍ ion,
superstition, and the effecι ⸍⸍ ιιves, in
certain cases with tragic re. ⸍⸍κεs a hard, serious and
critical look at a society wracked by illiteracy, ignorance
and superstition, in which drunkards, beggars, prostitutes
abound. The very nature of the society, the author seems to
suggest, does not allow for any escape, for the few who
tried are destroyed by jealousy and the workings of obeah."
   —Jacques Compton, author of a troubled dream

"A narrative of gigantic proportions."
   —Nicholas Jn Baptiste, Attorney at Law

"Very gripping & interesting ... a great one!"
   —Kristin Tobierre, corporate executive

"An enthralling story … a profoundly engaging and sub-
stantive novel."
   —Dr. Prosper Raynold, Miami University professor

"Crafted by the most articulately exciting St. Lucian crafts-
man of the written word I have met, The Stall Keeper takes
the town of Vieux Fort by the neck and shakes it vigorously,
releasing into the breezy Iyanolan atmosphere all of Vieux
Fort's idiosyncrasies … made me laugh, giggle, ponderous,
sad and glad, all at once, made me immensely proud to be
St. Lucian. In Dr. Reynolds, St. Lucia has produced another
writer of the calibre, or of even deeper essence than Nobel
Laureate V. S. Naipaul."
   —Peter Lansiquot, CARICOM economist & diplomat

Also by Anderson Reynolds

My Father Is No Longer There (memoir, 2019)

The Struggle For Survival: an historical, political and socioeconomic perspective of St. Lucia (nonfiction, 2005)

Death by Fire (novel, 2001)

Other Jako Books

A Lesson On Wings (poetry 2019)

The Brown Curtains (novel, 2006) Clive Sankardayal

Phases (poetry, 2005) Modeste Downes

Rhythms of the Ghetto (poetry, 2004) Ken Ballantyne

The Stall Keeper

Anderson Reynolds

JAKO BOOKS

New York, London, Toronto, Vieux Fort

Published in the United States by Jako Books, a division of Jako Productions.

 First Jako Books Edition, January 2017
www.jakoproductions.com

Library of Congress Cataloging-in-Publication Data

Reynolds, Anderson.
  The stall keeper / Anderson Reynolds.-- 1st Jako Books ed.
    p. cm.
  Summary: "A story of provincial bigotry, coming of age, religious experience and rivalry, the supernatural, fanaticism, and frustrated love and ambition, played against the wide open spaces and relics of Vieux Fort, a post-World War II American occupied Caribbean town"--Provided by publisher.
  ISBN-13: 978-0-9704432-6-7 (alk. paper)
  ISBN-10: 0-9704432-6-9 (alk. paper)
  1. Vieux Fort (Saint Lucia)--Fiction. I. Title.
  PR9275.S273R495 2006
  813'.6--dc22
                                        2006005272

Printed in the United States of America

The Stall Keeper

As the seven year old boy was about to straight-drive a ball from Ralph, his neighborhood friend, he heard his mother's call.

"Henry. Henry."

He dropped the bat immediately, the ball knocking down the wickets, and hurried towards his mother to create the impression that he was near and not at the back of the house playing cricket. But his legs gave him away.

"Boy, how many times must I tell you don't play ball in the backyard? You all mashing up all my garden. Look at your feet. Go wash yourself and come buy fish for me."

When Henry realized no beating was in store, he counted his blessings and hurriedly washed his feet under the standpipe.

"I want you to buy a three-pound tuna. I'm giving you five dollars, make sure you bring the correct change back."

"Yes, Mama."

"You know how you does stop and gawk at everybody you meet. None of that today. The sun already setting. I need the fish for supper."

"Yes, Mama."

Henry ran out of the yard and trotted down Walcott Lane towards Clarke Street, the town's main street. On Clarke he will take a left to the jetty and the fish depot.

As Henry ambled along, his slightly akimbo right arm swung much more freely and with much less control than his straight left arm. It was as if his right arm responded to a drum beat different than that of the rest of his body. He was born with a broken right arm that had healed crookedly. Since the arm had been too weak to support his weight, he never crawled. It was as if he had simply skipped a stage in human evolution. At ten months when his urge for mobility became paramount, the baby simply pushed up on his legs and got around by holding on to tables, chairs, walls, people, anything that enabled him to negotiate distance. People came from afar just to see the baby boy who refused to crawl. After a month or two of getting around by holding on to objects, the boy simply walked.

Henry didn't like the pushing, shouting, and jostling for position that accompanied buying fish from the fishermen at the jetty. Yet each time his mother sent him to buy fish he welcomed the opportunity. At the jetty there were always boat-boys hanging out. Their jobs were to help the fishermen drag their canoes onto the beach, carry fuel cans, boat engines, and other fishing equipment into storage, and to clean the canoes after the day's catch were sold. While waiting for the fishing canoes to come in, Henry loved to loiter where the boat-boys sat playing cards or dominoes for money. He drank the incessant cursing, the lewd description of sexual exploits, the loud intermittent cheating accusations, the occasional flashing of knives in preparation for a fight, the heated cricket and soccer arguments, the passing of the rum bottle. Henry envied the boat-boys' carefree and unbridled lifestyle. Something inside him connected well with them.

Henry was without a father. In fact, he had no memory of a father. Two days after his father and his father's best friend went on their usual Sunday morning swim off Enbakoko Beach to the Maria Islets in the Atlantic Ocean, a group of boys playing beach football found their bodies, white and bloated, on the seashore. Henry was eighteen months, yet right up to his fifth birthday, to the great consternation of his mother, Eunice, he was still walking up to men, asking: "Mister, are you my father?" At three and a half years old Henry gave his mother the fright of her life when he ran away from home and walked all the way to Enbakoko Beach in search of his father.

There was a man whom everyone, children and grownups alike, called Daddy Mano, who was forever giving children treats of candies and sweet biscuits. One day after receiving a candy from the man, Henry asked, "Daddy Mano, are you my Father?"

With great compassion and forbearance, Daddy Mano smiled down upon the four-year-old boy and said, "Sonny, I'm everyone's Daddy, including you."

Henry ate the candy, but it left a bitter taste. He didn't want to share his Daddy. He wanted a Daddy who would make tops, kites, and *kabowé* for him; a Daddy who would take him on top of the *kai planes*, airplane houses, to fly kites; a Daddy who would take him to the field to watch football and cricket even if his mother objected; a Daddy who would take him to the beach and teach him to swim. Instinctively, Henry knew that the only way all this could happen was to have a Daddy who was his and his alone. So his search for a Daddy continued.

A year or two after encountering Daddy Mano, Henry thought he had finally found a Daddy in the person of Ruben Ishmael, a school teacher, sports hero and one of the few persons outside his mother's church who visited her regularly. But no sooner had he started calling Ruben Ishmael "Daddy," than his mother put a stop to all this Daddy business. So now he was permanently without a father.

Henry's mother didn't allow him to go on the field to play or watch sports, so it was from Ralph, his best friend and neighbor, that he learned about Ruben's sport heroics. Ralph said that in one football match, Vieux Fort versus Micoud, Ruben took the ball in his defense, dribbled past the whole Micoud team, some falling flat on their back-sides, and then just touched the ball into the goal, touched it as if he were merely passing to a newly born baby. Ralph said that in cricket, once Ruben started to bat, no one could get him out; he would hit sixes and fours "black is white." He was right-handed, but when he got tired of batting he would switch to left-handed, and it was then people would see sixes and fours. Ralph's oldest brother played on the same team with Ruben. Ralph said that his brother said that if Ruben was a Bajan or a Jamaican or a Trini or a Guyanese he would have done play for the West Indies cricket team.

Every time Ralph related such stories about Ruben and what was happening in the world of Vieux Fort sports, Henry's wish for Ruben to be his father would grow stronger, and he would itch to go on the field to play or watch ball. Despite his akimbo arm, he would imagine himself playing on the Vieux Fort eleven football team, shooting the final goal in the final minutes of the match that would give Vieux Fort the victory over Castries. Or he would see himself captaining the West Indies cricket team, leading the West Indies to victory after victory.

Henry wished his mother allowed him the kind of freedom that Ralph and the boat-boys enjoyed. But no. His mother who worked as a cook at Vieux Fort's Cloud's Nest Inn, the only hotel or guest house in town, was a strict Seventh Day Adventist; a *Semdays*, who, since her husband's death, had become even more strict. Henry was only allowed to leave the house to go to school, to go to church, and to run errands. So besides the playing field, he couldn't go to cinema, he couldn't go to the Roman Catholic Church bazaars, he couldn't go to First Communion parties, he couldn't go to children's dances. His mother didn't even celebrate Christmas. From sunset Friday to sunset Saturday, Henry could do nothing but pray, study his Bible lesson and attend church. Not even his own worldly thoughts he was allowed to have. So the closest Henry came to realizing his sporting ambitions or even to watching a football or cricket match, was listening to Ralph's or sometimes the boat-boys' accounts of what took place.

Living on an island and in a town that was over 90 percent Roman Catholic, Eunice and the few other Seventh Day Adventists in Vieux Fort were like lone specks of rock in the middle of the Atlantic Ocean. Maybe it was to offset this overwhelming Roman Catholic tide that Eunice was so strict with her son. Right here in her neighborhood, not to mention the wider Vieux Fort, there was much evil to guard him against.

To her immediate left was Dantes and Ma Dantes. Every so often Dantes went out drinking and womanizing. Each time he returned from his debaucheries, Ma Dantes would corner Dantes and using all the weapons she possessed — fists, nails, pots, pans, graphic insults and curses — give him a sound lashing. Ma Dantes was a strapping, six-foot, two-hundred-pound woman. So Dantes, weighing less than a hundred and sixty pounds and weakened by nights of too much booze, was no match for her. After each encounter Dantes emerged bruised and bleeding, but he never learnt his lesson.

To her right was Rosalie, a twenty-six year old who was drunk most of the time. She wasn't much more than a living skeleton. But the real pity was her son, Stanley. He was two years older than Henry. Rosalie slapped, punched and kicked her son at the least provocation. So fearful was Stanley of his mother that he never tarried on any of her many errands. Every time you saw Stanley, he was on the run. Rosalie died at the age of thirty-five, and in time Stanley became a drunk.

Living directly across the street from Eunice was Reggie and Ma Reggie; their daughters, Olive and Rita; and their sons, Rony and Edwin. In the eyes of Eunice this was the most abominable family she had ever come across. Reggie and Ma Reggie, Reggie and his daughters, Ma Reggie and her sons, Reggie and his sons, Ma Reggie and her daughters, and the children and themselves were in constant racket. Their discords sometimes spilled onto the street — Reggie with cutlass running after his sons; Ma Reggie pulling up her dress in the middle of the street, sliding down her panties, bending over, and telling Reggie in no uncertain terms where he could lick her.

Next to that family a once halfway respectable family lived. The husband, Girade, died when Henry was four. Girade had taken a liking to rum. But there was a problem. Girade not once offered drinks to anyone, yet he always depended on others to buy him drinks. It was rumored that at a dance someone finally decided enough was enough and poured poison in Girade's drink. After his death his family went downhill. His wife, Pamela, became a drunkard. She died ten years later at the age of forty-eight. Miller, his eldest son, became a wharf rat, and his other son, Cecil, became a jailbird. His two daughters, Flora and Leona, would offer their services to the ever thirsty sailors, and when the sailors were scarce, they made their services available to the town's residents, though at much reduced rates. Flora's career as a prostitute would meet a disastrous end when the life boat carrying a group of prostitutes from a ship anchored some distance from the Dock capsized. Flora and the rest of the women on board drowned.

Girade's death didn't bother Henry much, but the all-night wake left a lasting impression on him. Throughout the night mourners drank rum and coffee and danced to the beat of the *tanbou*. Even in old age Henry would remember the dance moves and the beat and rhythm of the drumming that had kept him awake all night, and long after wakes in his country became just another *blocko*, another eating and drinking and loud contemporary music affair, his impression of a real wake remained the one that was held for Girade.

When Girade died, Henry's mother called him for admonishment.

"Henry, you see. This man's death proves what I've been warning you about. This was a hard-working man with a beautiful wife and four nice children. But he was there partaking of the pleasures of the flesh. Instead of staying home with his wife he was there drinking and fet-ing. Now his wife is without a husband and his children are without a father. Now, tell me, who is going to feed them? The man has brought death to himself and suffering to his family. You see, no matter how careful one is, the way of the world has only one ending—death and destruction. I hope you never forget this lesson. All around you are people in *bakanal*. But ten, twenty years from now see where they will end up."

It was a lecture Henry remembered deep into adulthood, and one he recalled every time he went to a dance, or to a party, or when he touched a beer.

Still, from Ralph he got another explanation for the family's downfall. Ralph told Henry that Mr. Dantes told his mother that one very warm night he was having trouble falling asleep, so he went to his balcony to catch some breeze. While there he saw a man whom he was seeing for the first time and who was carrying a large brown paper bag walked up to Mr. Girade's house, looked quickly on both sides, pushed his hand in the paper bag and threw something inside the house through an open window. According to Ralph, Mr. Dantes said that from that time onwards Girade and Ma Girade were always quarreling and fighting, and more and more Girade took to drinking until they finally poisoned him.

Lower down, closer to Clarke Street, was Ma Placide, Ralph's mother. Ma Placide was raising seven children all by herself. She did just about everything to make ends meet, including working as a maid, making charcoal, carrying bananas on banana day, making sea-egg cake or *chadon*, blood pudding or *bouden*, and pig-feet soup or *souse*, and rearing pigs in the horse-shoe-shaped earth mounds that the Americans used as camouflage hangars during World War II and which Vieux Fortains called *kai planes,* meaning house of planes. When Ralph, Ma Placide's last child, was a little over a year old, Placide abandoned his family and emigrated to America. His family was never to hear from him again. The story was that Placide left his wife because she had an ongoing affair with one of the American World War II veterans who visited St. Lucia every once in a while. People said that, according to Placide, the two last children, Ralph and his sister before him, weren't his. They were just too *shabine*, redskin, to belong to him.

This, in the main, was the nature of Eunice's neighborhood.

Looking back, among the people who lived on his street, Henry could think of only a handful who were respectable. Nurse Elra, a single mom, lived two houses to the right of his home. Henry thought she was almost as strict with her daughter, Michelle, as his mother was with him.

Another of the respectable persons was Miss Bernadine, a retired school teacher. Miss Bernadine was raising three of her grandsons—Keith, Kerwin and Kenneth. She held such a tight rein on them that the boys never played with the neighborhood children and they acted like they rarely met people. Church and school were the only places to which Henry saw Miss Bernadine going. To him it seemed that the teacher's only pastime was staring at the world from behind her glass window.

Henry's impression was that there were two kinds of people living on his street. There were the drunks, the vulgar, the obnoxious, and the unmannerly whose lives spilled onto the street, and who were in the overwhelming majority; and then there were the few respectable people like his mother, the nurse and the teacher.

The more restrictions Henry's mother placed on him, the more he wished he was of a non-respectable family, and the more he was drawn towards them and to what his mother called "the world." The world of the boat-boys, the world of cricket and football players, the world of steel-pan, sca, rocksteady, calypso and cadence music, the world of Eugene.

Yes, Eugene! The man who talked, walked, and behaved just like a woman. The only man Henry knew who was a stall keeper, one who made a living selling fruits and condiments out of a tray. However much the boat-boys intrigued Henry, for reasons that had eluded his mother's comprehension, the man they called Eugene intrigued him more. To gaze at the man who was a woman, to listen to his conversations, his nasty tongue, was the other reason Henry welcomed the opportunity to go buy fish, even if that meant disrupting his ball game, and suffering the fish stampede.

HENRY APPROACHED THE JUNCTION where Walcott Lane met Clarke Street. The man was there, the stall keeper, the man with the long *dògla* hair reaching to his back, and a nose with upturned nostrils that seemed to occupy his whole face. He was seated in his usual place, behind his two large trays that overflowed with mangoes, oranges, ripe bananas, sugar apples, golden apples, Shirley biscuits, chewing gum, everything. He was flanked by two other stall keepers. Women. Henry was in for a treat. He quickened his trot, then crossed Clarke Street. For disguise, he went over to the standpipe, a few feet from the stall keepers, and acted as if he were drinking water. Henry looked sideways at Eugene. Eugene's nails were polished and well trimmed. His legs were smooth and hairless, and appeared to have been oiled.

The stall keeper to the left of Eugene said, "Eugene, what you wearing for carnival?"

"Child, this year I eh jumping up in no carnival. I go be there watching the *bakanal* and making money."

"You saying that now, but I bet you come carnival day you go be the first person jumping up behind the band."

Just then a woman in shorts reaching no further than her buttocks, and walking as if the whole purpose of walking was to make her buttocks jump from side to side, was about to pass by on Clarke Street across from the stall keepers. Eugene got up from behind his tray, exposing his stout, reddish legs. Short khaki pants were all Henry had ever seen him wear, as if his legs were on permanent display. He was the only man Henry knew who never wore long pants. Henry himself couldn't wait to grow up to start wearing long pants.

"Christine, you don't know me anymore? You passing there with your nose in the air. What happen, since you start seeing that American sailor, you don't know me anymore?"

Henry drank every word. The shrill, quarrelsome voice never failed to surprise him; it wasn't the kind of voice he associated with a man.

"Eugene, look at you, eh. You putting all my business out. Is rush I rushing, or else I'd come chat."

"Come here girl. What rush you in so?"

The woman with the short shorts walked across to the stall keepers.

"Girl, how things? With that sailor things nice by you? Give me a dollar, nah."

 "Things eh too bad. You know these Americans. They eh stingy like the English."

"Child, child, child. I won't keep you. Go on. You say you in rush. Stop by on your way back."

Lapping up the conversation, Henry drank some water to disguise his curiosity, and he looked around as if expecting his mother to be there watching.

 As the woman walked away, Eugene said, "Some women have it too easy. All they do is make some sailor look their way and money come tumbling down."

"You don't lie," said the stall keeper on the left.

"Maybe," said the one on the right, "but I hear that other one, Caroline, is pregnant for a sailor."

"That true? Tra la-la," said Eugene. "Is she going to keep it?"

"Yes, the imbecile is saying, 'what God giveth, she keepeth.'"

"Eugene, that child going to be as reddish as you," said the woman on the left.

Just then a bareback, barefoot fisherman with knotted muscles, and skin and hair made yellowish by the combined action of sea and sun, approached Eugene's stall.

"How much is the mango julie?" he asked.

"You know the price well, you know damn well it's ten cents."

"Ten cents for that? You must be going out of your mind."

"Man, go to hell."

"Shut your ass, *salòp*, *malmanman*."

"Shut my ass? Why don't you go tell your mother the price she charges for a *bonm* is too high?"

The man walked off.

"That's what's wrong with Vieux Fort people," said Eugene.

"Is freeness they like," said the stall keeper on the right.

"Eugene, maybe he mistake you for an American," said the other stall keeper.

"Well, tell them for me the days of the Americans are long gone, and they eh coming back," said Eugene.

Now Henry was making no pretense of drinking water. He stared right at Eugene, missing nothing. When Eugene was quarreling with the fisherman, his animated face, his large upturned nostrils, the rapid movement of his hands, his swift neck movements, and his reddish brown skin, reminded the boy of the fire in his mother's oven.

"*Semdays*, what you watching at? Go on 'bout your mother's business. You know how Ma Auguste doesn't play with you," said Eugene.

"Eh-eh, Eugene, the boy likes you. He sees a nice *jal* like you there," said the woman to the left.

"I eh looking nowhere, is water I drinking."

"Is water you drinking? Come here," said Eugene.

With downcast eyes, Henry reluctantly approached Eugene.

"So *Semdays* boy, why you always looking at me? You like to see me? You think I'm pretty?"

Henry looked up. Eugene was wearing silver, leaf-shaped earrings. Several strands of hair stood under his chin. He was thinking, he has beard! He has beard!

"Eh, boy? Answer me."

"Is water I drinking."

"What's your name?"

"Henry."

"Your mother know you does watch me like this?"

Henry provided no answer.

"How is your father, Mr. Ruben?" Eugene asked mischievously. Word had gotten around that something was cooking between the *Semdays,* holier-than-thou woman, and Ruben, the darling of Vieux Fort. So much so the boy used to call him Daddy. But when the gossip got too much for the *Semdays* woman, she put a stop to the boy calling Ruben Daddy.

"Mr. Eugene, Mr. Ruben eh my father. My father die already."

"Oh, sorry. Mr. Ruben is such a good man. Your father was a good man too, though." The stall keepers struggled to hide their laughter. Then, as if to make up for his mischief, Eugene said, "You like plums?"

"Yes, Mr. Eugene."

"Eugene, see what he called you, 'Mister'," said the stall keeper on the left.

"Well, look a plum, and stop staring at me when you see me."

Henry hesitated to take the plum.

"What happen, you scared of my plum? You think I go poison you?"

"My mother say I mustn't take things from strangers."

"But your mother didn't tell you it's not mannerly to stare at people. And the number of times you been watching me from across the street, I still a stranger?"

"Take the plum, boy. Not fish you going and buy? By the time you reach home the plum done in your belly. What will your mother know?" said the stall keeper on the right.

Henry took the plum. On the way down Clarke Street to the jetty he bit into his plum. It was sweet and juicy. Juice rolled down his fingers. He couldn't remember when last plum tasted so sweet.

When Henry arrived home, his mother and Ruben were crouched in the garden, uphill beyond the house, weeding rows of tomatoes. Born and raised in the rural hamlet of Debreuil, Eunice was now far removed from the farm but the farm could not be taken out of her. Every square inch of her yard not used for walkways, cooking, laundry, and a pit latrine was under cultivation. At any given time her yard was home to some combination of corn, sweet potatoes, lettuce, cabbage, pigeon peas, carrots, peanuts, tomatoes, and sweet pepper. She had two great passions in life — gardening and serving God. And in her mind the two may be distinguishable but not separable. Not when the Bible spoke of vineyards, the garden of Eden, the tree of life, the tree of good and evil, be fruitful and multiply, the parables of the sower and of the fig tree, and the harvest truly is great but the laborers are few. Clearly, sowing seeds, nurturing plants, reaping the harvest, was a manifestation of service to God, was symbolic of spreading the Gospel of Christ and winning souls for the Lord. So, as if of

a Divine calling, Eunice tended her garden joyfully, loving-
ly, tenderly.

Earlier, with half her mind on Ruben as he talked about
the conduct of his students and the other half on whether
the boy will get fish today and on the caterpillars infesting
her tomatoes, Eunice had picked up what she thought was
a stone only to discover that it was soft and wiggly.
Violently, she threw it away and let go one scream that
made Ruben think that she had suddenly fallen victim to a
heart attack. "What is it?" he asked.

It was a toad. This was the one setback Eunice faced
with her gardening. Like her mother and her grandmother
she was terrified of toads, the very sight of them froze her
blood and set her heart racing. Yet, as if in their blood, all
three women loved gardening much beyond the mere provision of food.

Deeply concerned, Ruben held her hand, patted her
back and murmured, "You alright? You alright?" But the
fast pounding of her heart, her quickened breath, her damp
hair in his face, and the scent of her receding perfume got
him excited. In the middle of Ruben's excitement, as if
sensing his confused intentions, Eunice moved away from
him and said, "I'll fix it. I'll well fix it."

She marched downhill to the house and returned with a
cup of salt. From a distant she threw salt on the toad; it
took off as if it were on fire. This was how she dealt with
trespassing toads. She used more salt on them than in her
cooking.

In an attempt to calm Eunice, Ruben said, "Eunice, you
know toads are not that bad. They prey on the insects that
infest your plants."

Ruben then went on to explain how one's attitude
towards toads and other such harmless creatures were
dependent on one's culture. He said that English children

were brought up on stories about toads turning into princesses, so they saw toads as magical creatures, and one would be hard pressed to find an English person who wasn't fond of toads. But in St. Lucian folklore toads were what people turned into when they wanted to harm someone or scare them out of their wits. So it wasn't surprising that St. Lucians looked upon toads with disgust and sometimes fear.

Ruben said, "I have an English friend in Castries, a biologist, who actually rears toads in her yard as one would any other pet. She feeds them and built several pools of water for them to keep cool. It was there that I first found out that toads ate ground provision. The woman's yard was so crowded with toads that to avoid stepping on them I had to be careful where I placed my feet."

None of this moved Eunice. In fact, just imagining the woman feeding the toads set her blood crawling. As far as she was concerned she could do without the help of these ugly creatures. And culture had nothing to do with anything. After all, wasn't this one of the plagues God had set upon Pharaoh to let His people go?

Eunice said, "Ruben, I don't care what you saying there. I don't want these ugly creatures in my garden. Let them take care of somebody else's garden. Not mine. And if you think these creatures are so lovely and harmless, let me tell you what one did to my mother when I was small. She was in her garden on the hill above the house, and suddenly a huge frog the size of a breadfruit jumped in front of her. She screamed and took off and ran down to the house. You wouldn't believe what the wicked frog did next! It ran down after my mother."

Ruben laughed and laughed, and then said, "But, Eunice, the toad must have been even more terrified of your mother than she was of it. They tried to get away from each other at the same time, and since downhill was the fastest way of escape, they both ran towards the house, and so it appeared that the frog was chasing after your mother."

Ruben laughed and chuckled some more.

Eunice said, "Ruben, you talking as if you was there. And you can laugh all you want, but when I tell you these creatures evil, they evil."

Ruben's chuckle changed to a lingering smile. He admired Eunice's love of gardening. This was another one of the things that to him made her so endearing. As for him, he was happy to leave all this gardening business to other people. His one attempt at growing, raising something had met with dismal failure. He loved mango julies, and as any farmer could tell him he was not alone. On any farm, no matter what other mango trees there were, the birds would first attack the mango julies. Eight years before, Ruben had secured several mango julie plants that he planted in his back yard. All but one perished. He pampered it, placed cow and sheep manure all around it, watered it morning and evening. With all this care and nourishment the tree grew beautifully, and after seven years under Ruben's watchful eyes, the mango tree burst into blossoms and the blossoms gave way to young mango julies. Ruben felt so proud. No less proud than a father giving his beautiful daughter away in marriage or a father attending the college graduation of his first born. On afternoons he would sit with a book under the tree, sipping homemade juice, and breathing in the scent of the blossoms.

Then without notice, without any warning, without any premonition, the tree began to wither. First, all the mangoes dropped off prematurely; next the leaves dried up and they too fell; then the branches broke off and the top of the trunk toppled. Ruben brought in a government agronomist but he could only provide speculation. "Maybe there is some poison in the soil; maybe the roots of the tree have reached sea water; maybe the tree has been attacked by an unknown fungus." The agronomist's soil and other lab tests produced no new light. In less than a year after Ruben's beautiful mango tree had blossomed, it was dead. His friends told him that someone had put obeah on the mango tree.

Obeah or not this was the first and last time Ruben attempted to grow or raise anything. Nonetheless, he took so much pleasure watching Eunice tend her plants that helping her in the garden was one of the things he looked forward to when he came calling.

OUT OF BREATH FROM HIS RUSH HOME, Henry called to his mother, "Mama, I get the fish." Eunice and Ruben, their hands stained with dirt, came down the hill.

While washing her hands at the standpipe, Eunice said, "Boy, what took you so long? I'm of a mind to give you a good whipping."

"Mama, when I reach, there was no boat, and when a boat came, there was big rush for fish. I lucky to get fish."

Eunice said, "Give me the fish. Give me, with your lying." She turned to Ruben, "You don't want a boy? I've never seen a child lie so much."

Ruben chuckled and after washing his hands and drying them on his pants he affectionately passed his hand over Henry's head and said, "The boy is all right."

Eunice placed the fish in a large pan half-filled with water and sat outside on a pile of stones and began to clean it. Some fish scales flew onto her arms and her bodice. Ruben stood next to the pile of stones, and Henry, his mind bursting with questions, sat next to his mother. From the tone of his mother's voice he knew she wasn't too displeased. He fired his first question. "Mama, when was the time of the Americans? Are they coming back?"

"Coming back! Boy who you been listening to? Whoever told you that, tell them the Americans eh coming back, so Vieux Fortians better get off their behinds, and stop watching the streets."

"Mama, when did they come? Was I born yet?"

"Henry, you were born in nineteen-fifty-seven, the same year that the Americans left for good. How old are you now?"

"Mama, I'm seven years."

"You see, it's been seven years since the Americans left, so let Vieux Fort people stay there and wait."

"Mama, what did the Americans do?"

"Boy, what's with you and these Americans?"

"Mama, I just want to know."

"The Americans came during World War Two and build the base. Before they came is sugarcane Vieux Fort was covered with. You see where the Square is?"

"Yes, Mama."

"Well, that's where the factory was."

"Mama, what they do in the factory?"

"Sugar, of course, and rum and molasses."

"But Mama, Adventists mustn't drink rum."

"That's right, and you must never forget that. You see Mr. Popo, the *wonmyé* who always sleeping in the gutter?"

"Yes, Mama. The other day I saw him, he was stinking like a toilet, flies was all in his mouth, and a dog came and pee on him. The children shouted, '*Popo, santi caca*! Popo, smelling poop!'"

"Boy, I tired telling you don't come here repeating things you hear on the street. And boy, what kind of story is this? You sure you see a dog pee on the man?"

"Yes, Mama. Ralph was there. If you think I lying, ask him."

"Nowadays, everything is Ralph, Ralph. Anyway, I hope you not one of those calling the man name."

"No, Mama, I does just look at him, I doesn't call him any name."

"Well, good. Take long looks at him, because that's what will happen to you if you ever put that abomination in your mouth."

Ruben laughed and said, "The children are right. That Popo sure smells like poop."

Ruben and Henry watched Eunice split the fish's belly. She removed the guts, gills and eggs and scraped the inside to extract any remaining unwanted tissue. She cleansed the fish with water and lime and sliced it into steaks. The smell of fish filled the yard and caught the attention of the cat which drew in for the kill that was already dead.

Henry said, "But Mama, you haven't told me anything about the Americans and World War Two."

"Boy, you think I working for you, you giving me Johnson like that. I told you the Americans came here during World War Two and they establish the base."

"Mama, what's World War Two?"

"What kind of question is that? World War Two was a world war."

"But, Ma, what did they do? Who did the Americans fight? Was there a lot of shooting and fireworks?"

Eunice laughed and said, "That imagination of yours will get you into trouble one of these days. But stop asking me questions. I'm not from Vieux Fort. Ask Mr. Ruben, he is the teacher and he is the one from Vieux Fort."

Henry turned to Ruben, "Please, Mr. Ruben, tell me about the Americans."

The Stall Keeper

Ruben didn't mind at all. Compared to Eunice, whose only fond memory of the American occupation was that her husband was alive and she and him were together, he welcomed the opportunity to talk about Vieux Fort and the Americans. The boy's excitement and enthusiasm were contagious and reminded him of when he was growing up. He mirrored the same curiosity and the wanting to know that he himself had displayed at that age. Besides, history was one of his preoccupations, particularly the history of Vieux Fort and the legacy of the American occupation. Recently he had read all the back issues of *The Voice* newspaper spanning the time of the Americans. People blamed the present laissez-faire attitude of Vieux Fortians on the Americans, but for the past year or so a theory that explained the predisposition of Vieux Fortians, which involved much more than the Americans, had been brewing in his mind. He was just waiting for slack time to put down his theory in an article for *The Voice*.

Ruben was twelve years old when the Americans came. He was too young to work for them, but not too young to profit from their presence. The money that the magic words, "Hey, Joe, give me a black penny!" elicited from the soldiers, and the expired cans of food that they threw away and over which he and other children fought, was the difference between him and his siblings going to bed on a full stomach or on a stomach empty save for a cup of warm sugar water spiced with lime peel or lime or orange leaves. He knew men who made so much money just hanging around rum shops and getting women for the Americans that they took to lighting their cigarettes with flames from their dollar bills. Some, calling themselves "one-day millionaires," took great pride in saying "no stale money in my pocket, Jack." And to prove it they made sure all monies made in a day were spent in that day.

Accepting Henry's invitation, Ruben took a seat besides him on the pile of stones.

He said that the Americans changed Vieux Fort. Before they came, Vieux Fort was dead; there were no jobs and people went hungry. But soon after the Americans arrived, money started flowing and Vieux Fort came alive. The place became overcrowded with people. They came from everywhere, even from as far as Barbados and St. Vincent. The Americans cleared and drained the mosquito-infested mangrove swamps at Pointe Sable and Savannes Bay. They built a modern and fully equipped hospital, now known as St. Jude's, but back then it was called Fort Queen. They built concrete runways, and quarters for over 5000 soldiers, huge warehouses and a laundry that required hundreds of people to run it. The Americans constructed the *kai planes* in which they hid their planes from enemy air-raids. They established an electricity power plant, a sewerage system, and water reservoirs near the hospital and on the hilltop overlooking La Tourney. They also established a fire station, built the dock, and two tunnels, one running from Beanefield to St. Jude's Hospital and the other from the airport to Clarke Street.

Ruben said that some people say that the Americans also built an undersea tunnel running from Moule-a-Chique to the Maria Islets. But he didn't think so, because there was no proof of that and he has never come across that in his readings. He said that the Americans left in 1949 but when they came back in 1955 they established radar systems on Moule-a-Chique and on Morne Le Blanc, overlooking Laborie. Ruben said that according to some of the reports he has read, when all was said and done, the Americans had spent over ten million US dollars on the base and on their other constructions.

While Ruben went on about the Americans, Eunice seasoned the fish steaks with salt, curry, garlic, onion and seasoning herbs. Then she powdered the steaks with white flour. She poured some coconut oil in a frying pan, and placed the frying pan on a coal-pot with smouldering coals. Tiny bubbles soon began appearing in the oil. Careful to avoid hot oil splashing on her hand, one by one she slipped the fish steaks onto the frying pan. The fish steaks hissed in the boiling oil. The cat meowed for his share of the spoils that was looking and smelling more appetizing by the second. Henry was savoring every bit of what he was hearing about Vieux Fort and the Americans.

Ruben paused. The back of Eunice's beautiful neck and her profile, more befitting a twenty-one year old than the thirty-something year old woman that she was, caught his attention. At this moment he would have liked nothing better than for this woman to be his wife. It occurred to him that seated like this on the pile of stones, talking and carrying on, they were practically a family.

Eunice was several years older than Ruben, but that made no difference to him. In fact, he preferred older women. For three years he had been trying to find his way into this woman's heart, but the most he had accomplished was the privilege, like today, of visiting her without invitation. He had taken it as a good sign when her son started calling him Daddy, but she had quickly put a stop to that. Nonetheless, he knew what was required of him to be more than a mere friend to this woman. She was a Seventh Day Adventist and he was a Roman Catholic, so in her eyes he wasn't a Christian, he was yet to experience baptismal rebirth. She will not be unequally yoked. So for him to stand any chance of becoming one of her passions, he had to join her church. Yet how could he when that meant acquiescing to the notion that Roman Catholics were not

Christians; when that meant giving up the fellowship of the Roman Catholic Church that from childhood had nurtured his passion for learning; when that meant giving up the trust of and solidarity with Vieux Fortians who looked to him for leadership and guidance; and, most critical of all, when that meant giving up cricket, the greatest of his passions, because his cricket matches took place on Saturdays and Sundays and it was forbidden for an Adventist to play sports on Saturdays. He wasn't willing to give up all that, at least not yet, so his relationship with this *Semdays* woman with a twenty-something year old body, who loved gardens but feared and hated toads, was in stagnation.

Ruben said, "This isn't all the Americans did. The Vieux Fort River used to run into the Atlantic, across to where they call Lonely Tree, higher up Enbakoko Beach. But to build the airport, the Americans changed the course of the river to where it is today, at the Bacadere."

Eunice said, "Ruben I don't think you have that one quite right. The river didn't flow into the Atlantic. After leaving Beausejour it swung out towards Mankotè Hill and back to the Bacadere. So really what the Americans did was to straighten out the river."

"I'm not sure that the river didn't use to flow into the Atlantic. I will have to do some more research on that," replied Ruben.

Henry said, "But Mr. Ruben, how can they move a river? Only God and Prophets like Moses and Joshua can do that."

Before Ruben could answer, Eunice said, "Henry, you need to pay closer attention to your Bible. Joshua wasn't a prophet, he was a soldier. Anyway, sometimes people does want to play God. But little do they know that it's God who let them have their way. But you know what? Sometimes even if God let you do certain things, He does still turn around and show you who's really in charge. When there is a very bad hurricane, the river does forget about where the Americans had forced it to go, and it does cross the airport and go right back to where God had intended for it in the first place."

Turning to Ruben, Eunice said, "Do you remember the two Americans who climbed those coconut trees and could think of nothing better to do than go walking on the branches?"

"Yes," chuckled Ruben. "When any four year old could have told them a coconut branch can't even support the weight of a child, much less that of a grown man."

"I've never seen a people as stupid and crazy as these Americans," said Eunice.

"Mama, what happened to the Americans that walked on the coconut branches?"

"The same thing that'll happen to you if you go climbing a coconut tree. They break their necks," answered Eunice.

"And how about the man the Americans shot dead when he tried entering the base without permission?" said Ruben.

"No, no." said Eunice. "The soldier didn't shoot the man because he entered the base. After all, the man was working there. What happened was that the man's dog followed him inside the base. The soldier told the man that dogs aren't allowed so get the dog out. The man did as he was told. But as soon as he turned his back the dog followed him. So for the second time the soldier told the man to get rid of the dog. Again, the man put the dog out. But again the dog followed him inside the base. It was at this point that the soldier shot and killed both the man and his dog."

"So this was how it happened. The man lost his life on account of a dog?" said Ruben.

"Yes, eh, these Americans thought they owned the world."

"Mama, what did they do to the soldier?"

"People say that they placed the man in chains and forced him to walk on all fours while dragging a big iron ball behind him. Then they sent him back to America. That's what people say. But for all you know they didn't give the soldier any punishment. Probably, they simply transferred him to some other base in some other country. After all, to these Americans we were nothing. There was this drunk soldier, cursing and making a lot of noise in town. So a policeman came and asked him to stop disturbing the peace. The soldier slapped the policeman and continued making his noise, and that was that."

"Mama, the police didn't arrest the soldier?"

"Arrest! The soldiers always had guns, and the policemen only had batons. And you know how St. Lucians coward. Soldiers used to come to town and burst bullets in the air, and nothing to that."

Ruben said, "You know, people made up all kinds of stories about the man the soldier killed. Some say when they arrived at the cemetery to bury him, there was no body in the coffin."

"Trust Vieux Fortians for making up stories," said Eunice.

"One thing, though, those blackouts really got me scared. Every time the sirens went off for a blackout, I swore the Germans and Japs would bomb us."

"Blackouts, Mr. Ruben?"

"Yes, the blackouts were to prevent enemy planes that wanted to bomb us from seeing where St. Lucia was. At the sound of the siren, everybody had to put out their lamps and the power station would shut off. Lucky for us there was never any bombing, but at the Castries Harbor

German submarine boats, U-boats they used to call them, torpedoed and sank two ships."

"I'd forgotten all about that," said Eunice. "There was a song about it. How did it go? Let me see. 'The submarine coming, right in the habor, to bomb Lady Nelson, and torpedo Umtata ...' That's not all they used to sing. Ruben, don't you remember the rest?"

"No, I didn't even know there was such a song."

"Mr. Ruben, did people die? Did they ever catch the Germans?"

"Some people got killed. But, no, they didn't catch the Germans. But in the end the British and the Americans beat the Germans and Japs."

Chuckling, Ruben said, "These Americans may have been crazy, but they sure liked to spend and give away money. As children, no sooner we said, 'Give me a black penny, Jack!' than they would spray money at us and laugh and watch us scramble and fight each other for it. You know, when young children saw a plane flying overhead they used to shout 'Give me a black penny, Jack!' with the total conviction that the people in the plane would throw money down for them."

"The Americans sure spoilt Vieux Fortians," said Eunice.

"You can say that again," said Ruben. "They sure spoilt us children into thinking money could be had for nothing."

"Not just children. At Cloud's Nest where I work the hotel can never have enough towels. Steal the maids does steal the towels like that. For the amount of towels these people does steal, I does wonder what they doing with all of it."

"I won't be surprised if they stealing them to sell," said Ruben.

"Well, that's another thing you can blame the Americans for," replied Eunice.

THE AFTERNOON WAS QUICKLY DISAPPEARING. The sun was only a few feet away from touching the Caribbean Sea. Ruben said good bye. He patted Henry's head and he briefly caressed Eunice's back.

As he walked away, Eunice couldn't fail to notice and admire the broad, upright shoulders; the effortless walk. Besides herself, she was spending more and more time thinking about this man. Thinking about what it would be like to sleep in his arms, to wake up in the morning and make him breakfast, to be able once in a while to lay down all her burdens at his feet. Since the death of her husband, a part of her — the womanly part, the romantic part, the soft part — had died. But this school teacher, this athletic man who walked on springs, had awakened things in her. Now she was dreaming more about him and less about her dead husband. She was having all kinds of impure thoughts of him, thoughts of the things he could do to her, thoughts a Christian woman like herself had no business having, especially about someone who wasn't her husband, who couldn't be her husband. She would get up in the middle of the night and pray for strength to resist the Devil. She would force herself to conjure the image of her deceased husband and ask him for the strength to be loyal to him. What would the church say if they were to find out that she, the staunchest member of the church, was so vile inside? She couldn't very well marry him. He wasn't an Adventist. She will not be unequally yoked. If there was to be any future for them, he would have to be baptized and join the church. She couldn't marry him, but pray as she might she couldn't stop the impure thoughts and feelings. She couldn't stop waking up all moist, soft, and womanly. If she had the strength, she would have stopped him from visiting her. But how could she when his visits had become the highlight of her life, when his presence made her feel so alive, so womanly? No. She couldn't stop him from visiting. She welcomed his visits, but she discouraged any touching, any show that what was between them was more than just casual friendship. What she was able to put a stop to, however, was her son calling him Daddy. She had to. Next thing people saying she's playing holier-than-thou and there she was cheating on her husband. No. She couldn't have that, so she stopped the boy from calling the man Daddy, but she couldn't stop the man from making a home in her heart.

As EUNICE TURNED THE STEAKS OVER, the begging cat rubbed against her thighs. She shoved him off.

Then, disturbing his mother's reverie and taking her completely off guard, Henry asked, "Mama, why is the *malmanman* acting like a woman?"

Eunice answered, "Boy, if my hands weren't in the fish, I'd give you one slap behind your head. Never let me hear you say that word again. I tired of telling you when you hear people of the world talking, close your ears. If you don't watch yourself, you will become just like Vieux Fort people. And enough questions for today. Go pick up your Time Tables and let me finish the fish."

Henry kept his mouth shut. He didn't tell his mother about the woman who was going to keep the sailor's baby. Neither did he ask his other question: If the *malmanman* is a man, why is he a stall keeper?

He left his mother sitting on the stone pile, but not to pick up his Time Tables. His head was filled with the stall keeper called the *malmanman* and with the story of the Americans. It was a toss-up which fascinated him more. He walked absentmindedly in the backyard. How he wished he was there in the time of the Americans. They did so much for Vieux Fort. How he wished he was there to help them build roads, airports, hospitals, schools, docks and jetties for Vieux Fort. If he were there, he would have helped them fight the Germans and Japs. Henry picked up a piece of wood, and pretending it was a gun he aimed and said, "I would have ratata, ratata, ratata them."

Then a brilliant idea hit him. He will write a letter to the Americans asking them to come back and help Vieux Fort people. He tore a sheet from his exercise book and wrote:

Dear Mr. Amercans:

Tanks a lot for all the help you all has give to Vieux Fort. But we stil need you. Vieux Fort people poor, lazie, they curse a lot, some are postiutes, they like sailors, most are Roman Cathlics, they don't keep Sabeth. They waiting for you to com agin. Please com back and help us. This time I will help you. If any Japs or Jermans come trouble you, I will help you shot them down.

From the botom of my hert,
Henry Auguste

Henry read the letter over. It met his satisfaction. He took a used envelope, crossed out the old addresses and for his forwarding address he wrote: "Mr. Ameicans, United Sates of Ameica." And for the return address: "Henry Auguste, Vieux Fort, St. Lucia." The following day, as soon as school was over, he rushed to the post office, slipped the letter in the mailing slot and hurried home.

ALL THAT TALK about the Americans brought Eunice back to her husband, Raphael, who was chosen for her by God. She couldn't think nor talk about the Americans without her husband invading her thoughts. She was sixteen years old and married six months when she and Raphael arrived in Vieux Fort and she first laid eyes on the Americans. By then rumors about the Americans abounded. The unbelievably high wages they paid; their recklessness, drunkenness and wild spending; their weakness for prostitutes; and that their presence would bring down the wrath of the Germans and Japs on St. Lucia.

So understandably Eunice was wary of meeting the Americans, dismayed of their heathenism, afraid that the Japs and Germans would bomb Vieux Fort. Still, when Raphael returned from a trip to Vieux Fort where he had found a place to stay and secured a job with the Americans, not as a mechanic helper as he had hoped but as a carpenter helper, and had suggested that he should go alone and she could join him later, she rejected the idea outright. If the Americans were such easy prey to Vieux Fort's prostitutes, how could she take a chance on her husband being there alone in the midst of all this temptation? Next thing he returns home corrupted and with empty pockets! After all, it was less than a year since he had joined the Adventist Faith, and had joined only after she had made it clear that she would not be unequally yoked. So who was to say alone in all this hedonism he wouldn't backslide? What sense does it make throwing a lamb in a lion's den? No. She had to go along. Together they would save more quickly and get out of Vieux Fort sooner.

Sitting on the stone pile, frying fish under the fading afternoon light, Eunice smiled as she remembered Raphael's excitement about moving to Vieux Fort and working for the Americans. He talked for whole days about the money he would make. Money to build a home of their own, money to buy land to plant his own sugar-cane to sell to the sugar factory, money to buy nice clothes, money to even buy a nice horse carriage like those of the *bétchés*, the white people. After a while Eunice got so fed-up with Raphael's incessant talk of money, money, Americans, Americans, that at nights she feigned sleep just to get him to shut up.

On the second Sunday in June 1941, three months after the Americans started constructing the base, the young couple embarked on the nine-mile trek from Debreuil to Vieux Fort. Taking advantage of the coolness of the early morning, they left Debreuil at 5AM when there was just a mere hint of an approaching day. Once on the road, save for their youth, their glowing love, and the bounce and anticipation in Raphael's stride, there wasn't much about them to attract the envy of an onlooker. The grip Eunice carried had a rat-bitten hole through which some of her meager possessions were threatening to reveal themselves.

The one under Raphael's arm had no handle, and the latch had gone bad so he had tied a string around it to keep it closed. The thread-bare, patched-up clothes they had on were their town and church clothes, and their few remaining clothes, which they were carrying in their rat-bitten grips, were little better than rags. Most pitiful of all was that they made the trek barefooted to save on the one pair of shoes they each owned.

But none of that bothered Raphael. His mind was in the future, not the present. Bad as it may be, why dwell on one's current disposition when a storehouse of riches would soon open up? Or, as Eunice would put it, why worry about one's worldly possessions or one's fate on earth when there was a place in the Kingdom of God waiting?

As they stepped out into the predawn, Raphael said, "Eunice, doesn't this feel like the first day of creation?"

Eunice would have rebuked her husband about being careful not to blaspheme against God, but she too was caught up in the excitement of starting a new life with the one she loved, the one given to her by God, and of seeing the world. For her moving to Vieux Fort was tantamount to going overseas. The closest she had been to the town was the neighboring village of Laborie. She hadn't laid eyes on Castries, the capital, either. So although Eunice had her own apprehensions she would have been lying if she were to say that she wasn't looking forward to seeing Vieux Fort and all what the Americans were doing to the town. Her excitement mixed with fear of the unknown caused her to pause before rebuking her husband, and in that pause she took in the cool, dew-wet, slowly disappearing dawn, the emptiness of the road, the quiet interrupted only by roosters, barking dogs, and the sound of wind in trees, and it occurred to her that this must have been how it was with

Adam and Eve alone in the garden of Eden. Still, rather than voicing such thoughts and giving encouragement to her husband in his manner of speaking, she just smiled and said, "Raphael, trust you to come up with something like that."

As if hearing her thoughts and not her words, Raphael said, "Darling, it's like the world was created just for the two of us."

"Raphael?"

"But it's true, darling. Don't you feel it?"

Then as if to make sure his wife not only felt it but heard it, Raphael began to whistle a tune whose rhythm seemed to match that of their bare feet on the dirt path leading out of Debreuil to the main road that would take them to Vieux Fort.

When they turned left on the road to Vieux Fort, day was fast breaking, and the world had begun to stir. Smoke was beginning to rise from the huts scattered across the countryside, a few farmers were on their way to tend their animals, neighbors could be heard shouting morning greetings, crowing roosters were rudely and incessantly announcing their presence.

Taking a respite from his whistling, Raphael said, "Ah, darling, we make it. We make it. The first thing we going to do when we reach Vieux Fort is to throw away the rags we wearing and buy us some nice clothes and shoes. Darling, believe me, in next to no time we will have enough money to buy clothes, shoes, suitcases, and much more to our hearts' content."

"Raphael, don't you think you ahead of yourself?"

"No, darling. In Vieux Fort I see men lighting cigarettes with dollars. I see the Americans throwing quarters and dimes for children. Some people don't even have to work to get rich. They simply have to stick around the Americans when they come to town."

"Yes, I've heard of them. The loose women who does sell themselves."

"Darling, don't be so pessimistic. With both of us working for the Americans, in next to no time we'll save enough to come back and build a nice house, buy plenty of land, so rather than slaving on the estate for the *bétchés* we'll grow our own cane to sell to the factory. We'll be hiring people to do the work, so we go be just like the *bétchés*. We'll have horses and carriages just like them. You know, darling, come to think of it, we may even be able to get a Jeep."

"A Jeep!"

"Yes, darling, a Jeep. With all the American dollars floating around, who knows?"

"But Raphael, where does God come in all of this? I haven't heard you mention one word about Jesus and the Adventist Church in Vieux Fort. Raphael, in Vieux Fort you know we must be careful not to go astray. Remember Sodom and Gomorrah. Remember what the Bible say. Money is the root of all evil."

"Off course darling, of course we'll be going to church and sing praises to the Lord for blessing us so bountifully."

Again, Eunice came close to rebuking her husband. She had a problem with the thought that the only reason for serving God was to receive blessings from Him. In her mind one should glorify God and do His bidding simply out of love for Him. But overwhelmed by her husband's undaunted optimism she simply said, "We shall see. We shall see."

Soon, as if giving proof of his sincerity about praising God, Raphael hummed *Blessed assurance, Jesus is mine*. After a while Eunice too started humming. And so it was that Raphael and his wife, dressed in clothes not much better than rags, walked barefooted to Vieux Fort, carrying their borrowed, rat-bitten grips.

COVERED WITH DUST and resembling a pair of throw-away persons, the young couple found the once sleepy, fishing and sugarcane factory village of Vieux Fort in upheaval. The Americans had begun digging and turning the landscape upside down. Everywhere buildings and roads were springing up, and although it was Sunday American jeeps, dumper trucks, tractors, and bulldozers were on the move. People were arriving from as far as Castries and Gros Islet, from every nook and cranny on the island, from rural enclaves with names known only to their inhabitants, from the neighboring islands of St. Vincent and Barbados, in twos, in threes, in gangs and it seemed sometimes in whole villages. Among them carpenters, masons, joiners, blacksmiths, farmers, laborers. Name it, and the Americans had a job waiting. But not everyone came to work for the Americans. Some came to offer special services: beggars, drunkards, pimps, and prostitutes from the four corners of the island and beyond arrived in droves.

Overnight Vieux Fort became an overcrowded boomtown. Its weekday population quadrupled from 2000 to 8000. With no corresponding increase in the number of residential dwellings, there was a serious housing shortage. The only accommodation that Raphael had managed to find was a room in a house that was once a two bedroom, but to milk as much rent as possible the owner had split the bedrooms in two to create four rooms, each four feet by five feet. Yet the half rooms were being rented at twice what the full rooms fetched before the coming of the Americans.

Eunice didn't know it, but the reason Raphael had suggested she join him later was because he was hoping that by then he would have found better accommodation. She was appalled. Six feet tall, Raphael had to lie down curled up to fit the half room. Despite the exorbitant rent, the demand for housing was so great that rooms were being rented by shifts. Since they shared the half room with day-shift renters, Raphael and Eunice had to vacate the half room by six in the morning and they could return no earlier than six in the evening. But the size of the half room wasn't the worst of it. The small coconut fibre, lice-infested mattress they shared with the day-shift renters was dirty with perspiration and whatever else they could only guess. At nights mice and cockroaches crisscrossed the room like cars on a highway, and just about every other day Raphael killed a centipede crawling out from under the mattress. The stench of urine and slop vases permeated the neighborhood. If it wasn't the mice, cockroaches and stench, then sounds of drunkenness, and quarrels and fights among neighbors and between spouses kept them awake deep into the night.

Even so, Eunice and Raphael had to consider themselves lucky. The less fortunate had to make do with cardboard shacks erected on the edge of the mosquito infested swamps that made up the Mangue and the Bacadere. Others resorted to napping in rum shops and sleeping in fishing canoes, outhouses, kitchens, balconies, bushes, and under houses on pillars.

So great was the pull of workers from the sugar factories to the American military base, that taken by surprise the sugar factories complained that the Americans were doing great harm to the island; they were killing the mainstay of its economy. To the great dismay of workers, the Americans responded by paying lower wages than they had intended. Nevertheless, despite their concessions to the plantations and sugar factories, the wages the

Americans paid were still higher than anything workers had previously earned, so they continued to flock Vieux Fort, leaving the sugar factories with little choice but to endure serious labor shortages.

The authorities were also taken by surprise. Garbage disposal, sewage treatment, and water supply couldn't keep up with the burgeoning town. The vast majority of people had no toilet facilities and running water. The town had no choice but to resort to an open pit public toilet. Garbage piled up in yards and on streets and festered. Human feces accumulated under adjoining bushes. Eunice saw a dead dog remain in the middle of Clarke Street for days until the wheels of American vehicles reduced it to powder. Vieux Fort became a haven for rats, mice, and cockroaches and was soon plagued with tuber-culosis. Worse, in the last quarter of 1942 typhoid fever spread its claws and claimed 47 lives. Yet it would have taken many more lives hadn't the authorities quickly dis-covered that it was due to the proximity of the town's drinking water to the open sewer system.

Vieux Fort wasn't the only town to profit from the Americans. Prostitution became so rampant in the town that venereal diseases reached epidemic proportions. So much so that the Americans, the original source of the dis-eases, began bypassing Vieux Fort altogether and sought their pleasures in the neighboring village of Laborie. Playing one-upmanship, the Vieux Fort prostitutes changed their hair and dress styles and even their accents and presented themselves in Laborie as fresh, unspoilt ladies ready to satisfy the Americans' every whim.

Shoving off the begging cat that was again rubbing against her thighs, Eunice removed the steaks that were done from the frying pan and replaced them with fresh ones. She shook her head as she recalled her husband's talkativeness and stubborn optimism. She had thought that after their arrival in Vieux Fort and after Raphael had started working with the Americans his talk of money and the Americans would, if not stop, at least subside. But that was when the talk really got started. And indeed there was much for Raphael to talk about. The french fries and hamburgers he was seeing for the first time and which the Americans shared with him, the car magazines and comic books they loaned him, their talk of New York, Chicago, Boston and other American cities where the lights never dimmed and where the action never stopped. But most of all the American jeeps and trucks that he hopped on as soon as he entered the base to take him to whichever house he was working on.

The Americans liked him. But what choice did they have? How could they not like someone so upbeat, so optimistic, so willing? The Americans liked him so much that they were teaching him to drive. Teaching him to drive! Imagine that. Here he was, before the arrival of the Americans thinking in terms of horse carriages, yet as if by magic he was driving jeeps.

Returning tired to her pest-infested half room from a whole day of working for the Americans as a kitchen helper and a cook in training, a job she had secured a month after her arrival in Vieux Fort and that would serve her well after the Americans left because it enabled her to find a cooking job at Vieux Fort's Cloud's Nest Inn, Eunice had to contend with a husband speaking not only in greater volumes than before, but Yanking even more than the Americans. But that wasn't the worst of it. Ever so often she would detect alcohol on his breath and the taste of it in his mouth. Soon, added to the alcohol, his mouth stank of tobacco. Her constant scolding and nagging changed not a thing. Asking him how could he profess to be an Adventist, a Christian, and be drinking and smoking like this made matters worse, because he would smile and say something like, "Shit, honey, don't mind me. I'm just fooling around." Before the coming of the Americans Raphael didn't drink, smoke, or utter one curse word. But now he couldn't open his mouth if "shit" didn't come out. As soon as he arrived home from work his first words were something like, "Shit, honey, I'm really beat today." It was as if he created sentences just to be able to put "shit" in them. Before long, Raphael stopped going to church, and would only start back again with the birth of his son in 1957, the same year that the Americans packed up and left for good.

For years they had been praying for a child. But each time when it seemed God had answered their prayers, Eunice miscarried. After the fourth miscarriage, she had just about given up hope and concluded that the Lord didn't see it fit for her to have children. Pregnant for the fifth time and bowing to the will of God she waited for the miscarriage she knew was coming. None of her previous pregnancies had gone past three months, so when four months passed and there was no passage of blood that would signal God's will, she began hoping, praying that she had been wrong about God's intention. This fifth time the baby stayed, and when she gave birth on a Tuesday morning in March, two months before the Americans left for good, unmindful of the baby's broken arm that would render him unable to crawl and would earn him the name *bwa kochi*, her husband was so overjoyed that he promised to reconsecrate his life to God. A promise he had kept up to the morning of his death by drowning.

One area Eunice couldn't fault Raphael was his optimism, zeal and commitment to saving his money and improving their station in life. He would tell her, "Shit, honey, don't worry. Before long we'll be out of this stink hole and have our own home. The Americans told me that after the war instead of carrying all the vehicles back to America, the army will sell many of them to the locals. So, shit, honey, if we play our cards right and save enough money, we'll have a house and a jeep all to ourselves."

Bypassing the "shit," Eunice would be thinking: with rent and prices so high, when will they have enough saved to buy land and build a house, much less get a jeep? It was only in 1947 that Raphael, with his newly acquired carpentry skills, would build something resembling a proper house. Before that he took an intermediary step. Seven months after their arrival in Vieux Fort, with pieces of lumber discarded by the Americans, he built a hut in the Mangue in the middle of the cardboard shacks. The Mangue flooded after every downpour, so although the house was on pillars water threatened to seep through the floor. Undaunted, to Raphael his makeshift structure signaled that he was on his way up. With no rent to pay they could save more and achieve their goals more quickly. It may not be long before he is driving his jeep. So what if for now they had to use slop vases that had to be emptied under the bush, walk a good distance to get water from the standpipe, and being in the Mangue they had to be constantly treading mud. They were still better off than in Debreuil where for mere pittances he had worked on the River Doree Sugar Estate, cutting and transporting cane, helping to fix and maintain the factory machinery, and caring for the horses and cleaning the stable in the off-season, and where he and his wife lived with her parents and in earshot of the whole house when he was fulfilling his husbandly duties. After all, they started out with borrowed, rat-bitten grips, each a pair of shoes that was practically worn out, and the only halfway decent clothes they owned were what they had arrived with on their backs. Yet, if truth be told, the halfway decent clothes weren't much better than rags. In Vieux Fort, in next to no time, they each owned three pairs of shoes—a work shoe, a church shoe, and a town shoe. And talking about clothes, for church alone they each had three change of clothes. And how about the transistor radio he was able to buy from the Americans for next to nothing? If that isn't progress, if that isn't the good times, what is?

THE GOOD TIMES ARE HERE. Money, rum, music and merriment are flowing. Rum shops and dancehalls can't open fast enough. Forget about the congestion, filth and diseases; the good times are here. Can't you feel it? Can't you smell it? Can't you taste it? The newness and freshness that's in the air. Lay down your burdens, for it's a time of freedom, a time of liberation, a time of celebration. The Americans are here, they have brought beer, pop, blues, country and western, the sky is the limit. Get in your pants and miniskirts, grab a man, let the good times roll.

The good times are here. If you can't get on the American payroll, or you prefer to do your own thing, don't worry, for money is flowing and the locals have acquired the American taste for the good life. They are now one-day millionaires with no stale money in their pockets. See them lighting their cigarettes with flaming dollars. All manner of tailors, cobblers, charcoal makers, stall keepers, shop keepers, rum shop keepers, broom makers, bakers, wood cutters, and whatever else you have to offer are wanted.

Fishermen are wanted—pot fishermen, "seine" fishermen, row boat fishermen, flour-bag-sail fishermen, fishing-gun fishermen, rod and sinker line fishermen. Whatever the catch— tuna, kingfish, dolphin, red snapper, black fish or pilot whales, green sea turtles, leatherback turtles, hawkbill turtles, "chadon" or sea urchins or sea eggs, lobster, octopus, "lambi" or conch, crabs, whelks, and mangrove oysters—it will not go to waste.

The Stall Keeper

One thing though, remember to save the best — the tuna, kingfish, dolphin and lobster — for the Americans, for they pay top dollar.

Farmers, you too are wanted. People cannot get enough mangoes, oranges, grapefruits, golden apples, plums, pawpaws, plantains, breadfruits, breadnuts, white yams, yellow yams, kouch-kouch, dasheen, tannia, lettuce, cabbage, tomatoes, carrots, peanuts, coffee, cocoa, farine, cassava bread. No need to come all the way into town, you will be met halfway. Just remember, though, save the best for the Americans for they pay top dollar.

The good times are here. Even if you can't get on the American payroll and you don't wish to do your own thing, don't worry because "Give me a black penny, Jack," or if Jack doesn't hear or is pretending not to hear "Give me a black penny, Joe" might do the trick. For there are five, six thousand Joes and Jacks with much too much money than they know what to do with. And what do they need money for, anyway, if tomorrow they will be called to Europe to meet their deaths? Besides, why let the drunkards, pimps and prostitutes claim all the spoil.

And if Joe and Jack didn't do the trick, don't worry. Sit tight by the American garbage dump. These wasteful Americans throw away every and anything, and some things you wouldn't believe. Like spring mattresses that beat out the "kabann" or even the coconut-fibre mattress any day, any time; clothes that are better than what they sell in the stores; corned beef, canned sardines, powdered milk that the wicked Americans say have passed their expiration date, whatever that means; whole bags of flour, sugar, oatmeal that the sinful Americans say have been contaminated, with what, I don't know. And it doesn't matter, because contaminated or not they beat out by a long shot the dirty rice and sugar, and the maggot filled oat meal, corn meal, and flour that you get from the stores. And don't worry about things running out, because the delight, amusement and befuddlement in the eyes of the Americans as you scramble for their throwaways, suggest there is no end to what these abominable Americans will *throw away for the simple pleasure of watching you scramble. One thing though, be prepared to fight other poachers for these American spoils.*

The good times are here. Forget about working ten-hour days in sugar factories and slaving in mosquito, rat, centipede, snake, and whatever else infected canefields. Haven't you heard? "Tan èslavaj ja pasé," The time of slavery has passed. Now is the time of the Americans and they are paying top dollar for less. The good times are here. Forget about your "vòltivè" and coconut branch thatched huts with mud as flooring. Haven't you heard? You are in the time of enlightenment! The good times are here. Why go all the way down to the river, fetch water in calabash gourds and carry it all the way back to your hut to fill up clay goblets, all this to be able to drink bilharzia-infested water? Come to Vieux Fort, the Americans have provided chlorinated, bilharzia-free drinking water. Don't worry about the typhoid epidemic, this was just a one-time mishap. The good times are here. Why are you still cooking your food on "boukan difé," when the Americans are throwing away kerosene stoves? After all, you are not, never were, and never will be a buccaneer. And why are you still cooking your food in "kanawis", eating out of calabash bowls with wooden forks and spoons, and drinking out of cups fashioned out of evaporated milk cans when there are aluminum pots and pans, enamel plates and cups and silver forks and spoons?

Don't worry if you can't afford these things, just wait long enough at the American garbage dump and all things will come your way. After all, wasn't it the good book that said, blessed are they who wait for they shall inherit the earth, or is this a mis-quote? Never mind.

SATISFIED THAT THE FISH WAS DONE, Eunice placed the steaks one by one in a bowl. For supper she and her son will have fish, bread and cocoa tea. The rest of the fish will be used for preparing tomorrow's lunch. It seemed to Eunice that when people talked about the Days of the Americans, they only mentioned the good times, the time when all roads led to Vieux Fort, when without a doubt Vieux Fort was the center of economic, social and entertainment life on the island. But few dwelled on what happened afterwards when the good times came to an end, an end that had come rather quickly. Nor did they dwell on how the Americans had turned Vieux Fort into a Sodom and Gomorrah of beggars, drunks, pimps, and prostitutes.

Ruben was sympathetic towards Eunice's misgivings. His research had shown that by April 1941 the Americans construction of the base was already in full swing. Fourteen months later, June 1942, the zenith of the good times, they had 4496 workers in their employment. Soon after, employment began to drop such that by the end of 1945 there were no civilians on the American payroll. Four years later, in 1949, the Americans closed shop and the soldiers packed up and went home.

In Ruben's assessment, the good times, which had lasted for at most eighteen months, were over. Vieux Fort fell into despair. The once fashionable, American give-away clothes grew threadbare and patched up. Dilapidated houses and garbage-filled vacant lots looked on miserably. Ruben and other Vieux Fort children, burdened with parasite inflated stomachs, walked the streets barefooted and in rags. People who were lucky enough to have family land in the interior left to become peasant farmers. Those with the contacts, ambition, and wherewithal emigrated; some to post World War II England, others to the gold mines of the Guianas. Many stayed put and for their survival fell back on occupations closer to nature: fishing, wood cutting, charcoal making, broom making. Some prostitutes changed their ways, but since habits are hard to change others switched their attention to the occasional ship that called to port filled with deprived sailors. And, as Eunice saw it, many others simply sat by the roadside and waited for the Americans to return and the good times to roll again.

Thanks to the Cold War the Americans did return in 1955, but compared with their previous coming this time the bang was but a whimper and their stay was even shorter. Two years later, in 1957, they were gone and apparently for good. This second time, as if to appease and not disappoint those who had waited for their second coming, the occupiers built a secondary school in Vieux Fort, and, according to rumors, to continue where they had left off the Americans wanted to transform Vieux Fort into a metropolitan city far surpassing Castries, the seat of government. Besides having spent so much time in Vieux Fort, it was easy to see why the Americans would have wanted to target the town for such a project. For surely Vieux Fort, more than any other part of the island, would have reminded them of their vast western plains. When the Americans left without fulfilling this promise, the rumors added that the British, the owners of these lands and the masters of its people, opposed this American generosity out of fear that the Yankees would take over their fair island. The rumors also said that Castries folks, wary of Vieux Fort surpassing their town in importance, objected to this American intervention even more strongly than had the British. So according to the rumors, unwanted and unappreciated, the Americans were left with little choice but to leave.

Some said that watching the Americans leave this second time around and realizing that if not for the greed and selfishness of Castries and the British the good times might have continued forever, Vieux Fortians fell into even greater despair and hopelessness than the first time, prompting an observer to ask, "After the closing of the Base, what?"

At least one Vieux Fortian, Emmanuel Prescott, a great philanthropist, didn't take this lying down. He was a short man, five feet, four inches; East Indian, maybe mixed, but nonetheless predominantly East Indian. His chubby frame, pot belly, and flat-footed, off-the-back-foot walk made him a natural Father Christmas. But that wasn't the only way he fitted that description. He was a meek man of great patience, forbearance, generosity, and a fighter for those who couldn't help themselves. He would stop and chat with the youngest of children, and the poorest and most downtrodden of the town's dwellers.

The most enduring picture of Emmanuel Prescott was of him handing out candies and sweet biscuits to children, an activity he conducted almost daily and that had earned him the name Daddy Mano, which had confused Henry into thinking that Daddy Mano was or could be his daddy, a confusion that had quickly led to disappointment when the philanthropist told Henry that he was everybody's daddy, and not his and his alone as Henry had wished.

Commiserating the state of Vieux Fort after the departure of the Americans, Daddy Mano wrote both the British prime minister and the president of the United States of America letter after letter demanding that England and America pay Vieux Fort for the exploitation of its land and people, or at the very least fulfill the American promise of transforming Vieux Fort into a metropolitan city. He argued that Vieux Fort was just as deserving as Europe for American post World War II reconstruction funds. Time passed. The island obtained Associated Statehood. Daddy Mano became a politician. He won elections, he lost elections. The country gained its independence from Britain.

Daddy Mano died. Posthumously, an annex of Vieux Fort was named after him. Yet the Americans, much less the British, save for the school they donated, didn't remit a cent.

With thoughts of Vieux Fort and the Americans lingering, Eunice raised herself off the pile of stones. She couldn't help but be negative and pessimistic about Vieux Fortians. To her, they just sat there as if waiting for the Americans to come back. As if the Americans were some kind of Messiah. "The Americans, my foot," she whispered. "They had better get up from their behinds and go look for something to do. What good did the Americans do in the first place? I know of only one Savior, and He is sitting on a throne in Heaven. It's His second coming, and his alone, I'm waiting for. They came with their loudness, drunkenness and loose money, turning Vieux Fort into a stink hole of drunks, prostitutes, beggars and garbage. *Chups.*"

That awful night on her way home from a Wednesday night prayer meeting flooded her memory. It was the time that Raphael had stopped going to church. She had begged him, "Let's go to church," but the only concession he had made was that he would come and meet her after service and walk home with her. As she had anticipated, Raphael didn't keep his promise. On her way home she got caught in a drizzle, so, without an umbrella, she walked as fast as her feet could move to get home before the drizzle turned into a downpour. She was about to bypass a rum shop on Clarke Street when a tall, drunk American soldier stumbled out and nearly bumped into her. Before she could go around him, he raised up his puffed-up eyes, held Eunice by the shoulders, partially to make his advance and partially to steady himself, and said, "Hey darkie, five Yankee dollars for your cherry." She pushed his hands away and ran all the way home. Never before and never after would anyone make her feel so cheap, so dirty. Up to today she could still recall his awful, alcoholic breath, his bloody eyes, and his repulsive, slurry voice.

Eunice never told Raphael about the incident. In fact she was glad that Raphael wasn't home when she arrived. She would have had to explain her state of distress, and she was sure he would want to accost the soldier for insulting his wife. The soldiers owned the town. Against them the police were helpless. Once, shortly after a group of policemen had for one reason or the other roughed up a lone soldier, a jeep full of soldiers arrived at the police station seeking revenge. Facing such an onslaught, the best the police could do was hurry and close all the doors and windows of the police station. The soldiers vented their anger by firing their guns into the air for an interval of over five minutes. The whole town, including Eunice, was terrified. If even the police could not deal with the soldiers, then Eunice could well imagine the danger Raphael would put himself in by accosting the drunk soldier.

Eunice thought of the story about the Vigier woman whom people said a jeep full of Americans had accosted on the road. They had dragged her into the bushes to have their way with her. She wasn't a young woman. She was well past her forties. In fact, she was already a grandmother. In desperation, the woman pulled down her top to expose her flabby, wrinkled breast. She couldn't speak English, but she did her best. She said, "I is grandma, me *tété gwiji.*" Meaning, I am an old woman, my breast is already shriveled, why waste your time. This was how the woman escaped from being gang raped.

Besides this incident, throughout the American occupation of Vieux Fort, the stories piled up of how the soldiers chased after women to rape them. Apparently, it made no difference to the soldiers whether they paid for it or took it by force. It got so bad that after a while the only women who stepped out after dark were prostitutes and those like Eunice who believed they were protected by God Himself.

The Americans my foot, thought Eunice. What if they built roads and airports? How has that benefitted Vieux Fort people? How is that going to undo the damage they have done to Vieux Fortians? Can a rape be undone? Can innocence be reclaimed? Can they give people back their sanctity? Is it any wonder that most Vieux Fortians can do nothing but *bacchanal* and watching the streets? Now, tell me, wouldn't Vieux Fort be better off if the Americans had never shown their dirty, white faces? After all, what does it profit a man to gain the whole world and suffer the loss of his soul? And, even so, what did Vieux Fort profit?

Once when Eunice was carrying on like that about the Americans, and in the same breath kept bringing up her husband, Ruben said, "But Eunice it seems you blaming the Americans for the death of your husband?" She denied it vehemently, but Ruben wasn't far from the truth. Eunice's bitterness towards Vieux Fort and the Americans was somehow linked to the death of her husband. It seemed that at some subconscious level she blamed his death on their move to Vieux Fort. She missed him so much. Up till now she couldn't fully accept that he was dead; that she would never lay eyes on him again; that they would never again stroll hand in hand on the beach; that never again could she wake up in the morning and lie on top of him, forcing him to get up; that he would never again hold her at the waist with his left hand, draw her to him with the knowledge that she was all his and his alone, and look into her eyes as if there were no one else in the universe. She missed him. She missed him badly. The only way she was able to carry on with her life was never to fully accept that he was gone forever, to trick herself into believing that he had simply emigrated to, say, England, to work and save money in order to take better care of his wife and son.

She had given Ruben a hell of a hard time before she had finally accepted him as a friend. Him not being an Adventist wasn't the only reason she had treated him so coldly. The other reason was that to admit that she liked Ruben, to allow him into her life, was to accept that her husband was truly dead and was never coming back, something she couldn't do, something she had needed to continue holding on to life.

Soon after she buried the husband God had given to her in dreams, she had made plans to leave Vieux Fort behind and return to Debreuil. But then she had a dream. In that dream she was there watering her garden, which, on account of all the care and attention she was giving it, was bluish green. Then an angel of the Lord took Eunice on her wings and flew over a desolate area where the vegetation was dry and shriveled. The angel said, "These too are in need of water." She had the same dream several nights in a row. Finally, it dawned upon her that God wanted her to stay in Vieux Fort to bear Him witness. So despite her begrudging of Vieux Fort, she obeyed God. Before that dream Eunice saw her religious experience more as a personal relationship with God and less as the spreading of His word. But after the dream, she became much more active in the service of the Lord. At crusades her voice began rising above that of the rest of the congregation. She became much more receptive to accepting positions in the church. The only time Vieux Fortians saw Eunice without her cloak of aloofness was when she was out there collecting Ingathering, and when along with one or two of her Sisters in the Faith she went about giving house to house Bible lessons. To Vieux Fortians it was an amazing thing how the aloof, head-in-the-air woman they met on the street could change into the charming and engaging woman they found on their doorsteps, Bible in hand. They would quickly invite Eunice in, more curious of the messenger than the message. They must have no doubt likened her dual personality to that of the politicians who only came down from their high horses during election time. Of course, the politicians came to win votes, she to win souls.

Nonetheless up to this day Eunice remained perplexed. Why should God have offered her Raphael, only to take him away so soon?

With lingering thoughts of Vieux Fort, her husband, and the Americans, Eunice, followed by the cat that was still waiting to partake of the kill, entered the house. As the cat was about to enter after her, Eunice turned around and pushed it out with her foot. "Not inside you coming," she said. "What, you think I owe you? Mice running everywhere in the house, but you eh catching not one, and you there begging, begging. Wait there. See who will feed you. Tonight you can starve for all I care."

DARKNESS WAS BEGINNING TO DESCEND UPON VIEUX FORT. The street lamps were turned on. The street dogs were preparing for their dominion of the night. The last fishing boat had already made its way to shore. Anticipating supper, Henry came in and sat at the dining table, and was ready to ask his mother another avalanche of questions.

HENRY'S FASCINATION and interest in Eugene, the stall keeper, were insatiable. He and Ralph were standing at the rusted zinc fence surrounding his yard, watching the business of the street, when Eugene passed by with a large tray heaped with fruits and condiments on his head. It was banana day and Eugene was headed for the dock to sell to the men unloading bananas.

"Look the *malmanman*," whispered Henry.

They watched Eugene. As usual he wore khaki shorts. His rounded buttocks were swinging from side to side. To the boys he walked just like a woman. They crept out of the gate and followed Eugene at a safe distance, and, holding their giggles, began to walk and swing their buttocks just like him.

Unfortunately, shortly after they had walked out of the gate, Eunice arrived in the back yard just in time to see their impromptu caricature of Eugene.

They were funny. They were really funny. A hint of a smile crossed Eunice's face. But not for long. This was exactly the kind of thing she was trying to guard her son against. Why doesn't he imitate the preachers in the church? When he's in church, he utters not one note of song, but his mouth does be wide open staring at people. Why is it that it's only the things of the street he's interested in? They were funny. They walked just like the man. But she felt she had no choice but to beat the street out of him. He wasn't going to end up like Vieux Fort people. One way or the other she was going to keep Vieux Fort out of her gate. With those thoughts, Eunice's voice cracked the air like a whip. "Henry, what are you all doing? Come here this minute."

Wanting no part of what he knew was coming, Ralph ran home. Henry raced just as fast back to his yard. But that didn't save him. His mother placed his neck between her legs and whipped his buttocks thoroughly. Henry wasn't sure which was worse: the suffocating feeling of his neck between his mother's thighs or the sting of the tamarind whip? His wail could be heard far down Walcott Lane.

Yet the whipping did nothing to quell the boy's curiosity. Instead his unwavering fascination with Eugene led him a couple weeks later to one of the treats of his childhood. He was on his way home from school when he noticed a crowd of people at the junction of Walcott Lane and Clarke Street where Eugene usually set up his trays. Henry quickened his steps, and upon reaching the crowd squeezed through just in time to see the man stall keeper get up from behind his tray and slap a woman stall keeper. The woman flew at Eugene with the ferocity of a tigress, her nails becoming claws. In the process she tipped her tray over, fruits and condiments spilled onto the ground and rolled into the nearby gutter. Over the spilled fruits and condiments the two tangled, aiming at each other's face, scratching and pulling hair. Soon one fell on the other, knocking down one of Eugene's trays, his merchandise traveling the way of that of his foe. The crowd got larger, pushing Henry closer to the action. Spills of laughter shut out the screams, grunts, and curses of the combatants. Eugene was fighting just like a woman. No fist, no judo, just the flailing of arms, the lashing of nails and the pulling of hair. In the midst of the laughter, Henry heard a spectator say, "*Gadé malmanman-an goumen*, Look at the she-man fight." So enthralled was the crowd, no one offered to break up the fight. It was the police who came and separated the two tigresses. Henry went home convinced the *malmanman* had won.

At school Henry couldn't stop talking to his other classmates about the man stall keeper. They argued. What kind of man was the stall keeper? Did he have a wife, or did he have a husband? During one of their discussions, Henry asked his often repeated question. "Is the *malmanman* a man or a woman?" And just when the discussion was about to take its usual circular course, an older boy, three classes ahead of Henry and his friends, joined the conversation.

"Don't be stupid," said the older boy, "of course he a man. That's why they call him *malmanman*, a man who acts like a woman."

"When he start acting like a woman?" asked Henry.

"Since he small."

"How you know?"

"Stupid. Everybody knows the story about Eugene. They say when he was small, he didn't play marbles, cricket, football, topee, nothing boys did. All he wanted to do was play with dolls and play rounders and netball with the girls."

"Play netball! That's a girls' game."

"Isn't that what I saying, *Semdays*? They say Eugene used to put on his mother's panties and bra, and he finish his mother's powder on himself."

"You lying, you lying," said Henry.

"If you all tweenies don't shut up, I eh telling you all nothing."

"Shut up, *Semdays*," said one of the boys.

"They say when the children playing house, is only the mammy Eugene wanted to play. Vex that made Eugene's father! Vex! The father, they say, was the strongest, baddest man in town. People called him Big Man. He was a giant, and his eyes were always red, red as blood. Even grown men were afraid of him. They say during the time of the Americans, the soldiers who even the police were afraid of, Big Man used to beat them five, six at a time when they came to town to drink and look for women."

"And the soldiers didn't shoot him?" asked one of the boys.

"How can they shoot him when he's a giant?" said the older boy.

"Well, in the Bible David slay a giant," said Henry.

"This eh the Bible, *Semdays, bwa kochi*. So, as I was saying, Eugene's father was a bad-john. He was a fisherman too. They say hurricane or no hurricane, he went to sea. And he never came back with empty boat. Anyway, Big Man vexed at Eugene. So vexed, Big Man stopped Eugene playing doll, playing rounders and netball, and forced him to go and play with the boys. He took all Eugene's dolls and burned them in a bucket. They say Eugene cried for days.

"You know Eugene eleven years and he couldn't swim! So one day Big Man took Eugene to the jetty and throw him in the water. Eugene beat water, and he crying 'Save me! Save me!' He go down once, and he come back up. He go down again, and still the father eh coming to save him. Until finally the father jump in the water and dive for him.

"But the biggest joke about Eugene is when time for him to go to the Boys' School. They say in the morning of the first day of school Eugene glad. His mother taking him to school. Eugene glad, he skipping and singing. But when Eugene see which school they taking him, he start crying, telling his mother this eh his school. Guess where Eugene wanted to go to school? He wanted to go to the Girls' School."

"The Girls' School? Who would ever want to go there?" said Henry.

"Well, *Semdays one week, read the Bible upside down*, this is where Eugene wanted to go. They say he cried all morning. They give him sweets, Shirley biscuits, guava jelly. But is cry, Eugene crying. Lunchtime come. Eugene goes home for lunch. When he come back for the day, guess where he going? The Girls' School. When he entered the class, all the girls started to giggle, so the teacher turn around from the blackboard to tell the girls to shut up. And she sees Eugene sitting there as if he a girl. The teacher say, 'Boy, what you doing here, are you out of your mind?' Eugene say, 'Miss, I come to school.' The teacher say, 'That I see. But you are in the wrong school. You are a boy, aren't you?' Eugene say, 'No,.. ah, ... yes.' The teacher say, 'Oh you are not sure, no wonder, no wonder. Well, whatever you are, you are not a girl. You belong to the Boys' School.' So the teacher half drag, half walk, a crying, screaming Eugene back to the Boys' School."

"So how he became a stall keeper?" asked Henry.

"That was after his father died. His father drown at sea. This was what save Eugene. His father would have killed him. After his father died his mother kill herself. She mixed rat poison in her juice. And then Eugene's Aunt from

Laborie come to live with him. The aunt used to sell by the road in Laborie, so she take Eugene out of school for him to help her sell. She make Eugene sell all over the place. Happy Eugene was happy! Happy he didn't have to go to the Boy's School any more. The aunt died but Eugene eh stop selling up to now."

The school bell rang, signaling the end of recess. The boys departed. But this was not the end of Henry's preoccupation with Eugene's story. For the rest of the day his thoughts remained on the stall keeper.

DAWN WAS FAST APPROACHING and the roosters were conducting their morning symphony. Needing no clock or watch or rooster to wake up, the fishermen were far out at sea in search of the day's catch. Overpowering the roosters' morning ritual, the intoxicating aroma of the Caribbean Sea and the mantra of its waves lashing on the seawall had many Vieux Fortians in deep slumber. But in this predawn no oceanic potion, or sleeping pill, or day-before exhaustion was strong enough to keep Ruben in bed. For he had spent the better part of the night mulling over his decision and today was the day he would let Eunice know of that decision. So there he was, in pajamas, dawn breaking upon the horizon, seated on the floor at the back door of his rented house next to the seawall, peering into the Caribbean Sea, listening to, tasting, breathing it, unmindful of its morning chill.

All night he had weighed the decision in his mind. What will Father Pierre and the rest of the Roman Catholic (RC) Church say? How will this affect his teaching job at the RC

Boys' School? Clearly, this will destroy any chance, however slim, of him ever becoming headmaster. How will his friends, especially members of his cricket and football team, take it? How will Vieux Fortians look at him? Most of his cricket matches took place on weekends, so how can he continue playing? No matter, he had waited long enough. Three years to be exact. Neither he nor Eunice was getting younger. If he wanted children with her he had to act now. His mind was made up. He will baptize, join the *Semdays* church and marry the woman who for the past three years had kept him sleepless, tormented, and frustrated. The woman who was suffocating his sleep and occupying every minute of his day.

As Ruben waited next to the seawall for the world to light up and for him to begin life anew, to be born again as the Adventists would say, his mind traveled back to when he first started taking notice of the woman who, now that he would take the baptismal plunge, would no doubt become his wife. Vieux Fort was a small town where everybody knew each other, so from childhood he knew Eunice and her husband. But they were Seventh Day Adventist people. They lived a life of seclusion. They didn't go to cinema, dances, First Communion and Christmas parties. They didn't come to the plays and other cultural activities that Father Pierre organized, nor the calypso and carnival queen shows, much less the carnival parades and jump up sessions. So he had always viewed Eunice and Raphael and the handful of Adventists in Vieux Fort from a distance. The drowning death of Raphael and his friend had been a great tragedy. It remained the talk of the town for several years. Yet, even so, Ruben had not taken particular notice of his widow.

All this changed on a Wednesday night three years back when their paths crossed as if for the first time. There she was, holding her son's hand, heading to prayer meeting. And he, having just showered and freshened up from a tough yet victorious football match, tired but feeling on top of the world, was heading to the steps of Damascus Guest House to hang out with the boys, where the football match would be replayed over and over again.

This wasn't the first time he had seen Eunice hurrying to church. It seemed to him every time he saw her she was hurrying to church as if there wasn't enough church to go around so she had to get there quickly to secure her share. But this Wednesday night in August he wasn't sure what was different about her that attracted his attention. Maybe that night the light from the street lamps was shining from a slightly different angle, highlighting and accentuating her slender neck, her haughty, no nonsense, no time to waste African beauty. Or maybe the blue and white embroidered dress she wore flaunted, without her aware-ness, the fact that despite her thirty-something years everything on her — shoulders, breast, buttocks — was still standing up straight, at least as straight as those of a teenager. Or maybe that night the spirit of God was ablaze in Eunice, transforming her into the gloriously enchanting woman that he saw. Or maybe it had nothing to do with Eunice, but all to do with his state of mind at the time. Maybe having beaten Drifters, his archrival, three goals to one — and the two goals he scored were two of the most beautiful goals you would ever see — he was a bit more generous and agreeable than usual and so was seeing everyone and everything in a softer light. Or maybe hav-ing just got over an eighteen month relationship with a woman several years his senior who had finally decided he was too young for her so sooner or later he would dump her for a younger woman, he was open to suggestions. Or just maybe the night before he dreamt (a dream that had not entered his conscious mind and therefore he would not recall) of a beautiful woman favoring Eunice and in that dream a voice sounding very much like the voice of God proclaimed that this woman was to be his wife. Whatever. This Wednesday night in August on his way to spending yet another evening with his buddies to replay the football victory and to rehash what they had rehashed yesterday, day before yesterday, last week, last month, and last year, even, because with men things never change, he was smitten and his life was never to be the same.

He said, "Hello, gorgeous, how are you this evening?" She didn't answer, she didn't even look his way. Instead, as if he represented a danger, she gripped her son more firmly and quickened her already hasty pace.

He said, "Can I come to church with you?"

"You welcome to church anytime. But you not welcome to come with me."

"Why not?"

"Mister, leave me alone, I'm late for service."

Knowing full well that she doesn't come by the field to watch football or cricket, he said, "Did you see the match this afternoon? We beat Drifters three-one?"

She didn't answer.

"You should have been there, this was one of the best matches in the history of Vieux Fort football."

"Mister, I don't have time for things of the world."

"How come, when God Himself said that man should not live by bread alone, which if you change it around means that man needs bread to live, and if you generalize the meaning of bread, it would include recreation and entertainment, because all of that is part of healthy living, help relax the mind and reduce stress."

Eunice chuckled. "Mister, leave the name of the Lord out of your nonsense. The Almighty doesn't take kindly to blasphemy. Be careful He don't strike you dead."

"So can I come and chat with you some more about God and the Bible?"

"No, you cannot. I don't have time."

"But I does see you going around giving Bible lessons."

"Mister, I does be on the Lord's mission. And I don't invite people I don't know to my home."

"So you mean to tell me you don't know me?" He said jokingly.

But sure she knew him. Everybody in Vieux Fort, from the youngest child to the oldest grandmother, knew him. He was Vieux Fort's darling boy, its brightest star. He was the best footballer in Vieux Fort, the best batsman Vieux Fort had ever produced, and in the opinion of many Vieux Fortians he was by far St. Lucia's best cricketer: by far its best batsman and one of its three top pacers. Each year the selectors in Castries would call him up for national cricket and football trials, but each year Vieux Fort would be disappointed. A man who in their eyes should be on no less a team than the West Indies cricket team was being told he wasn't good enough to make the national team. The once or twice he made the cricket team he didn't bowl a ball nor score a run, for he was selected as an extra, to warm-up the bench, to substitute in the field, or to be the "moose boy" of the team; and, in the eyes of Vieux Fortians, to appease them, to avoid Vieux Fortians stoning Castries teams when they came down to Vieux Fort to compete. So each year Vieux Fort would be in uproar. "Castries people think Castries is St. Lucia."

Still, say she wasn't a sports fan, which she wasn't, she couldn't have missed the fact that he was a teacher at the RC Boys' School. A post he had held since the age of fourteen, making him the youngest person ever to have taught at that school. And who in the town wasn't certain that on account of his talent and teaching performance he would become the next headmaster? Of course, what the town may not have known and what Eunice certainly didn't know was that the headmaster held a grudge against Ruben. So, no matter how deserving, he would never become headmaster.

At eight Ruben had wanted to join the Roman Catholic Church's youth choir and learn to play the piano. The headmaster was not only a leading member of the church but he was the choir leader and music instructor. Learning of Ruben's interest, he invited Ruben to his home for private lessons. Upon Ruben's arrival the headmaster fed him Shirley biscuits and Ju-C, and then sat him down to the business of learning music. Ruben's eyes were focused intently and innocently on the smooth, well manicured fingers of the headmaster as they caressed black and white piano keys, when he felt a hand slipping into his pants and then fondling his privates. Shocked, without thinking of consequences and definitely without looking at the headmaster, Ruben yanked out the hand as if it were a snake about to strike him and ran out of the house and all the way home. When he got home and told his mother the best way he could about the hand that slipped where it didn't belong — "Mama, the school master touch my *kòkòlòk*" — he received his second surprise of the day. For his mother said, "Boy, what kind of *papicho* you telling me? I send you to school to learn something, and you coming in front me with *papicho*. And your father eh even feeding you. I giving you one slap behind your head."

Now, it wasn't that Ruben had never heard of the headmaster's mischievousness with boys. Some of the boys attending school and those no longer at school were not exactly shying away from laughing and joking that music lessons, arithmetic lessons, Ju-C, coconut jam, guava jam, turnovers, Shirley biscuits, *lababad*, and shillings and pence weren't the only things the headmaster was giving. But it was one thing for others to talk laughingly and jokingly about it, but a whole different story when you find the same hand that was supposed to be teaching you music notes and putting sums on the blackboard, slipping in your pants as if this were all part of the package, as if this were yet another lesson to be taught and learned. Besides, it was difficult to look at the headmaster and see any evil in him. He wasn't a big, tall, intimidating man with a fierce face or satanic eyes. On the contrary. He was a short man with rounded features, soft and inviting eyes, and a cherubic face. So in spite of the talk about the man's naughtiness, Ruben was taken completely off guard.

The headmaster, on the other hand, would not forgive nor forget. On meeting Ruben his cherubic face and soft eyes would suddenly turn sour and baleful. If the headmaster had had his wish, he would have forced Ruben to repeat standards (grades), or worse expel him. But Ruben's brightness was legendary. Although he was in an educational system where it seemed the whole purpose of exams was to fail students and not to test their knowledge, no matter the subject it was a rare event when Ruben scored less than a hundred on an exam. Teachers unabashedly admitted that Ruben was the smartest student ever to have graced their school. These same teachers, having heard repeatedly from their mothers and grandmothers that fruits don't fall far from their tree, and growing up having been inundated with sayings like: *was sé moun sa la modi*, these people's lineage is cursed; *sé kon sa was sé moun sa la yé*, this is how these people's lineage is; and *sé moun sa la sòti was entélijan*, these people come from an intelligent lineage; would shake their heads wondering where the boy got his brains from. Ruben couldn't blame them for their puzzlement. It couldn't be said that he had inherited his gifts from his father, for his father was illiterate and wasn't around his children to encourage them in the way of education. Neither could it be said that he had inherited his gifts from his mother, for she wasn't any better educated than his father, and scrounging around keeping starvation at bay she had neither time nor inclination to foster education on her children. It couldn't be said that his home and community environment was what gave rise to his gifts. On the contrary, with a two bedroom shack devoid of books, but housing eight people, not counting frequent and changing overnight masculine guests, his home couldn't pass as a haven for such nurturing. Nor could his community, because in this regard there was little to choose between his home and those of his neighbors. The teachers may have been tempted to point to his early association with Father Pierre and the Roman Catholic Church. But that would be putting the egg before the chicken, the cart before the horse, rain before clouds, or fire before lightning, because it was in recognition of his gifts that Father Pierre had taken him under his wing and given him access to a feast of books. It seemed that at four, with very little input from anyone, Ruben simply picked up a book and started to read and never bothered to put the book down.

It was much easier to explain how he became a sports figure. Because for the longest while Vieux Fort with its abundance of flat, grass-covered, rolling land ideal for playing fields, had been a hotbed of sports. Vieux Fortians may have been landless, but they could always find a flat, grass-covered piece of ground for playing ball. So in terms of sports, Ruben, though more talented than most who came before him and most who would come after him, was coming from a long line of excellent athletes. Thus, while his mental prowess remained a mystery, his athletic powers could somewhat be explained.

The headmaster couldn't expel nor force the pride and joy of the school to repeat grades without drawing undue attention to himself. Instead, what happened was that Ruben devoured his lessons so ferociously that teachers had him skipping grades. So by the age of twelve he had completed standard six, the highest primary school grade. At the time there were only two secondary schools on the island, St. Joseph's Convent (an all girls' school) and St. Mary's College (an all boys' school), both of which were in Castries, two hours drive away. In those days to attend secondary school one either had to have well-to-do parents, or a godfather pulling strings; and it didn't hurt if one were clothed with light skin, "fair skin," and hair that was at least halfway straight, "nice hair." Ruben had neither. His skin was undeniably black and his hair was anything but straight. His father barely knew of his existence, and with eight children of eight different fathers his mother was of no greater help. Besides, even if he had been admitted to St. Mary's College, how could he attend? With transportation as it was, traveling to Castries everyday was out of the question. But where in Castries could he stay? For Ruben to have attended St. Mary's College, the headmaster or someone of similar clout would have had to play a big hand. But having had his hand rudely pulled out from where it had no business in the first place, the headmaster refused to lift the hand that would have helped Ruben fulfill his academic potential. Too young to leave school, Ruben repeated standard six twice, during which time he functioned as an unpaid substitute teacher. At the end of Ruben's second year in standard six, three teachers retired. Desperate to fill the positions, the headmaster had little choice but to hire Ruben.

Ruben didn't attend secondary school, but he made the best use of what he had received. Under his coaching the Vieux Fort RC Boys' School became legendary. Year after year, in both cricket and football, they walked over the rest of the primary schools on the island. In time when the national team became more receptive to players from the out districts, his protégées would go on to dominate the national football team.

But sports were by no means the only sphere of Ruben's activities. He was one of the leading actors in the three or four plays that Father Pierre staged each year. The church and the Town Board depended heavily on him to help organize, among other things, bazaars, talent shows, carnival and calypso competitions, and queen shows. Forever with a newspaper in his back pocket or in his shirt pocket (when he was wearing a shirt jac) and a transistor radio glued to his ears (listening more often than not to the BBC), Ruben was Vieux Fort's information bank, its research officer, its news reporter, its access to what was happening in the outside world.

For example, he was the most reliable source of West Indian cricket scores and records. He was the first to bring news of a West Indian or African territory fighting for its independence or about to become independent, or news of civil wars, tribal wars and whatever other wars going on in the world. He was the one who would educate people (at least those who were interested in such things) on the racial revolts in England and the Black Panther, Black Power and Civil Rights movements in America.

Added to that Ruben was a prolific writer. His articles appeared regularly in *The Voice* of St. Lucia, and through the years he would craft calypsos for several Vieux Fort calypsonians, some of whom would go all the way to winning the crown. Through his association with Father Pierre, Ruben developed a love and passion for history. He read world history, Caribbean history, and he relished the few books on St. Lucian history that Father Pierre had collected during his European travels. It was as if unable to satisfy its intellectual cravings via higher education, Ruben's mind munched on whatever it could find.

Given all these engagements, even a reclusive Adventist like Eunice would have known Ruben.

Nonetheless, smitten on a Wednesday night in August, Ruben, the pride and joy of Vieux Fort, set about making sure the *Semdays* woman with the four year old boy really got to know him. He told her about himself, his teaching, his football and cricket exploits, and so on, as if she didn't already know. When they arrived at the church, he said, "Goodbye my darling." Her son who up till then was in search of a father answered, "Bye-bye, Mr. Ruben." But she never answered, nor did she bother to turn her head and acknowledge his departure. After all, she did not know him.

That night when Ruben joined his friends at the steps of Damascus Guest House, they laughed and made fun of him. "*Gason*, don't tell me you after that frigid, holier-than-thou *Semdays* woman who already has a child and who could be your mother. I keep warning you. Leave these old women alone."

He laughed with them but his mind was on how was he going to get this *Semdays* woman? It was true, though. He liked older women. But it wasn't just that. Both physically and mentally he had always been more advanced than his peers. He found boys his age and younger silly, immature, boring. So growing up he was always hanging out with boys five, six years older than himself. Even so, in cricket and football he was in the strange situation of being so much better than everybody else that not even those older boys provided him with serious competition. Similarly, he found older women to be more attractive, more interesting, and better able to keep his attention. The problem he usually faced with this peculiarity of his was that oftentimes the older women distrusted his motives; they were leery of a man who, as they saw it, could get any woman he wanted, yet was coming after them. They refused to believe that his interest was genuine beyond getting them in bed. And the few who were inclined to take him at his word were convinced something was seriously wrong with him.

The next time Ruben met Eunice and tried to hold conversation, she said, "Mister, what's your problem? Why you keep troubling me? Don't you see I'm older than you? Didn't your mother teach you manners?"

He said, "No, it's just that I want to spend some time with you and get to know you better."

"Well, mister, I don't want to know you, so leave me alone."

He kept talking but Eunice walked on as if he didn't exist, and for months when he came chatting her, she wouldn't look at him nor say a word to him. Soon he began to wonder whether he was wasting his time. Maybe he should leave this *Semdays* woman alone. What did his mother use to say? "What sense does it make throwing stones at the sun?" But at nights he had a difficult time sleeping. The woman was on his mind.

It wasn't until over a year after Eunice had first caught his fancy, on that Wednesday night in August, that he made a small breakthrough when one Sunday night he caught up with her on her way to service. This time, before he said a word, she said, "I see, you can't stop troubling me. Then maybe you can do something for the Lord. It's

Ingathering month. We're collecting money for the needy. Give something to the Lord."

He said that he didn't have money on him, but he would make a donation next time they met. But he didn't wait for a chance meeting. He went to her home. Upon his arrival, before she could open her mouth in rebuke, he told her he came to give her his ingathering. This did the trick. She offered him lime juice, and while he drank it the transformation from the aloof, leave-me-alone woman to the engaging campaigner for the Lord that Vieux Fortians had often noted when she arrived at their doorsteps, Bible in hand, materialized. She said, "Mr. Ruben, the Lord needs you. It's time you leave the world behind and come serve Him."

This was one of the things that irked Ruben about Adventist and the other Protestant denominations. They were insulting Roman Catholics at every turn. According to them Catholics were heathens, abominators, worshippers of idols. They bear the mark of the beast. Surely, if they didn't repent of their evil ways and be baptized, they would go straight to hell. To Ruben it seemed the whole mission, the whole existence of what he considered these bastardized protestant denominations was to convert Roman Catholics to their faith. And the irony was that everyone of them preached that the only way to heaven was through their brand of gospel, and all others were false prophets, devils dressed in white robes. All this when the Roman Catholic Church was the first Christian Church, the one established by Christ Himself. True the Catholic Church had plenty of members who were Christians only in name. But the same could be said of all other churches. And what about all the pious, dedicated Roman Catholics? Nonetheless, Ruben saw an avenue whereby he could continue seeing this *Semdays* woman. Whatever she said he shouldn't take her too seriously.

He said, "But Eunice, I already have a church. I was born and raised in the Catholic Church, so was my father and mother. Why should I leave my Church? One is as good as the other. All preach the same thing. All are serving the same God. The important thing is to belong to one."

"Wrong. We don't preach the same thing. You all don't keep the Sabbath. You all worship idols. You all fornicate. You all go to dance, drink rum and smoke cigarettes. You all eat any number of unclean things. Pork, *bouden, souse, mashwen, chadon.* You want me to continue?" She stopped and stared at him, her eyes burning with the spirit.

He smiled and said, "But Eunice, what's wrong with a little vice? Once both the man and woman are willing, what's wrong with that?"

Her spiritual fervor changed to anger. "Mister, I eh in your *papicho.* Leave my yard, because I eh standing around and listen to people blaspheme against God."

He said, "I'm sorry. I was just joking. Of course the Bible is against fornication. I'll come to church next week to learn more about God."

And so their relationship germinated from a rat-bitten seed to a seedling, to a thriving sapling, and several months back to a full grown tree when one early evening, after sharing her supper, on his way out he held her hands and kissed her and she had not resisted immediately and when she did it wasn't to express disgust or that he had insulted her but to tell him with a hint of regret that she was an Adventist, she could not marry a nonbeliever, she would not be unequally yoked, so friends were all they could ever be. From that time onwards their conversation was increasingly laced with an undercurrent of unmet desire. She was wrong. The tree was on the verge of blossoming. They had become not just friends but lovers. The only thing was that the love-making was taking place only in their dreams and daytime fantasies. He tried his best to shift their love-making from the realm of magic, dreams and fantasy to reality; from a tree about to blossom to one laden with ripening fruit.

One Saturday he had accompanied Eunice and her son to Sabbath service. After service, they walked home with the boy in between them holding their hands. Despite the long service and her empty stomach, Eunice glowed with the spirit. Watching her, a thought, an epiphany, flashed through Ruben's mind: they were a celestial family. So seizing the moment he said, "Eunice, I love you with all my heart, lets get married."

She said, "Ruben, I like you too. But as I told you before, I can not, I will not be unequally yoked."

Her son, afraid of missing an opportunity to get a father for real, came to Ruben's aid. "Mama, why don't we leave *Semdays* and join Catholic, so you can marry Mr. Ruben, I will have a father and you will have a husband?"

Instantly Eunice's spiritual glow gave way to anger. She said, "Boy, if you see today wasn't Sabbath, I would give you one slap behind your head, that would make you hear and understand. And when you hear big people talking, keep your mouth shut."

Lying there in bed waiting impatiently for day to open its eyes, Ruben smiled as he thought of that Saturday, the way his beloved had changed so suddenly from a glowing celestial being into a wrathful defender of her faith. But his smile quickly disappeared with the memory of the first and only altercation he had had with Eugene, when the stall keeper had brought up talk that amounted to the soiling of Eunice's name. Ruben and Eugene were well acquainted with each other and knew of each other's history going back to their parents. But they weren't exactly friends, for they had little in common. Ruben's life was centered around school, sports and the Roman Catholic Church. Eugene, on the other hand, was the antithesis of a sportsman, he could barely read and write, and as he often said, "Me and religion don't mix." Nonetheless, during the mango season Ruben's love of mango julies brought him in almost daily contact with Eugene. For whatever the basis of comparison—taste, size, texture, or rosiness—Eugene's mango julies were far superior than those of his competitors. So Ruben obtained his supply of mango julies from no one else but Eugene.

One afternoon when Ruben came buying mango julies, Eugene said, "Eh-eh, Ruben, you eh hear what they saying? They saying you is the *Semdays* woman's child father."

Ruben said, "Eugene, I just come here to buy mangoes, not to listen to what Vieux Fortians have to say."

"But they say the boy calling you father?"

Despite his great annoyance, Ruben was forced to laugh. "Eugene, I'm surprised at you. No one knows better than you how malicious and *malpalan* Vieux Fortians are. They know damn well that even before the boy knew himself he used to go around asking men if they were his father. That's if he hasn't asked you that. After all, the boy can't stop watching you and does everything he can to be near you."

Now it was Eugene's turn to laugh, only his laugh was womanish, louder and lasted longer. "Ruben, you joking. Look at me, you think any boy would mistake me for his father?"

Ruben said, "Frankly, I don't care what people say about me. They can all go to hell for all I care. But they must leave the name of the woman alone. They know damn well this isn't a woman in slackness."

"O.K., but where there is smoke, there is fire. People also saying you and the *Semdays* getting married. That true?"

"That's not your damn business," said Ruben and he walked off.

Afterwards, the more Ruben thought about his bout with Eugene the angrier he became. Because what Vieux Fortians were implying was that Eunice had been sleeping around with him while her husband was alive. This he couldn't take, people thinking that this pious, this virtuous woman, who at the drop of a coin would turn into an avenging tigress in defense of her faith, could have ever cheated on her husband. Ruben stayed several weeks away from the stall keeper, suffering inferior mangoes from other vendors, until one day he was walking up Clarke Street, his head straight ahead to make sure his eyes never wavered in the direction of where Eugene sat behind his stalls, when Eugene shouted, "Ruben, I have plenty nice mango julies, you don't want any?" Ruben's love of mango julies combined with the apologetic, pleading voice of the stall keeper made him succumb. So that very day he abandoned his embargo and returned to feasting on the best mango julies to be had in Vieux Fort. But never again was Eugene to bring up any topic with him about Eunice.

There were other memories that Ruben would rather forget on this his morning of momentous decision. He squirmed in shame as he recalled the string of loose women, all several years older than him, he had slept with in an attempt to get Eunice off his mind when it appeared that he was never to claim her as his. Sex with these women had been anything but satisfying. Instead of making him forget Eunice, it had made him appreciate and desire her even more. After each such encounter he felt vile and guilty of having sullied the woman he wished to be his wife.

All this was history now. It didn't matter what Vieux Fortians or anyone else thinks. His mind was made up. He will wait no longer. The tree will bear fruit. He will not follow in the footsteps of his father. He will not end up like him: old, sick, alone in a hut, and with children scattered all over the place. What was his father's excuse for this pitiful ending? He was illiterate, yes, but his industriousness had more than made up for that. He went to sea, he cut *bois campèche* to make coals and to sell to bakeries, he made fishnets out of bamboo and *tibonm* sticks for himself and to sell to other fishermen. They say Vieux Fortians are lazy, but who could have outworked his father? Hard work that had not gone unrewarded. His hands were always in money, but he was the biggest fool Vieux Fort had ever seen. He squandered his money on prostitutes, card games, cockfights, rum for the crowd, cookouts where the pots were often too small to hold the whole pig or goat he had slaughtered, on *gadès* to ensure that the sea rewarded him bountifully and for protection against the harm those jealous of him might send his way. The fool swam in his own ignorance, making Vieux Fortians change his name from Stephen to *Labondans*, squanderer. The most wicked thing of all was that while the fool was wasting his money on strangers, his several sets of children, fifteen in all, and their mothers were going to bed hungry. The man throwing away money and with children scattered all over the place, died alone in the one-room shack that he had built on land belonging to the Anglican Church with the first set of big money he had earned as a young man of twenty. The same shack that had made most Vieux Fortians think of him as a very progressive young man, building his own home at an age when most boys were still living with their parents. Funny thing, thought Ruben, attitudes and indiscretions that pronounce a child cute and endearing, may render an adult shameful and unmannerly. So the shack that as a young man had made his father seem ingenious and ahead of his time, in his old age provided yet another example of a man who, in the eyes of Vieux Fortians, had *mal twavai*, worked badly.

No. He wasn't going to end up as his father. And he surely wasn't going to put any woman through the hell his mother had gone through keeping himself and his seven half brothers and half sisters alive. If not for the Americans and Father Pierre and the Roman Catholic Church, he might not be alive today.

No. From a little boy he had made up his mind that he would marry and have three children with his wife. And these were all the children he would ever have. And he would stay with his wife forever, and take care of her and his children. He had found the woman whom he wanted to marry, have those children with, and live with until death interfered. True, he hadn't bargained that she would be a *Semdays* and that she would be well in her thirties and with a child already. But life wasn't perfect. It was all about give and take. He will join her church. Since she already has a child, they will plan on having just two. In a way this wouldn't even be a compromise. After all, he was already thinking of the boy as his son, and the boy was already call-ing him Daddy, that is before his mother had put a stop to that. In return for whatever compromise he had made, he will gain a beautiful, principled woman, the love of his life, a woman with whom there will be no need to worry about *ki les ka jwé an pla'y*, who was playing in his plate.

Not bad, not bad at all. Yes, as soon as the sun unburied itself from under the Atlantic Ocean, he will visit her, unveil his decision, then they will start making wedding plans.

SINCE WRITING THE AMERICANS, Henry waited impatiently for their return. Meantime his interest in what they left behind gathered momentum. It was as if he were seeing the *kai planes* , the dock, the jetty, Beanefield Airport, and the lighthouse for the first time. These to him were fire-proof evidence that the Americans were once here, evidence of World War II, evidence of the goodness and greatness of the Americans, evidence that as sure as he knew he was Henry they would return.

But Henry had a problem. His mother's tight rein denied him easy access to these American legacies. He saw the dock only when he went to New Dock Beach with his mother, but she would not allow him to walk on the dock alone, and she herself rarely ventured on it. Henry saw the *kai planes* from a distance, on his way to and from church. In fact the jetty, which sat right next to the fishing depot and which Henry had mistakenly attributed to the Americans, was one of the few American wonders (in his mind) that, on account of his fish-buying errands, he had easy access to. Yet his mother had forbidden him ever to go on the jetty.

That was soon to change because Henry's wonderment of the Americans boiled over to the point of surmounting his fear of the rod. When he went to buy fish, he ventured out on the jetty and was quick to find out that walking the wooden pier wasn't the piece of sugar cake he had imagined. There were cracks between the planks and it seemed that with any misstep down through the cracks he would fall. So Henry walked the jetty with his head down, his eyes glued to the cracks that seemingly spelt his doom. With great abandon boys his age and younger ran up and down the pier and took dives off it, yet every step Henry took was like an eternity. This was one piece of construction for which he wasn't singing praises to the Americans. In time Henry learned to breeze down the jetty, but at first walking on it seemed a life and death proposition.

Emboldened by his jetty escapade, Henry came up with a bright idea. Why not *mawon lékòl*, run away from school, and go and explore the *kai planes*? He shared his plan with Ralph to whom the *kai planes* held little appeal for he was not as intrigued as Henry about the Americans and he went to the *kai planes* often and at will. His family reared pigs under the bush in the *kai planes*, so twice a day they went there to feed the pigs *manjé kochon*, pig food—boiled green bananas and leftover meals. And during kite season Ralph and his brothers, using the top of the *kai planes* as launching pads, spent whole afternoons there flying kites. Besides, unlike Henry, Ralph had freedom. Once he didn't stay out for more than half a day at a time, he was more or less free to go on the field to play ball, or on the dock and the jetty to swim, or even as far as Enbakoko Beach. And often he would tag along his older brothers to such far-off places as Bwa Chadon along Vieux Fort's Atlantic coast, and L'anse Bayson and Enbakoko Dan on the Caribbean coast. So what did it for Ralph wasn't the *kai planes* but the *mawon lékòl*. School was a plus for Henry because it was a means of feeding his unquenchable curiosity and an opportunity to venture out of the house without a beating waiting for him when he returned. Ralph, on the other hand, saw school as a nuisance and welcomed any opportunity to *mawon lékòl*.

The day of the *kai planes*, after lunch, instead of returning to school Ralph and Henry cut across the Mangue and New Dock Road. Once on the pasture on which sat the *kai planes*, dodging sheep, goats, cows, horses and pigs feeding on the pasture, Henry broke into a run, his crooked arm swinging wildly. Taking up the challenge, Ralph followed him. The boys raced to one of the *kai planes*. As they approached, a flock of black birds feeding on the fruits of the gum trees (inside the *kai plane*) and the seeds and worms in the waste of the pigs (housed under the gum trees), took flight. Anticipating lunch, a colony of pigs raised a cacophony.

Inside the *kai plane* a paved road was visible under the bush. Unmindful of the overpowering stench of the pig pen, Henry said, "Ralph, it's true, it's true! Look at this airport under the bush! It's here the Americans used to hide their planes from the Japs and Germans." Without waiting for a reply, Henry scrambled to the top of the *kai plane*. From up there the pasture, dotted with grazing animals, spread out around him. But the pasture wasn't a farm. Many of the town's residents owned some livestock and since most of the plain was government land, all were free to graze their animals. These animals were a blessing to their owners. When times were hard they had the animals to fall back on, or on feasting occasions such as Christmas and weddings they need not wander far for meat.

Sometimes these animals served higher purposes. There was this man with a few cows and sheep but otherwise poor. His daughter had by a thin margin failed her secondary school entrance exams. Desperate, but realizing there was still hope, the father, like Abel, brought the headmaster a gift of several sheep. And like God, the headmaster accepted his gift and admitted his daughter. Among his ten children this daughter was the only one to receive a secondary school education.

West of Henry, beyond the pasture, was the Mangue; beyond the Mangue was Clarke Street and the main part of Vieux Fort town, beyond which was the Bacadere and Enbakoko Dan; to the east was Enbakoko Gui and the Atlantic Ocean; to the South: Moule-a-Chique, New Dock Hill, and the Caribbean Sea; to the North the "Base," or Beanefield Airport. Facing the hill rising above Walcott Lane, Henry looked towards his home. There it was: the red and green house. He then shifted his attention to the lighthouse. It stood on the highest point on Moule-a-Chique, the tallest peak in the Vieux Fort area. The lighthouse seemed to wave at Henry, and at this moment he would have given anything to get up there.

The boys scampered from one *kai plane* to the next, each an exact replica of the other. At the third one Henry said, "I want to pooh."

"Me too," said Ralph.

As they stooped to relieve themselves, anticipating a treat, a sow surrounded by seven piglets and partially concealed behind a low-lying tree branch drew closer and waited. No sooner had they pulled up their pants and moved away, the sow pounced on their feces. Henry said, "Mama! That pig really greedy. That's why pig not good to eat."

"Eh we does eat pig," said Ralph.

"The Bible say don't eat pig. It too nasty."

"Shut up, *Semdays one week, read the Bible upside down.* Pig is sweet."

"You shut up. You Katolik."

"*Bwa kochi*, I giving you one kick."

The two boys got into a shoving match, then in the distance they heard the faint sound of the school bell signaling school was over for the day. Thoughts of a beating if he were to get home late made Henry forget about his religious beliefs.

He said, "School let go already. Let's hurry."

On the way home Henry couldn't stop talking about the Americans, the *kai planes*, the airport, the dock, the lighthouse, the radar systems. Then another brilliant idea hit him. He asked Ralph, "You go to the lighthouse already?"

"If I go there? I go there a lot with my brothers," lied Ralph. His brothers had never taken him as far as the lighthouse. When he begged to go with them, they would tell him that he was too small.

Henry said, "You lying."

"No, I eh lying. It's true, I go there with my brothers all the time"

"Let's *mawon lékòl* and go there," said Henry.

"Yes, let's go Monday."

"Yes, Monday."

SAVE FOR INTERMITTENT PLATEAUS, it was a steep uphill climb to the lighthouse. Nevertheless, Monday, the boys skipped afternoon school and made their way up New Dock Road and onto the Moule-a-Chique road. It was an hour and fifteen minutes past noon and the unmerciful sun was shining directly upon them. Soon they were perspiring profusely. The road first swung right, keeping on the Caribbean side of the peninsula. At the first plateau they stopped for a breather. Ralph sat in the road and aimlessly threw stones at the bushes. Henry kept standing and looked upon the waters of the Caribbean. Several pairs of scissor birds were soaring across the sky. Out in the open sea, at the horizon, he could see a faint silhouette of the neighboring island of St. Vincent, twenty-one miles away. To his left was the L'anse Bayson Beach where his mother's church sometimes held beach picnics. To his immediate right was the dock, straddled by a large Geest banana boat. Further left, beyond the dock, was the jetty in the mouth of Vieux Fort town. Seconded between the dock and the jetty was the fish depot, a fleet of twenty or so fishing canoes sheltering under sheds fashioned out of coconut leaves and held up by wooden stakes. Brightly colored and with names like *In God We Trust*, *Praise The Lord*, and *Jehovah* the canoes were equal in beauty to the Caribbean Sea.

Suddenly Henry heard the whirring sound of an engine rising from the sea, and then he saw a fishing canoe speeding to shore. He shouted, "Ralph, look!" Ralph stood up and gazed at the canoe that was creating a splash and a trail of parted water behind it. As the canoe drew nearer, they could see that it was barely able to stay above water, a sure sign that it had a good catch.

Thanks to the richness and calmness of the Caribbean Sea, canoes such as the one Ralph and Henry were watching (equipped with outboard motors hugging their back-ends and manned with crews of two or three men) have made Vieux Fort the center of the island's fishing industry. Although fishing fleets repeat themselves at each coastal village or town, nowhere was the catch as bountiful as those adorning the seafront of Vieux Fort. People traveled as far as forty miles, from the northern end of the island, to buy fish in Vieux Fort. The richness of the surrounding waters, however, wasn't the only factor that explained the prominence of fishing in Vieux Fort. Back in the days of the Vieux Fort sugar factory, an unspoken but nonetheless binding agreement between factory supervisors and tradesmen seeking work was that upon employment the tradesmen would provide their supervisors with a female relative. Refusing to succumb to this kind of prostitution, many Vieux Fort men took to sea.

During the second half of the year, fish was so plentiful in Vieux Fort that sometimes due to a lack of refrigeration the fishermen would have to just about give the fish away. Even so, the fishermen didn't leave things to chance. In late June, at the beginning of the fishing season, they turned to none other than Saint Peter, the fisher of men. A few days before Saint Peter's Day, they dry-docked their canoes, turned them upside down, removed the old paint, sealed all cracks with flax and putty and aluminum sheets and then gave the boats a new coat of paint. Then on the Sunday closest to June 29, Saint Peter's Day, the fishermen in somber gray suits and their women in black dresses attended mass. After mass, the priest, armed with his Holy Bible, holy cross, holy water and acolytes, led a procession of fishermen and their families to the fleet of freshly painted canoes. Before mass the women would have placed freshly cut bouquets of bougainvillea, oleander and other flowers on the canoes' boughs. Sprinkling holy water on the canoes, the priest blessed the fishermen, the ocean, and their canoes and prayed for a season bountiful in fish but devoid of mishaps. After the dedication of the canoes the fishermen and their families offered themselves to Saint Peter by way of a lavish feast.

During the fishing season the fishermen might not need the priest's blessings for a bountiful harvest, but since the fishing season corresponded with the hurricane season, they definitely needed his blessings for a season devoid of mishaps. The Caribbean Sea can be deceiving. Sometimes, especially during the hurricane season, it behaved with as much fury as the Atlantic Ocean. It has claimed the lives of quite a few fishermen. Some disappeared never to be found; others washed ashore.

When Henry was twelve the Caribbean Sea would present him with one of the most traumatic events of his life. After an evening of partying, a sailor from a cement boat anchored some distance off the dock was taking a group of prostitutes back to port on a small lifeboat when, according to the sailor, the Caribbean suddenly got angry and the overcrowded lifeboat capsized. The sailor said that he tried his best to save the women, but the Caribbean had become too rough and there were too many women for him to cope with. In fact, he himself had barely survived the ordeal. All the women drowned. In the morning one of the women, white and bloated and completely naked, was washed ashore at the fishing depot for all to see. Henry was among the crowd that gathered to witness the spectacle. The prostitute was the same woman with the short shorts whose conversation with the stall keeper Henry had overheard at the standpipe five years before. Flora, Henry's neighbor and daughter of Girade, the man who was killed when he drank a poisoned shot of rum, was also among the women. But her body was never recovered. Staring at the washed-up, naked body of the prostitute gave Henry an inkling of the manner in which they had found his father. He cried off and on for the whole day, and for months he was unable to erase from his mind the picture of the dead prostitute.

The explanation of the sailor may have satisfied the authorities, but it didn't prevent Vieux Fortians from speculating. Some said the sailors wanted the women for next to nothing, and when they refused to offer themselves so cheaply, the sailors decided to throw them overboard.

Some others said that this was the doing of one of the older, over-the-hill prostitutes. Jealous of the earnings of the younger prostitutes, she had put obeah on them.

The boys followed the canoe all the way to the depot and then they continued on. The road swung left towards the Atlantic Ocean and then rose steeply. The mountain was clothed with a profusion of cactus, palm trees, *bois-campeche*, *bois d'orange*, *tibonm*, white cedar, gum trees, and other deciduous trees that were threatening to engulf the road. Some of these plants provided livelihood for many Vieux Fortians. The palm leaves, or *latannyé* as they were called, were plaited into brooms; the *bois-campeche* or log wood, though one of the hardest woods to chop, was prime wood for bakeries and for making charcoal; the *tibonm* was excellent for fencing.

The uphill climb was laborious. The boys' uniforms were soaked with perspiration. It was as if they had just jumped whole suit into the sea. Ralph said, "Let's go back, it too hot and I tired."

Henry said, "Eh-eh, it eh hot, is the sun that shining."

"*Semdays*, off course it's hot."

"It eh hot at all, it's hell that's hot."

"Shut up, *Semdays*."

Pointing to the bush, Henry said, "Look, mangoes!"

A short distance into the woods a mango tree burdened with ripening fruit rose above the vegetation. The boys hurried through the bush, saplings, twigs and branches slapping them in their faces, scratching their arms and legs and tearing at their shirts. The woods were filled with the scent of *tibonm* flowers. The call of ground-doves, hummingbirds and blackbirds crowded out the sound of the sea several hundred feet below.

But apparently birds weren't the only creatures that occupied the hill, for suddenly the woods became silent, and directly ahead of the boys stood a herd of sheep. The boys came to a standstill. They couldn't believe their eyes. They knew goats roamed the hills, but never would they have imagined that there were wild sheep under the bush. They had always associated horses, cows and sheep with pasture, not running wild under bushes. Dumfounded and hypnotized they held their breath and stood still, staring at the incomprehensible; the incomprehensible staring right back at them. Then in a flash, as if satisfied that this was enough suspense for a day, the herd disappeared, leaving the sound of their departing hooves as the only evidence by which the boys could convince themselves that they had not been dreaming, and indeed had come face to face with a herd of wild sheep. Henry said, "Wait when I tell my mother that!" And right away he knew that unless he wanted a serious beating, this was one experience he could never share with his mother. But all wasn't lost, because he said to himself, "Oh, I'll tell Eugene, I bet he doesn't know about these sheep." The boys feasted on mangoes, and what their bellies couldn't hold they put in their pockets.

Heavier now than when they started, they resumed their journey, for the moment forgetting about the heat or aborting the mission. They slowly climbed the hills and took a breather at each plateau. About two hours after commencing their journey, they found themselves at a plateau that offered an uncluttered view of not only Vieux Fort but all of its surroundings. They stood gazing at the landscape. A few hundred yards off the Atlantic shore stood the Maria Islets, home to the island's unique species of whiptail lizards, imortalized in *The Adventures of Lennie Zandoli* by Victor Marquis. A swim to these islets has tested the manhood of many a Vieux Fort youth. It was this swim that had led Raphael, Henry's father, to his death.

Patches of white spray, interrupting the blue of the Atlantic, were betraying its anger. The trade winds coming to the island by way of the Atlantic vexed the ocean. So in a timeless ritual, wave after wave drew water inward from the beach, gathered strength, height and rage, for the simple pleasure of splashing across the beach with the roar and fury of a lion, while the foam, the byproduct of the attack, simmered in the sand. Despite the fury the trade winds caused, in a land where the temperature rarely fell below 75 degrees Fahrenheit and often climbed above 90 degrees, and where residential air conditioning was nonexistent, the trade winds mixed with ocean salt blowing over Vieux Fort were a welcomed air conditioner.

The year before, Henry had visited Castries for the first time. He had been so excited about the trip that he was barely able to sleep the night before. At three-thirty in the morning, just when it seemed he was getting into deep sleep, his mother woke him to get ready to catch the Castries bus, which would leave no later than four-thirty. Henry fell asleep as soon as he got on the bus, and it had taken nothing less than the wintry chill of the Barré de l'Isle to get him out of his slumber. Two hours after he boarded the bus in Vieux Fort, he arrived in Castries sleepy and sickly. The capital fell far short of the thrill and enjoyment he had anticipated. Its heat, humidity, poor ventilation, and human and vehicular congestion had only added to his discomfort. His mother bought him cake and a Ju-C. Things he ordinarily relished. But he was barely able to chew and keep down the cake and soft drink. The happiest part of his stay in Castries was when he and his mother boarded the bus at one-thirty to head back to Vieux Fort. Yet he was even more miserable on the trip back than on the morning drive. The many twists and turns and ups and downs encountered on the way, the heat and crowdedness of the bus, and the mixed aroma of its cargo (sacks of sugar, flour, and barrels of salfish) brought him close to vomiting the cake and Ju-C he was barely able to swallow. Thanks to the trade winds, it was only on approaching Vieux Fort, when a sudden blast of Atlantic breeze slapped Henry in the face, forcing him to breathe the poignant aroma of seaweed and taste ocean salt, that he revived. Since that initial experience, Henry would always hate going to Castries, and no matter how far he traveled and to how many places he would interpret this in-your-face blast of salt-laden, Atlantic breeze as Vieux Fort's way of welcoming him home.

From the foot of Moule-a-Chique the beach stretched northward as far as their eyes could see. Though as one traveled along the beach its name changed from Enbakoko to Sandy Beach, to Lonely Tree, to Bois Shadon, to Boriel Beach and then to Aupicon, it was the longest uninterrupted sandy beach on the island. Bois Shadon, meaning sea egg forest, was a favorite picnic spot, especially for families with young children. They need not worry about their children drowning, for the water remained shallow far out to sea, barely reaching the waist of a six year old.

The mangrove swamp along the northern end of Vieux Fort's Atlantic beach and beyond was the largest on the island. This despite the fact that large portions of it were destroyed when the Americans drained some of the swamps and used others as shooting ranges and dumping grounds. Besides serving as an important fish hatchery, the mangrove forest continued to be an important source of firewood, and provided the raw material for charcoal, fish nets, fencing and the building of huts.

The Atlantic coast also boasted other useful vegetation. All along its border, sea-akee or "fat poke", sea-almond or *zanmann* and sea-grapes or *wézen* tangled, and in season provided a feast for those who cared to join. Further inland, colonies of coconut trees, some reaching the gods, announced the island's tropical status. The coconut grove called Enbakoko Gui held plenty of fear for Ralph and Henry and other Vieux Fort children, for it was notorious as a place where old Indian men kidnaped children for the Devil. Why Indian? was a question that never entered Henry's mind.

During the rainy season the Atlantic Beach and its accompanying vegetation were blanketed with the migratory *pitjwits* or sandpipers. Generations of sling-shot-carrying Vieux Fort boys have been a menace to the *pitjwits*. Yet year after year, like the turtles that spawn on the beaches of the isalnd, including Pointe Sable Beach, the *pitjwits* returned. Hunting these birds with sling shots was yet another pleasure Henry's mother was denying him.

To the left of the Atlantic coast, the boys could see the town and the plains of Vieux Fort interrupted only by the Vieux Fort River, Beanefield Airport, the *kai planes* and the hills of Derriere Morne, Morne Beausejour, and Mankotè or Beanefield Hill. Roughly four square miles, these plains made Vieux Fort one of the few stretches of land on this volcanic, mountain dominated island where one didn't feel suffocated by mountains and where one could look ahead for more than half a mile without one land mass or the other blocking one's view. At the northern end the plains gave way to the hills that formed the rural villages of Piero, Morne Cayenne, and Belvue. To the far west, near the village of Laborie, the land rose from the Caribbean Sea, first gently then steeply into Morne Le Blanc and then cut east across the landscape to give rise to Grace. Rising above and beyond Morne Le Blanc and the hills of Grace, Belvue, Morne Cayenne and Piero was a mountain range that appeared to be touching the clouds. West, beyond this mountain range, rose the twin peaks of Gros Piton and Petit Piton.

The boys were awed by the expansive scenery that lay before them. If they had been slightly older and had traveled to other lands, they would have no doubt proclaimed this land as beautiful. But having no basis for comparison, and not yet fully able to appreciate the majesty of what lay in front of them they simply looked on in silence.

The sound of an airplane approaching Beanefield airport from the Atlantic interrupted the silence and shifted the boys' gaze. They followed the airplane to the landing strip.

After the airplane landed, filled with the view, they moved on. At the foot of the last incline that would take them to the lighthouse, Henry saw a building partially hidden by bush. He said, "Ralph, look an American building, let's go see it before we go to the lighthouse."

The building once housed American radar equipment, but now it was gutted. Vieux Fortians had carried away all the lead, plumbing, ball bearings and everything else that they could make use of. Still, Henry was awed. This was more proof that the Americans were once here. He said, "*Gason*, you see all what the Americans did. They made the dock, the jetty, the airport, the lighthouse, St. Jude's Hospital, the secondary school, and everything. These Americans were really good."

"But they didn't make the Catholic Church, and the Health Center, and the Boys' School, though," said Ralph.

"*Gason*, what you talking about? That's nothing."

"*Semdays*, of course it's a lot. You don't know nothing."

"Stay there with your *maji*, nonsense. The Americans are coming back. Wait and see."

"You lying, "*Semdays*. Who told you that?"

"Of course they coming back. Just the other day I send them a letter asking them to come back and help Vieux Fort. Stay there, when they come I go be working for them."

"With your old *bwa kochi*?"

"I eh go even answer you, because is jealous you jealous."

The boys left the building and climbed the steep hill that led to the lighthouse. They arrived breathless, disturbing the sleep of the watchman. He stood up. Tall, slim, dressed all in khaki. Looking at their torn and soiled school uniform, he said, "What the hell you all doing here? Shouldn't you all be in school?"

"School let go already, mister," said Ralph.

Gaining full comprehension, the man laughed. "They send you all to school and you all *mawon lékòl* to come all the way up here. If I was your father, I would cut you all backsides."

Henry flinched. He said, "The mister, we just came to see the lighthouse the Americans make."

"Who told you the Americans build the lighthouse?"

"The mister, of course they make the lighthouse. They make the dock, the base, the hospital, the fire station, the secondary school, the jetty. They make everything in Vieux Fort."

"Boy, the Americans did a lot but they didn't build the jetty, and they surely didn't build the lighthouse."

"Then, the mister, who did?"

"The English, if I have to guess."

"You see, *Semdays*," said Ralph, "the Americans didn't make everything."

"Forget about who built it," said the watchman. "You are in it, you have seen it. Now hurry home before it gets dark and *jan gajé*, evil witches, come after you all."

"Can we walk around the lighthouse before we go?" asked Henry.

"Go ahead, but hurry."

They circled the lighthouse. From there they had a commanding view of both the Atlantic Ocean and the Caribbean Sea. Rugged cliffs dropped precipitously into the ocean. It was as if they were at the end of the world. And indeed they were at the end of the world called St. Lucia, for they were at the southernmost tip of the island. The heights and the precipices made them giddy. Henry looked up to gaze at the lighthouse's steeple. To him it appeared that the steeple's tip was in the clouds.

He said, "This must be taller than the tower of Babel. A little again and the lighthouse would touch heaven and God would make the Americans speak different tongues."

Ralph said, "*Semdays*, let's go before your mother beat you."

They said goodbye to the watchman and began their descent. It was already five-thirty. The sun had lost most of its heat and was already at the horizon preparing to bury itself beneath the Caribbean Sea. The boys were hungry so they made good use of the mangoes they were carrying in their pockets. The downhill trek was much easier and faster than the uphill, but they had far to go. As night approached the sound of crickets and frogs took over where the birds left off. In the distance Vieux Fort lighted the sky. The darker it got the more frightened the boys became.

Henry said, "I eh afraid of *jan gajé*, Jesus will protect me." But both boys jumped at every sound that rose from the bushes.

As if talking would keep evil away, Ralph began telling stories about the various evil beings — *jan gajé, maji nwè, ti boloms* — known to terrorize people. Stories that he had gotten from his mother. And once started he couldn't stop talking. Yet with each story, Henry, despite his faith in Jesus, grew more scared.

According to Ralph, his mother said that when her mother was a young girl she had to walk all of the five miles from Desruisseaux to Micoud to school. Now in those days few people had watches and clocks so they told time by roosters' crows. One morning his mother's grandmother mistook the cocks' crow to mean five-thirty instead of three-thirty, so she woke her daughter to begin the trek to school. On her way to school the daughter was a bit worried that she wasn't meeting any of her usual walking companions. But she said to herself maybe they were late. After walking for about half an hour, at the Desruisseaux Gap she met a very tall white man on a very big horse, the biggest horse she had ever seen. Yet the man was so tall his feet were dragging on the ground. Right away the daughter knew this was no white man but a *jan gajé*. Ralph said, "Run she run! Run she run! Until she reach the school house."

Ralph said that in the old days people used gold coins for money and they didn't bank their money. Instead they put their gold coins in clay jars that they buried under the ground. They did so particularly in times of war, when the British were fighting the French, to keep their money safe from soldiers. But oftentimes these people died before telling anyone where they had hidden their money. So sometimes the Devil gave people these hidden treasures in dreams. Ralph said that long before he was born his aunty, his mother's oldest sister, had a dream in which she was told that on Sunday at noon she must go under the golden apple tree next to the spring that sent cold water in the morning and hot water in the afternoon. Under that tree she will find a silver fork. Dig there and she will find a jar of gold, but when she goes for the money she must bring Ralph's mother with her. The aunty went for the money at noon on Sunday, but instead of bringing along Ralph's mother, she went with her husband. As they approached the golden apple tree, they heard a loud sound of something descending into the earth. They found the silver fork under the golden apple tree, they dug at the spot where they found the silver fork, but all they found were pieces of a broken clay jar.

Changing course, Ralph said, "Do you know who is the richest man in Vieux Fort?"

"Mr. Ramsipaul, of course."

"I bet you don't know how he get so rich," challenged Ralph.

"Of course I know. He was working for the Americans and he found a sac of gold in a cave the Americans discovered."

"*Semdays*, who told you that nonsense?"

"I hear the boat-boys talking about how Mr. Ramsipaul became rich. They say it was a French plantation owner who hid the money in the cave when England came fighting the French."

"No, stupid. It's the Devil that give it to him. They say Mr. Ramsipaul wanted to be rich so bad that he used to stay up all night thinking about how to get rich. Every night he took out his De Laurence and tried calling the Devil. But Mr. Ramsipaul English so bad the Devil doing as if he eh hearing him. Finally the Devil get fed up, he came when Mr. Ramsipaul called. But he vex. In a rough voice he asked Mr. Ramsipaul, 'Coolie, what the hell you want?' Mr. Ramsipaul say, 'Me wanta be rich. Me wanta be richest men in Vieux Fort. No, richest men in the whole status.' The Devil say to himself, 'Me eh bothering with that stupid coolie that can't even speak properly.' The Devil turned his back to go about his business. Mr. Ramsipaul say, 'Me gonna give all things you want, but please make me be rich.' The Devil asked, 'Anything?' 'Yes, Mr. Devil, me even be servant for life,' answered Mr. Ramsipaul. The Devil say to himself, 'Me eh want that coolie with his broken English to be my servant, hanging around me all day. But I go need a sacrifice.' The Devil tell Mr. Ramsipaul, 'At midnight, Friday next week, bring your brother to me at Enbakoko Gui, under the big *zanmann* tree, next to the burning coalpit.' Mr. Ramsipaul fell on his knees, and said 'Tank you, Devil. Tank you.' Mr. Ramsipaul went and see his brother bright and early in the morning. He tell his brother that he received money in a dream. The money was buried under the big *zanmann* tree, next to a burning coalpit at Enbakoko Gui. He said that they say he must go there midnight next week Friday to dig up the money. But when he comes for the money he must bring his younger brother. The brother glad he go get some money. Midnight Friday, with flambeaus, a pickaxe and a crowbar, they took off for Enbakoko Gui, under the big *zanmann* tree, next to the burning coalpit. When they reach, the Devil was there waiting. Mr. Ramsipaul say, 'Mr. Devil, me bring wah you ask for, now make rich.' When the brother hear that he pissed and pooped in his pants, and he took off running. But the devil was too fast for him. The Devil took him. After that Mr. Ramsipaul English got worse, but he became the richest man in Vieux Fort and I think in St. Lucia too."

"What did the Devil do with Mr. Ramsipaul's brother?" asked Henry.

"I don't know. Maybe he roast him in the coalpit."

"*Énben*, Mr. Ramsipaul really *méchansté*, wicked. God will surely *modi*, curse, him. In the Bible when God *modi* a man, He eh *modi-ing* just him, He does *modi* his wife, his children, his children's children, way down to the fourth and fifth generation. I go be rich. But I don't want nothing from the Devil. I'm going to work hard, obey God, and be rich like Job."

"*Semdays*, you always there with a *maji*. It's me that go be rich. I will be richer than Mr. Ramsipaul. When the Devil ask me what I giving him, I eh giving him no brother. I giving him a big fat pig. Pig sweet so I know the Devil go be happy."

For a while there the boys argued over who will get rich and by what means. Then Ralph went on to tell stories about coffins people found in the middle of the street in the middle of the night; *Ti boloms* calling people at night into the woods until they got lost; *jan gajé* entering people's homes as frogs, cats, and dogs for no other reason but to scare them.

Ralph told of a *jan gajé* that used to enter a house in Grace as a toad. The toad used to come and jump on the children's pillows. Each time the children would get up in the middle of the night screaming. One night, when the father had had enough of the *jan gajé*, he prepared a *fléwi*, a special spear used to *degajé* people and waited for the *jan gajé*. As soon as he heard the children's scream, he bolted to their bedroom and just in time to see the toad squeezing through a hole in the wall. He speared the toad, placed it in a bucket, threw kerosene on it, and set it on fire. Next morning the story spread throughout the country of a woman found in bed, burnt all over, a hole in the middle of her chest. They said that all morning, before the woman died, she *depalé*, confessing all the wickedness she had committed as a *jan gajé*, including turning into a toad and scaring children. The children's father had *degajé* the *jan gajé*, unwitched the witch.

On and on Ralph's stories went. Finally, Henry said, "Let's pray." The boys closed one eye for prayer and kept the other on the lookout for *jan gajé*. Henry said, "Lord Jesus, protect us from evil, from *jan gajés, maji nwès*, and *ti boloms*. Amen."

Despite Henry's prayer, when the boys heard a noise in the bush close to where they had got the mangoes, they burst into a run. And when they reached *fant kayè*, a rock crevice fifty yards from the junction of New Dock Road and Walcott Lane, known as a cesspool of all manner of evildoers, their terror reached new heights and their feet took wings.

MEANTIME, with a belt clutched in her hands, Eunice waited for her son to come home. Earlier, she had spoken to Henry's teacher about his whereabouts. The teacher had informed her that Henry hadn't returned to class after lunch, and that Friday last week he hadn't returned after lunch either. Eunice went to see Ralph's mother. Ralph was missing too. Eunice saw the picture. Following bad company, her boy was skipping school. Several years before, when the boy was no older than three and a half years, he had given her the fright of her life when he walked all the way to the beach in search of his father. When the stranger who had found Henry fast asleep on the beach brought him home, Eunice was so relieved that it had never occurred to her to spank the pitiful boy. But not this time. Not anymore. This nonsense has to stop. What if something happened to him? What if he went swimming and he drowned, his body white and bloated washed ashore? What would she do? How could she live without her son? She had lost his father, would she lose him too? No. No. No. This nonsense has to stop and stop now. The Devil is at work. Spare the rod, spoil the child. This time around she would beat him with no less than the buckle end of the belt. It was time he heard and understood.

The Stall Keeper

When Henry appeared at the door with his shirt torn and stained with perspiration and mango juice, Eunice asked no questions and uttered not a word. She simply forced the head of the already sobbing boy between her thighs, and using the buckle end of the belt gave him such a beating that when she released him he ran round and round the house screaming. Then, exhausted, he came in sobbing and dropped lifelessly on the floor. Soon he was snoring loudly. Eunice picked him up and carried him to his bed. She removed his school uniform. The boy's buttocks was bruised and swollen. Sobbing, Eunice rubbed him with coconut oil and put on his pajamas. Still sobbing, she lay down besides him. Morning found her cuddled next to her son. She could not remember falling asleep.

This was the last time Henry would *mawon lékòl*. For he could stomach the tamarind whip and the tail end of the belt, but not the buckle end, not metal on flesh.

EUNICE'S TOMATO PLANTS had produced the biggest tomatoes she had ever grown. So much so that just about everyone who saw the tomatoes had asked her where she got the
seeds and that she should save some for them. Even Ruben
who had seen the tomato plants from seedlings was
impressed. Yet not only were the tomatoes huge, but the
yield was so bountiful that Eunice was already anticipating
that even after giving some to Ruben, some to her church
members and some to a few of her neighbors, there would
be plenty left to sell. So one could well imagine the shock
on Eunice's face when upon slicing some of the tomatoes
she discovered they were rotten. She sliced a few more at
random. All the tomatoes were blighted. And as if this
wasn't enough, the night following this discovery the toad
she had thrown salt on invaded her dreams. The toad's
eyes were the color of fire, and its bumpy back was oozing
yellow puss. It was the puss that made Eunice realize that
this was the same toad she had assaulted with salt, the one
that had transformed itself from a stone. Looking directly

at Eunice with its fiery eyes, the toad laughed at her and said, "*Mové ou kwè ou mové, mwen kai wanjé-ou;* bad you think you bad, I'll fix you." And suddenly all the tomatoes in her garden turned into carbon copies of the menacing toad and all the toads started laughing and their laughter became a deafening scream that roused Eunice from her sleep.

Eunice could not stop wondering how tomatoes so rosy and blemish-free on the outside were so rotten inside? And what's this business of toads laughing at and threatening her? When she told her neighbors about her beautiful yet rotten tomatoes, the toad she had attacked with salt, and how that toad had tormented her sleep, they told her this wasn't a toad at all but someone jealous of her garden who had come to make sure the tomatoes didn't amount to much. Eunice didn't believe, couldn't believe her neighbors. She didn't believe in this obeah nonsense. Besides, even if obeah worked, she had her God to protect her. So instead of believing them, she scolded herself for confiding in nonbelievers. Her church elder had a knack for interpreting dreams. She took her worries to him. He told her something or someone was going to give her a big disappointment. Her elder's interpretation of the dream was more believable than that of her neighbors, but it didn't explain her corrupted tomatoes, and it opened up a new set of worries. The disappointment couldn't be the rotten tomatoes, or else she would have had the dream before she discovered the rot. So who, what would disappoint her so badly that she had to be forewarned by a nightmare?

Eunice had to take her dreams seriously because they had a way of foretelling the future or changing the course of her life. The day before her ten year old cousin drowned in the River Dorée when he went there to catch crayfish, seven-year old Eunice had a dream in which she had an insatiable thirst for water. The more water she drank, the thirstier she got, until she had taken in so much water that her stomach exploded. In the morning when she related her dream to her father, Editon, he said that she was just thirsty, and that the next time she had such a dream she should get up and drink some water. But two days later when the lifeless body of her cousin was found swirling in the river basin, her parents had to take notice.

Her parents took further notice when she dreamt of miles upon miles of rope coiling around her until she completely disappeared and all what could be seen was a huge ball of rope, like a beetle entombed by a spider. And then the rope uncoiled with the speed and suddenness of lightning, and suddenly she was dangling by her legs at one end of the rope and when she looked up the other end was dipping into the clouds. The following day they found a Debreuil man hanging by the neck from a branch of a mango long tree in the middle of his farm. The story was that the man had left his wife and seven children to go and live with a *djabal*, a girlfriend on the side. The wife went to a *gadè* to "fix up" the husband. The *gadè* cast a spell on the *djabal* to cause her to have wandering eyes. The *gadè's* ploy worked so well that the man hanged himself after finding his *djabal* in bed with another man.

The dream that finally made Eunice's parents pronounce her special was the one that foretold the forty plus people who perished when the boat taking them from Castries to Soufriere capsized just outside Soufriere. Every night of the week preceding the tragedy, Eunice dreamt of a basin filled with loud screaming water. To stop the screaming, which was so loud that it threatened to burst her eardrums, Eunice tried to dump the water. She lifted the basin, turned it upside down over her head, yet the water stayed suspended in the basin, as if glued to it. No matter what else she did to and with the basin not one drop of water fell out, and the screaming continued unabated.

Before this dream and the event it foretold, Eunice's parents didn't know what to make of their daughter. She was so shy that even at nine years old on meeting strangers she was still hiding under her mother's skirt. Eunice wasn't only shy, she was ultra sensitive. If someone stared at her too long and too hard she would cry. If a stranger spoke to her, "Little girl, what's your name?" she would burst into tears. If her parents spoke to her too loudly or too fast or too angrily she would weep. But after the dream that foretold the boat disaster, when people said things like: "What happen to that child she so afraid of people?" or "*En ben bon,* you all spoil that child bad"; or "Eh-eh, that child *dèkdèk*", Teresa, Eunice's mother, would take it as a compliment, and with a proud, knowing smile would say, "Nothing wrong with her, she just special." And then these people would scrutinize Eunice more closely, and indeed they would see something different about the little girl, something they couldn't quite put a finger on, but something nonetheless, which said that whatever it was, good or evil, they were better off leaving that child alone. For in a time when coffins could be found unattended on roadsides in broad daylight; when *jan gajé, maji nwè, ti boloms, gadès, tjenbwatè* and *vyé lam* could make one wish for death; when not having a *gadè* to offer one protection against people with dirty hands was downright irresponsible; when poison could get into one's food or drink by the most unsuspecting of routes, one does well to leave alone, or, better yet, stay far away from what one didn't understand. After all, it was difficult to distinguish between what would bring good and what would bring evil. The same church where one went for confession and absolution and assurance of a seat in God's Kingdom was where people with dirty hands went to collect holy water to do evil. The most beautiful and unassuming woman from whom a man could derive so much pleasure was the very one who would put obeah on a man to make him go mad, *dèkdèk*, or send him to an early grave, or both. A man's best friend, the one whom he welcomed to his home without any reservation whatsoever, and who in turn would do any and everything for him, was the very friend who would turn *maji nwè* at nights, push the man off his own bed, and do whatever he pleased with his wife. And in the morning the unsuspecting wife would get up with only fatigue and scratches to tell that the night had brought mischief. The same Psalms the reading of which could elevate one to God and provide protection against evil, could be used for one's downfall. *Glo moun mò*, the water that was used to cleanse the dead ensuring they arrive in heaven sparkling clean, because after all cleanliness was next to godliness, was the most potent of ingredients people used to harm their enemies. And what could look more helpless and harmless than a baby? Yet it was the very thing — *ti bolom* — that someone could send one's way to do one in.

Eunice was special but nonetheless it bothered her parents that her dreams or visions were never clear or detailed enough to allow them or anyone else to take action to prevent whatever calamity the dream or vision was foretelling. It bothered her parents even more that her dreams were mostly about the foretelling of calamities. Why wasn't she receiving dreams that could profit them? Like where jars of gold coins were buried in the bowel of the earth? And how come she herself was never able to interpret her own dreams? Still, to Eunice's parents their daughter was special and they were willing to leave it at that.

Eunice's specialness was further unveiled when by the age of eight she revealed that she wanted to be a nun. It was a career aspiration no one could have guessed from the tantrum she threw upon her first close encounter with nuns. Yet the tantrum was by no means surprising, for given Eunice's shyness and fear of people it wasn't difficult to imagine the task Teresa had on her hands when time came for Eunice to attend the Roman Catholic elementary school at Choiseul where she would be in constant company of nuns. The first day of the school year that coincided with Eunice's fifth birthday, glad that at last she would get a break from this her last child who stuck under her feet everywhere she went, hindering her from doing her work (the child that came at the good and ripe age of forty, eight years since her last child, when she was convinced that her child bearing years were long over), Teresa heartily dressed her daughter and took her to school. On meeting the nuns Eunice buried herself underneath her mother's dress, and no amount of coaxing from the nuns or her mother could get her to come out. Finally, Teresa pulled Eunice out and gave her to the nuns, one of whom held Eunice's hand. By then Eunice was all in tears. As her mother turned around to return home, Eunice let out a scream that startled the nuns and caused the one holding on to her to slacken her grip. Eunice freed herself of the nun and raced after her mother. The nun, her robe and headgear under sail and her rosary swinging wildly, ran and grabbed Eunice. The girl screamed, scratched, jumped. The nun held on tight.

All day Eunice cried. The nuns tried to placate her with sweet biscuits, guava jam, a glass of powdered milk, but is cry Eunice crying. Eunice's river of tears and the unending stream of mucus from her nose made a mess of her dress. When Teresa came after school to pick up her daughter, the nuns were compelled to tell her that maybe her daughter wasn't quite ready for school. So Eunice stayed at home, glued to her mother, for another year. The following school year her mother tried again. The results were almost the same. All morning Eunice cried, but as she weakened, between involuntary sobs she began to take notice of the long, white, flowing robes of the nuns, the black rosary and the silver crucifix hanging round their necks, their high pitched voices that tickled something inside her, especially when they sang. Eunice's curiosity got the better of her. She took a vacation from her crying and misery to spend time contemplating the strange nuns, particularly the white ones. Angels was what came to her mind when she gazed upon them. Every morning that Eunice's mother dropped her at school she threw up a tantrum and then her fascination with the angels would take over. So it got to the point where she stopped crying altogether and started looking forward to school, not out of a quest for knowledge, or a desire to be with her little schoolmates, but to be in the presence of angels, who by then were so fascinated by how fascinated the little girl was with them that they had singled her out for special treatment. They sang to her just to watch the total contentment on her face, they gave her special treats of Shirley biscuits and candies, they let her finger their rosaries and sometimes even put them around her neck and delighted in the shy giggle that escaped the little girl who not too long ago couldn't stop crying. With all the nuns around, school began to offer Eunice a glimpse of how heaven must be, and their favoritism forced her to accept that indeed she was special. Before long Eunice harbored a secret. She wanted to be a nun. But not just any nun. A white nun. Because they were the ones who fascinated her more, they were the ones who conjured images of angels in heaven.

At thirteen, when everyone had accepted that Eunice was special and would become a nun, she had a dream. In that dream she was on her way to Sunday mass, but it was midnight. Just when she was asking herself why was it morning and yet it was midnight, she heard joyous singing and the praising of the Lord. Then suddenly she heard joyous singing and the praising of the Lord arising from behind her, in the opposite direction from where she was going. Soon a large crowd approached and bypassed her on their way to joining the joyous singing and the praising of God. The last person in the crowd to bypass her was a little girl no older than five. The girl was a spitting image of Eunice when she was that age. The girl was enveloped in a bright shining light, and she said to Eunice, "Follow me, you are going the wrong way." Weeks went by but the dream continued to bother Eunice. Which wrong way she was going?

About a month after Eunice's dream the Adventists from Soufriere came and held a crusade in Debreuil at a dancehall turned crusade hall. Night after night, in twos and in threes and in whole groups, people from Debreuil and beyond emerged from the foliage with kerosene lamps and flambeaus to guide their feet, and gathered at the dancehall turned crusade hall. A few came to hear what these people had to say but with no intention of taking them seriously, because, after all, they already had a Church—the Roman Catholic Church. That's where they were born, that's where they were christened, that's where they made their First Communion, that's where they were confirmed and where they were married, and that's where they would be buried. Just like their parents, their grandparents and their great-grandparents. Most however didn't even come to hear what the people had to say. They came for entertainment, a break from their early-to-bed routine. Back then in a place like Debreuil where by seven o'clock the place was clothed in an uninterrupted darkness so dark that the night turned blue, one might as well be in bed by six. So the Adventist crusade, the first of its kind in Debreuil, was indeed a treat.

Eunice was at home in bed when she first heard the Adventist singing and carrying on. Set on being a Roman Catholic nun she had no interest in other denominations. But she swore she had heard that singing before. She bolted from her bed. This was the same singing she had heard in her dream. She stayed awake listening to the enchanting voices, and long after the voices had gone home she remained in a half dream, half awake state of mind; the singing and the dream intertwining, making a torment of her sleep. The following evening Eunice was one of the first to appear at the dancehall turned crusade hall. After that first night there was no stopping her. She showed up every night and soon she started attending the Saturday church services. Towards the last few weeks of the crusade, night after night, at the end of his sermon, while church members hummed a song, the preacher appealed to his congregation to walk up the aisle and give their life to Christ. Come lay down all their cares and worries, and Christ would give them rest. Each night one or two of the congregation walked up and surrendered their lives to Christ, in the process eliciting a loud "Amen" and "Praise the Lord" from the Adventist congregation. The preacher then prayed, praising God for the souls won, and asking Him to keep them on the right path. Each night some force kept commanding Eunice to get up and give herself to the Lord, but she resisted the force for she was already a child of Christ, she was already consecrated, dedicated and rededicated to the Lord; she was already destined to be a nun. At eight, in angelic white, she had taken her First Communion and embarked on her rite of passage to Christ. At eleven, under the attentive eyes of the Bishop who had come all the way from Trinidad for the occasion, she received her confirmation, rededicating herself to the Church and vowing to be a soldier for Christ. Everyone — her parents, the nuns, the priest — had already accepted that she would be a nun. But the voice didn't care, it had no respect for nuns, priest or parents. It got stronger each night. "Follow me, you are going the wrong way. Walk up the aisle, surrender your life to Christ." Giving Eunice no respite, the voice accompanied her home and tormented her sleep. Soon the voice became a loud, unending drum beat. So loud and persistent that, nun or no nun, Eunice could take it no longer.

On the first day of the last week of the crusade she obeyed the voice, and in step with the drum beat walked to the front of the dancehall turned crusade hall and gave in to the yearning, pleading, beseeching voice of the preacher. As he prayed for Eunice a deep peace settled over her and she knew the meaning of her dream. God never meant for her to be a nun. She will not set foot in a Roman Catholic Church again. She will give up her Holy Mary's; the sign of the cross; the rosary (a gift from one of the nuns) with which she prayed no less than six times a day; her Saturday trips to the confession box to confess sins that not even the priest could make out as sins; all her saints — Saint Peter, Saint Paul, Saint Gabriel, Saint Joseph, Saint Dominic Savio, and her favorite, Saint Maria Goretti. She had come home.

Everyone was stunned by Eunice's conversion. No one, her parents especially, liked it one bit. Everyone had gotten used to and comfortable with the fact that she would be, could be nothing else but a nun. Yet no amount of quarreling, no amount of nagging could dissuade Eunice from her newly found path. She was home. So finally, bowing to what they couldn't understand, her parents accepted defeat and consoled themselves with: "Well, she is special, what do you expect?"

At school Eunice was no longer the nuns' special student. She who had wanted to be a nun was a traitor, a Satan in a fragile body. Hard looks, intolerance and inattention replaced the special treatment, the gifts, the confidences. Things came to a head when, during one of the catechism classes that the priest sometimes held, the shy, insecure Eunice, who seemed in a perpetual shell, suddenly shouted: "You eh my father, the only father I have is the one at home and the one in heaven." And just as suddenly the classroom became quiet. Not one student shifted. The priest was momentarily stunned. In those days the nuns, priests and the Roman Catholic church were angels, God, and the Kingdom of God on earth. The Church controlled an incredible amount of property and all the schools on the island were under their supervision. The population was over 95 percent Roman Catholic. Just a generation before, priests passing on horseback were known to horse-whip anyone, including grown men with woman and children, if they discerned that the said person hadn't greeted them with sufficient humility and subservience. Upon meeting a priest, grandmothers with heavy loads on their heads would fall down on their knees in homage. As a legacy of slavery, many couples simply shacked up as opposed to marrying. Looking down upon this practice, the priests would enter villages and compel all shacking couples to enter matrimony. So prominent was that practice, that the population named that period *temp misyon*, the time of the mission. So for any adult or child, much less the shiest, frailest and quietest child in a catechism class, to defy a Roman Catholic priest was unthinkable. Eunice herself could not explain her outburst, except that some hidden force that she didn't know existed in her, over which she had no control, had taken over. Later her Adventist brothers and sisters would inform her that the force was the Holy Spirit.

The priest was speechless, but not for long. He called Eunice to the front of the class, made her put out her hand and gave her six strokes of the school's leather belt. And he went on to belittle her, to condemn her, to tell her if she continued along this path she was destined to hell fire. The already shy Eunice cringed into a shell that no matter how tightly closed she held it, it wasn't tight enough to save her from shame and embarrassment. She continued sobbing long after the priest sent her back to her seat. After that day the nuns had nothing but contempt for Eunice. Her fellow students taunted her: "*Semdays, one week, read the Bible upside down.*" And "Burn, *Semdays,* burn!" The news traveled throughout the land. A little *Semdays* girl from a hole in Debreuil who probably still wets her bed had the audacity and irreverence to tell the priest he eh a Father. What is the world coming to? After a whole year of that Eunice refused to go to school. Once again, pronouncing her special and accepting that she was the one with the map, the one with the dreams, her parents gave in.

At fifteen, Eunice's path would change yet again when she received a dream in which on a Sunday morning she, her mother and her mother's younger sister were in the River Dorée doing their week's laundry when lo and behold a boy with the whitest set of teeth she had ever seen walked across from the other side of the river and offered her a basket full of mango julies. Two Sundays later, Eunice and her cousins where bathing in the same River Dorée when a boy came, as if from nowhere, and approached them. Topless, the girls scrambled to their clothes and shielded themselves. Unperturbed, the boy approached,

his smile revealing teeth so white they sparkled in the sunlight. The sparkling teeth jolted Eunice's memory to her
dream. Her heart missed a beat. This was the same boy in
her dream. He had on a *jarry*, a stained blue terelene shirt,
and stained khaki short pants. The very same clothes he
wore in the dream. Shocked to see her dream in daylight,
Eunice wasn't surprised when among the five girls frolick-
ing in the river, all about the same age and being cousins
all looking alike, she was the one whom the boy with the
whitest of teeth looked at, and, with a smile as broad as the
Troumassee River, said, "You look as fresh as a fresh vegetable. What's your name?" Embarrassment flooded
Eunice's face. But her cousins who forevermore would
change her name from Eunice to "Fresh Vegetable" pelted
squeals of laughter.

Eunice's embarrassment turned to anger. "Boy, you
crazy or what?"

"No, I eh crazy. This isn't the first time I see you washing
and bathing in the river. I keep saying to meself, who this
angel? Where she from? But you never was alone, so I was
afraid to come chat you. But today I say to meself, I just
have to talk to this angel."

The girls released another squeal of laughter.

Eunice said, "Boy, I eh no angel, and I'm definitely not a
fresh vegetable. So get lost with your craziness."

But rather than losing heart, the boy smiled because
vexed, the angel who was still trying desperately to protect her nakedness, lit up the river. Savoring the unexpected treat in front of him, his smile lingered as if to make sure
his whiter-than-white teeth didn't go unnoticed. And
indeed they didn't, because while he responded to Eunice's
rebuke with, "Oh, this was just a way of speaking, this just
my way of saying you special," she couldn't help asking
herself, "What the hell was he doing in my dreams, and

how come his teeth so white?" The second question brought a half smile to her face, like someone harboring a perplexing yet pleasurable thought.

Mistaking her involuntary half smile for approval of him, the boy ignored the giggles of the four other girls and said, "I'm Raphael Auguste, what's your name?"

"Eunice Demacque," chorused the four cousins.

"Where you from?"

"Debreuil," they shouted.

"Shut up," said Eunice.

Glad for the help and considered properly introduced, Raphael went on about himself as if nothing interested Eunice more. He lived in Piaye, down by the mouth of the river. His father was a *seine* (net) fisherman, but he himself, although he sometimes pulled *seine* with his father, worked on the Balembouche Estate. True he helped plant and cut cane, but that wasn't his real job. He was good with machines, and he could work iron. In fact, all around, he was good with his hands. He could even do some carpentry too. He knew the workings of the sugar factory inside-out. During harvest it was his job to keep the machines running. He could fix anything. After the harvest he and the engineer would take the machines apart and clean and oil them so that come next harvest they would be in tiptop shape. His other big job on the estate, especially during the off season, was that he was in charge of the stable. He was good with horses. Yes. He could speak the language of horses. The horses obeyed him. When he gets rich, and rich he will get, he is going to have a stable and horse carriages just like the *bétjés*.

Preoccupied with the white teeth, the Troumassee-broad smile, the dream, and the question of how a person could be fresh as a fresh vegetable and that no one but a complete idiot could come up with something like that,

Eunice paid little attention to Raphael's boasting. But the preoccupation permitted her to stay still in front of Raphael and so left him with the impression that he had a captivated audience. So much so that when he was leaving he had the confidence to tell her that he would come back and see her next Sunday as if there was nothing better she would like. Eunice was so taken aback with all that had happened, that the boy was far gone when she shouted, "Boy, who you think you are?"

Raphael came the next Sunday, and many other Sundays. Most times Eunice was rude and insulting to him, but the dream, the cotton-white teeth, the Troumassee-broad smile, and the notion of being as fresh as a fresh vegetable prevented her from walking away from him. And this was all Raphael required. For he was a talker and he approached life with an undaunted optimism. As long as he had his desired audience he would keep coming. Soon, on Saturdays, he went all the way to the Adventist Church in Debreuil with the hope of seeing and talking to his angel.

The Friday evening of the first Saturday that Raphael came to church, Eunice dreamt of him. He was in church, and as soon as she arrived his sparkling white teeth emitted a light like a ray of sunlight, and the light circled around her head, went down to her feet, then back to her head, and then it streaked out through a window and as it left a voice said, "Whom God has chosen, let no one cast asunder." And later in her sleep, Eunice dreamt that she was in the River Dorée putting her clothes to dry on a big boulder. Suddenly the river became big and muddy and swept her into its current, and just as she had resigned herself to a death by drowning and was thinking that they will find her body like that of her cousin whose drowning was foretold in her dream, Raphael came galloping into the river on a horse as black as his teeth were white, yanked her out of the water, hoisted her on the horse and rode to safety.

After that Friday night, Eunice could no longer ignore Raphael. For surely God was telling her something. One dream, one occurrence, could be explained away as a mere coincidence, the result of something she had heard or read the day before, or the result of going to bed with too full a stomach. But not a succession of dreams. First, Raphael bringing her a basket of mango julies; then his teeth emitting a light that says he was chosen by God; and then he is galloping into a river to carry her to safety. Of course, God was trying to tell her something. Clearly, God had chosen Raphael for her. So the second Saturday that Raphael came to church, Eunice stopped seeing him as the stupid, boastful boy who had accosted her at the river with his fresh vegetable idiotic nonsense. He was now the man with the beautiful white teeth whom God Himself had chosen for her. And for the first time in her life Eunice started thinking of herself not as the little girl who had fallen in love with the nuns, but as a woman who could be somebody's wife and who could have his babies. Before then she looked upon boys as noisy, dirty, boastful creatures who should be ignored as much as possible. Marriage, the thought of falling in love with one of those unnatural creatures, had been completely out of the question.

This second Saturday, as Raphael approached Eunice, she gave him an encouraging smile, and gone was her arrogant, don't-bother-me stare. And, as if thinking that Raphael was reading her thoughts, Eunice was so embarrassed that she couldn't look at him. When he greeted and spoke to Eunice, her eyes were downcast. Still, when he said, "Eunice, can I have lunch with you?" She instinctively replied, "No."

"Eunice, I want to be friendly to you."

"What for? You not an Adventist."

"So, is that what it is? Is that why you doesn't want to talk to me?"

"I don't know. I'm going."

That Saturday night the dream with the black horse repeated itself, but this time with a twist. When she got on the horse, and as they rode away, the friction with the horse and the holding on tight to Raphael caused an excruciating pleasure that obtained relief only by an explosion between her legs. Eunice woke up in the morning wet and sticky, ashamed of her sinfulness, unable to look anyone in the eye, convinced that everyone in the house knew of her night of iniquity.

Sunday, Raphael appeared at the River Dorée to press his case. In his brief encounter with Eunice the previous day he had not failed to notice her welcoming smile, her shy, downcast glance and her barely audible responses. All signs that he had taken a step closer to winning his angel. Eunice sat on a stone in the river washing her clothes. She was one among several women doing their laundry in much the same way. Raphael sat on another stone in front of Eunice, and over the busy, melodic voice of the river, the sound of the women washing, and the calls of birds in the canopy of the lush vegetation, he told Eunice that he had no problems joining the Church. He loved her. He would marry her as soon as she gave the word.

Embarrassed by her night of passion, her night of debauchery, Eunice never looked at him, and she never said a word. She simply sat there and continued washing away as if the sound of soapy water spraying out of the bodice she was washing was all the reply required.

Unmindful of the soapy water spraying on him, as if taking her silence as a "yes," Raphael went on to tell Eunice how much he loved her, how he was going to spend the rest of his life making her happy. Yes, he would be baptized and join the church, and how lucky he was to have found his angel, his true love. "You are special," he said. "You know that, don't you? You are so special."

Night after night, dreams involving Raphael, in one way or the other, kept bombarding Eunice's sleep, and increasingly she daydreamed about her life together with Raphael. How many children would they have? How many girls and how many boys? Would they take after him? Would they get his beautiful teeth and his broad smile? How about his big, fat ankles? Why him? Why had God chosen him of all persons for her?

Unaware that in Eunice's eyes God had chosen him for her, and that she needed no further convincing, Raphael continued to talk her into marrying him, and he kept coming to church and visiting Eunice at the river.

Never saying a final "yes" to his marriage proposal, Eunice increasingly behaved like she had already said yes. She made time for Raphael, she sat beside him in church, and when it was time for him to head home she walked with him a little ways. Soon everyone understood that they were a couple. Five months after his first encounter with Eunice, Raphael got baptized, and then it was understood that they were engaged to be married.

But before the engagement could be considered official, he had to receive the blessings of Eunice's parents. A few Sabbaths following his baptism, after church service Eunice brought him home for exactly that purpose. Her father wasn't home. Teresa was seated in the doorway with a large calabash on her lap, shelling peas. Her face turned sour as soon as she set eyes on the boy accompanying her daughter, walking a walk that said that he and her daughter were sharing something that she could never be part of.

Eunice said, "Ma, this is Raphael, he joined the church just the other day."

"Good afternoon, Ma Demacque," said Raphael with his broadest smile, as if hoping his exposed whiter-than-white teeth would keep demons away.

Teresa grunted as if something unpleasant was caught in her throat.

Nonetheless, intent on his mission, Raphael took the plunge. "Ma Demacque, I love your daughter so much. I even love her more than myself. I come to ask for her hand in marriage. I promise to take care of her, to make her happy, to protect her even with my own life."

Teresa paid little attention to what the "nothing-to-do boy" was saying. Instead, still shelling peas, she watched from the corner of her eyes the pleading, vulnerable smile on her daughter's face, her nervous, involuntary holding of the boy's hand, and her uneasy, guileless posture. Teresa was caught off-guard, for she had never fully accepted that her daughter wasn't going to be a nun, much less anticipating that someday she would bring home a man, and would be standing in front of her, radiant but artless, defenseless but hopeful, innocent but expectant. Teresa was alarmed. The girl hadn't even turned sixteen. What did she know about marriage? Just the other day she was going to be a nun, now she wanted to get married. What was wrong with that girl?

When Teresa brought her attention back to the "nothing-to-do boy," she said, "*Ti neg, sorti douvan mwen, ek bitiz-ou-la*; worthless nigger, get lost with your nonsense."

So, with an embarrassed half smile, Raphael looked sheepishly from daughter to mother, and gently squeezing his angel's hand said his goodbye and walked away with his head bowed.

After he left, Eunice said, "Ma, why you insult him like that? I love him."

Teresa said, "Girl, you too young to marry. What's your rush? Marriage is forever, you know. Once you do it, there is no turning back. That boy has nothing, he can't take care of you. What's the matter with you, anyway? First you leave the Church to join the *Semdays*; then you don't want to be a nun; then you insult the priest of all persons; and now you eh even sixteen you want to marry. Is it because of this boy you join dem *Semdays* people? Is it dem *Semdays* putting you up to all this?"

"Ma, he wasn't in the church when I joined. He just got baptized a few weeks ago. And Ma, I love him."

"It's these damn *Semdays* causing that."

"Ma, it's God's will."

"No. God has nothing to do with that. It's dem *Semdays*. They have turned your life upside down."

"No Ma, God revealed his choice to me in a dream. I love him, Ma."

"You love him? Wait when your father hears this, you will see if you love him."

"But Ma I love him with my whole heart."

Early evening when Editon arrived home, Teresa allowed him to settle down with his pipe and then she presented him with Eunice's case.

"But Editon, you know that your daughter is set on marrying this *Semdays* boy from Piaye that don't even have two pennies to rub together? And yes, she had the guts to bring the boy home this afternoon to ask for her hand. And the shameless boy, spitting all over my peas, telling me how much he love Eunice, and all the while they holding hands and Eunice acting like a hen ready to lay eggs. Editon, you ever see something like that? I don't know what's wrong with the girl. I tried talking sense into her, but all she could say for herself is that she loves him and it's God's will that they get married. You ever hear stupidness like that? Editon, you have to talk to your daughter and put a stop to all this nonsense."

Puffing on his pipe, Editon listened patiently, so patiently that an onlooker would think that he was miles away from the conversation his wife was trying to draw him into. Approaching seventy, in the chill of early morning and evening every bone in his body ached. A testament to a life of back breaking work felling trees, sawing lumber, growing most of the food that entered his house, and planting and harvesting cane for ungrateful sugar estates. Smoking his pipe was one of his few reliefs from his aching bones. In fact, his pipe served more than just relief from pain, it was his way of meditating, of making peace with life, of making life tolerable, of making it easier to ignore or not make much of whatever his wife would say to him. For in his mind, if he couldn't dismiss most of what his wife had to say to him, his life would be miserable. So sitting outside on the root of the mango palwi tree whose branches were brushing the roof of the house, and watching night approach and with it the chill his bones complained about, he gave the impression that the whole world around him could fall apart but once he had his pipe in his mouth, he would lose not one ounce of contentment.

A long time ago Editon had stopped trying to predict what this strange daughter of his old age would come up with next. And now it gave him some pleasure just to see what new direction the girl would take. So this time around he paid attention to his wife, but only as an amused bystander with no intention of altering the scene before him.

After his wife had finished making her case, Editon puffed a few more times on his pipe and said, "But Ma

Demacque, if she say she loves the boy, then she loves him. Let them marry-eh."

Teresa said, "I knew I was wasting my time coming to you. Once you can smoke that pipe of yours, you don't care a thing about anyone, not even your own daughter. Let them marry? And the girl is barely fifteen. What kind of a father are you?"

At this stage in his marriage, Editon had worked things to a science. He knew just when in a conversation to stop listening to what his wife had to say. So without a change of expression, he pulled on his pipe and smoked his wife out of his consciousness.

It takes two to tangle. Teresa walked off with a loud "*chups*," and decided that since both daughter and father had lost their minds, she would go right down to the source of the problem. She would pay the Adventist elder a visit.

Arriving the following afternoon at the elder's home, Teresa found him outside, seated on a stool, sharpening a cutlass. The sound of metal on metal crawled her blood.

No sooner than they had exchanged greetings, Teresa said, "Mr. Beausoleil, don't tell me you all encouraging a girl who don't know a thing about life into marrying. You all must tell the girl she too young. Surely, these children can wait a few more years."

The church elder was a short man with an animated face whose expressions telecast what he had to say long before the words came out. He paused from sharpening his cutlass to listen patiently to Teresa, but he wasn't too sympathetic. They were in the business of winning and preserving souls for Christ. His Adventist congregation was like a tiny seedling in a huge Roman Catholic jungle. They had to win and keep souls any way they could. Besides, this wasn't the old days. Young people now-a-days have too much heat. True, Eunice and Raphael were very young, but it was better they got married than live in sin.

He said, "Ma Demacque, your daughter eh a child anymore. She old enough to make her own mind."

"Mr. Beausoleil, you call fifteen years old enough? The girl been nowhere, the girl is a little innocent. Just two years ago is a nun the girl wanted to be, and now she marrying. Don't you see something is wrong?"

"Ma Demacque, my grandmother was married at fourteen. So fifteen eh too young for a woman to marry."

"But, Mr. Beausoleil, that was in the old days when people didn't know better. Times have change. We no longer in slavery. People now more enlightened. We don't have to make the same mistakes our parents made."

"Ma Demacque, even according to your own Roman Catholic Church, once someone has received confirmation the way is open for them to get married. Eh, people does be confirmed by twelve, thirteen and sometimes even as early as eleven, and your girl is already fifteen going on to sixteen. So I don't understand what you telling me there."

"Tell me, Mr. Beausoleil, you have two young girls, would you be happy if they were to marry at fifteen?"

"Well, I will tell you this, I prefer them marrying at fifteen than living in sin. And let me ask you this, won't you prefer your daughter marrying at fifteen than coming home with big belly, and she eh even sure who the father is or the father saying the child eh his?"

After some more back and forth arguments with the elder, Teresa realized she won't get any help from this quarter. Daughter, father, God, Church, elder and love had combined forces against her. Facing such opposition she eventually bowed to the inevitable, and consoled herself with the thought that well, the girl was special. She was the one God visited in dreams. She must know what she is doing.

So shortly after her sixteenth birthday, Eunice got married to the man of her dreams, the man given to her by God. Now, two decades later, having buried the husband God had chosen for her, it occurred to Eunice that ever since she knew herself dreams had a way of marking, dictating her life. So in this her latest dream she couldn't help but wonder what God was trying to tell her? What was this business of frogs ridiculing and threatening her? What had she done to anyone to deserve that? Was the disappointment lying in ambush for her so terrible that nothing less than a nightmare was needed to warn her? And how could tomatoes so beautiful and appetizing on the outside be so corrupted inside?

THEY CAME. The event was scheduled for 7:30 PM, yet they started arriving at 6:30, an astonishing feat for a people who had made it their business to be late for any and everything. They came to the Town Hall, which also served as public library and concert hall, across the street from the Roman Catholic Church. They came ready for battle, their faces long as the fishing canoes adorning Vieux Fort's waterfront, but no way as welcoming. In fact, they were anything but welcoming: their faces mean and sour, their *chups* of anger, so loud and menacing, could have chased away a prowling tigress. They had read the flyers and posters hanging all over Vieux Fort and beyond. They had heard the radio announcements over and over again, in both English and Kwéyòl. Those who missed the flyers and posters and radio announcements couldn't have missed, even if they had wanted to, the loud proclamation of the town crier on a public address system earlier in the after-noon. "Vieux Fortians are Lazy: Fact or Myth? *Jan Vieux Fort Feyan: Lavéwité ou Mansonj?*" Most of them never got past the part that said "Vieux Fortians are Lazy, *Jan Vieux Fort Feyan,*" because by then their anger didn't allow them to continue reading or listening. So the part that asked, "Fact or Myth? *Lavéwité ou Mansonj?*" that would have softened their anger, never had a chance to do its job; thus they came vexed and ready for battle.

They had been a bit subdued when they found out the whole mess was organized by none other than Father Pierre, the most kind, humble and generous priest they had ever known. The priest who brought them plays that made them laugh tears, who organized bazaars with all kinds of amusement for children, who sponsored school spelling, essay, and debate competitions, who hired steel pan masters to teach school children how to play pan. The priest whose pronunciation was so horrible and whose English accent was so Latin-thick that it would have made little difference to his congregation if he had held his services all in Latin. The priest who, only after he had learnt and started speaking Kwéyòl, had been able to get the people to make sense of what he had to say. The priest whose whiskered mustache and narrow, squeezed-in face reminded the people of the *kwibich,* crayfish, they caught in rivers, and whose reddish face and hair reminded them of *fonmi wouj,* red ants, thereby compelling them to describe him as *pwet kwibich, fonmi wouj-la,* the crayfish, red ant priest, and causing people to travel from all over the south of the island to attend mass in Vieux Fort just to see this loving, red ant, crayfish priest who couldn't speak English. Looking at the pitiful yet kind priest, Vieux Fortians couldn't help but feel a tenderness toward him. So when they found out that this whole thing was Father Pierre's initiative, they had cooled down somewhat. But as they were dressing, preparing to come and defend their honor, priest or no priest, their anger boiled to the surface. "Who is this ugly, white man, who can barely speak English, coming here calling us lazy?"

They came. By 7:15 the hall was packed and overflowing with people. All seats were taken. Those who arrived after 7:15 had to stand, and those who came after 7:30 had to stand outside because all standing room in the hall was taken.

They came from everywhere: Mangue, Bacadere, La Ressource, Derriere Morne, Augier, Piero.

They came from all walks of life: fishermen, wood cutters, charcoal makers, broom makers, coal pot makers, stevedores, banana carriers, lawyers, auto mechanics, carpenters, joiners, masons, blacksmiths, nurses, maids, bookkeepers, stock keepers, beekeepers, shopkeepers, rum shop keepers, truck drivers, footmen, pit toilet and grave diggers, beggars, drunkards, prostitutes.

Eunice and Henry were there. So too were Daddy Mano and Eugene in his short, khaki pants, displaying his reddish legs. Even Popo, the town's most celebrated drunk, stumbled in bright and early at 7:00PM, reeking of alcohol and filth.

Eunice had been alarmed when Ruben informed her of his participation in this event. She associated all such activities with the Roman Catholic Church, and she would have nothing to do with anything that had to do with the Roman Catholic Church. Besides, she needed no debate or discussion to tell her what she already knew: Vieux Fortians were the laziest set of people she had ever come across; and the towel-thiefing maids at Cloud's Nest Inn proved what her father always used to say, "*moutjwé mwen an fenyan èk mwen kai moutjwé-ou an vòlè,* show me a lazy person and I will show you a thief." Still, what really made her apprehensive was that she saw Ruben as a tender lamb of the faith. His involvement in such worldly activities would do nothing but compete for his soul and weaken his resolve to get baptized and leave the world behind. He couldn't serve two masters. She said, "No, Ruben, let somebody else do it. I thought you had already left all this behind. You should forget about the world and start putting your talent in the service of the Lord."

"Come on, Eunice," answered Ruben. "This discussion is the first step in trying to bring change to Vieux Fort, trying to bring progress and development. And this isn't a Roman Catholic event, it is all part of a new government initiative. You yourself does complain all the time that Vieux Fortains are lazy, how they should stop waiting for the Americans and start doing things for themselves. Well, this is the start of helping Vieux Fortians to taking an interest in their town, to finding out what the problems really are, and to finding solutions for them."

Eunice wanted to tell him that what Vieux Fortians really needed was the Lord, not another discussion. But Ruben didn't give her a chance to speak, he went on to appeal to her to come and give him moral support. After all, hasn't he pledged to be baptized? Wasn't he going to join her church? So what harm could be done if she simply came and gave him some support? Even if she didn't care about the discussion, she could come for his sake. Didn't she care enough about him to give him that little support?

Put in those terms, Eunice couldn't muster further resistance, especially in light of an early Monday morning, two weeks before, so early that dogs were still asleep on the streets of Vieux Fort, when Ruben had come bursting into her yard, demanding to be baptized and demanding her hand in marriage, demands she had been so willing to give in to that she had nearly fainted and may have fallen if he had not caught her in his arms.

Anticipating trouble and not taking any chances, Father Pierre had invited two uniformed policemen. They were seated in the middle of the audience. The air was thick with animosity. One could see it, hear it, smell it, touch it, and if one cared to, one could even slice it with a butter knife.

The discussion panel was seated around the head table. On the right, businessman Sonson Springer, a staunch member of the ruling political party; on the left, Ferguson James, the opposition party's Vieux Fort candidate, defeated in the last general elections; in the middle, school teacher, actor, intellectual, and highly celebrated footballer and cricketer, Ruben Ishmael. Standing at the podium, to the right of the table, was the moderator, Father Pierre, with his thick Latin accent, and his reddish, whiskered face that seemed ablaze.

When people saw Ruben sitting there smiling at them, their faces grew longer and their *chups* louder. How could Mr. Ishmael get himself involved in this kind of thing? He was their brains, their St. Lucia and world news reporter, their champion, the one who made Castries football and cricket teams return to Castries with their tails between their legs. For many who couldn't read and write he was the one who read the letters they received from their overseas sons and husbands and who wrote the replies to these letters. So how could he sit there smiling at them as if he were a child about to receive guava jelly? One fisherman from the audience stood and shouted, "Ruben, traitor!"

"You can say that again!" said another.

Father Pierre launched the evening. "Brothers and Sisters, let's be tolerant and loving of each other as Christ is of us. I thank you for turning out in such large numbers. I thank the Vieux Fort Town Board for allowing me this opportunity to moderate this event. I am honored to be part of this important discussion. This is only the first of a series of discussions aimed at finding solutions to the problems Vieux Fort faces. At the end of this series of discussions we will be making recommendations to the government on the most critical bottlenecks to Vieux Fort's social and economic development. All this is upon the request of the government, so we hope the government is sincere and that it will uphold its end of the bargain and take onboard our recommendations in its national development plan. As we embark on this journey, we ask for your support and indulgence. Before we begin the discussion, let's bow our heads in a moment of silent prayer."

Father Pierre then introduced members of the panel. Each panelist would have fifteen minutes to make his case. The businessman, Sonson Springer, would speak first, then the politician, Ferguson James, and last would be Ruben Ishmael. At the end of the presentations the floor would open for questions and discussion.

Sonson Springer began. "Ladies and gentlemen, good evening. I feel both honored and privileged to be addressing you this evening. My hat goes off to Father Pierre for organizing not only this discussion but all of the many cultural, artistic and educational events that he has in the past sponsored, and to the government for its foresight in encouraging the people to come up with their own solutions to the problems they face. Ladies and gentlemen, Vieux Fort has a lot going for it. It has the most flat land on the island. The Vieux Fort River provides an ample supply of water for irrigation, commercial, and residential use. Taking advantage of Vieux Fort's flat land, at Beausejour the government has established the largest animal husbandry farm on the island. The rich waters surrounding Vieux Fort have made it the fishing capital of St. Lucia. Ladies and gentlemen, thanks to the generosity of the Americans, just recently the Vieux Fort Secondary School opened its doors to children from all over the south, making it one of only three secondary schools on the island. Again, thanks to the Americans, Vieux Fort has a network of roads second to none. It has one of the island's two major hospitals, one of its two seaports and one of its two airports. But there is more. As part of the government's new economic development initiative, there are plans to entice hotels to the Vieux Fort area, and to make Vieux Fort the industrial capital of St. Lucia by building factory shells and providing generous tax and other incentives for manufacturers to come and set up in these shells. The government also has plans to turn Beanfield into an international airport. But do you think Vieux Fortians are taking advantage of all these opportunities? No. They are sitting there blaming everything on Castries, the government and the English. They are sitting there as if waiting for the American messiah to come and save them. Ladies and gentlemen, anyhow you cut it Vieux Fortians are rude, lazy, tardy, and disrespectful."

The audience went into uproar. "Shut up, you thief! It's you keeping Vieux Fort back with your sky-high prices," said one man.

"Move your ass from there! The government doing endless *bòbòl* (corruption) with people's money, and you there talking shit!" said another.

"The man right," said Eugene. "Vieux Fortians like too much freeness, they need to get off their backsides for a change."

"Shut your ass, *malmanman*!" someone responded.

Suddenly Henry stood up and shouted, "Don't worry, Mr. Eugene, the Americans coming back to help Vieux Fort. I wrote them the other day to come help Vieux Fort."

Eunice looked at Henry with crossed eyes.

Forgetting Eugene and the businessman, the audience burst into laughter. Someone said, "Listen to the *Semdays* boy, listen."

Father Pierre stood up. "Brethren, please don't interrupt the speakers. You will have a chance at the end of their presentations to make comments and ask questions. Please, let's not turn this into a charade."

The businessman continued. "You all may not like what I'm saying, but it's the truth. Vieux Fort people want to come to work when they want, what time they want, and leave when they want. When they come to work, they just want to sit around doing nothing, yet they always quarreling for more pay, and before anything they cursing you. It is for these reasons you don't see any Vieux Fortian working in my store. I prefer to hire people from Augier, Desruisseaux, Micoud, Laborie, anywhere but Vieux Fort. Vieux Fortians are lazy, plain and simple."

"But who wants to work in your stinking store anyway?" Shouted someone at the back. "Who wants to work for your starvation wages?"

The businessman continued as if he were never interrupted. "Until Vieux Fortians get rid of this laziness and this attitude that someone owes them something, that everything has to be given to them for free, they can never progress. No matter what the government does for Vieux Fort, it is people from outside of Vieux Fort that will benefit, not Vieux Fortians."

After more booing and insults at the businessman, the politician, Ferguson James, took his turn. "Father Pierre, my esteemed colleagues on the panel, ladies and gentlemen. It's indeed a pleasure to be here. 'Vieux Fortians are lazy: fact or myth?' is an issue that's dear to my heart. For I'm one who has devoted his entire life to the development and progress of Vieux Fort. That's why my heart aches when I hear people saying Vieux Fortians are lazy. And it aches even more when it's Vieux Fortians themselves mouthing that stupidness. So this discussion tonight is a good thing. It's good that we Vieux Fortians are dealing with it head-on and once and for all. Now, I'm not sure about the sincerity of the government in giving the people a voice in solving their own problems. For all you know this may be yet another ploy to appease Vieux Fortians, while doing nothing for them. But, be that as it may, I welcome the opportunity to contribute my two cents to this debate. Ladies and gentlemen, as my fellow panelist has said, Vieux Fort is the fishing capital of St. Lucia. But tell me, is there any occupation harder and more dangerous than that of a fisherman? Over the years, how many fishermen do you know who went out to sea and never came back? So tell me, does that sound like an occupation for the lazy and the fainthearted? Ladies and gentlemen, let's be honest. The only occupation more dangerous than that of a fisherman is that of a soldier. How about the people eking out a living cutting campeche, the hardest of woods, all day in the hot sun to make coals and to sell to bakers? Is that an easy and lazy occupation? And how about the stevedores or the men loading the banana boat on banana day, or the women working all night like ants carrying bananas on the dock, is that lazy work?"

"Yeah, tell them. Tell them, brother," someone shouted.

"Ladies and gentlemen, here is the problem. A person comes into town and sees a group of guys hanging around the corner or even in a rum shop, having a drink or two and right away, because it's midday or mid-afternoon, the person jumps to the conclusion that Vieux Fortians are lazy and they are drunks, there they are in the middle of the day skylarking and in a rum shop drinking. But what such a person would not know is that these same guys may have spent the previous three days loading cargo on a ship; or they were at sea for the past five days; or were up at four o'clock that very morning, went to sea, came back with their catch by 12:00 noon, so when the visitor saw them hanging out at two-thirty having a drink, they had already put in a day's work. The other thing, ladies and gentlemen, is that Vieux Fort is a town, and in any town at any hour of the day you're bound to have people hanging out. For example, if you go to Desruisseaux and see no one idle by the roadside and you come to Vieux Fort and see a group of people hanging out, should you conclude that Vieux Fortians are idle and Desruisseaux people are hard working? No, ladies and gentlemen. No. The population of Vieux Fort is much greater and much more concentrated than that of Desruisseaux, so of course on any given day, at any given time, you are more likely to see people idle in Vieux Fort than in Desruisseaux. But this in no way means that Vieux Fortians are lazy and Desruisseaux people are hard working."

"It's these same country bookies coming to Vieux Fort and taking our jobs. Tell them it's time to go," someone shouted.

"Fellow Vieux Fortians, let me tell you. This business of Vieux Fortians are lazy is just the government's excuse for doing nothing for Vieux Fort. For keeping Vieux Fort back. For making sure Vieux Fort never surpasses Castries in importance. To enable Castries people to keep hoarding everything for themselves. If you think I'm just making up stories, listen to this. Way back in seventeen-sixty-three, one by the name of M. de Rochmore wrote, and I quote: '*It is essential that those two towns,*' meaning Vieux Fort and Soufriere, '*should not develop too much and compete with Carénage,*' later renamed Castries, unquote. Ladies and gentlemen, fellow Vieux Fortians, you see how long

Castries folks been trying to keep Vieux Fort back. It's hundreds of years, ladies and gentlemen, hundreds of years. And ladies and gentlemen, don't tell me that you all didn't know that the Americans had plans to transform Vieux Fort into a metropolitan city that would have put Castries to shame. But what happened? I will tell you what happened. The British and Castries people protested so vehemently that the only thing the Americans ended up building was the secondary school that my colleague here spoke so gloriously about. Yet, if not for the selfishness of the British and Castries people, the school would have been just the tip of the iceberg of what the Americans would have done.

"But that's not all, ladies and gentlemen. When the Americans were leaving they left two power generators for Vieux Fort. What happened to the generators? The government took them to Castries. The Americans left plenty of green hearthouses behind. Where are they now? They are all sitting in Castries because they were dismantled and sold to Castries folks.

"Ladies and gentlemen, I rest my case."

There was thunderous applause, plenty of smiles, and plenty of nodding of heads. "It isn't turning out too badly after all," the audience seemed to say.

It was now the moment of truth for Ruben. He gathered his notes in preparation for his delivery. But before he could say anything, someone shouted, "Here comes the traitor." Then surprising everyone for the second time and to the great consternation of Eunice, Henry stood and shouted, "Mister Ruben eh no traitor." The audience burst into laughter.

Someone shouted, "That *Semdays* boy is good, you know. I must remember him for when I need a lawyer." This was followed by another burst of laughter. Then the audience quieted down in anticipation of Ruben's presentation. What will it be? Fact or Myth?

Ruben was ready. He had made it his duty to be ready. History and politics were among his great loves. Starting at fifteen he had read everything he could find about St. Lucia. During his summer teaching breaks he would visit the Central Library in Castries and spend days at a time reading old issues of the Voice newspaper dating back to the late 19th century. On his European travels, Father Pierre, himself a history and archaeology enthusiast, brought back several books on St. Lucia and the West Indies. These Ruben had read over and over again. Added to that, Ruben was always holding court with the old folks in Vieux Fort, cajoling, teasing their memory to cough up their recollection of the past. So despite Ruben's limited schooling, the priest would have been hard pressed to find someone more conversant with the history of Vieux Fort and St. Lucia. In fact, although it was Father Pierre and the Vieux Fort Town Board who organized the discussion, it was Ruben who inspired the topic three weeks before when he came seeking Father Pierre's opinion on an article he had written for the Voice. An article that attempted to explain the backwardness of Vieux Fortians.

Father Pierre thought it was very fortuitous that Ruben would come up with his theory of Vieux Fort at the same time that, as part of a comprehensive social and economic development plan, the newly elected government had embarked on an island-wide initiative where the various districts were to hold discussions to identify the key problems and limitations they faced, and come up with possible solutions and recommendations. Since Father Pierre had such a long history of social and cultural development in Vieux Fort, the town board had enlisted his help in organizing these discussions. When Father Pierre read Ruben's article, he had no doubt what should be the focus of the first discussion. He would let the people give their views on what's wrong with Vieux Fort. But he knew since this wasn't a piece of drama, or a dance where there were music, rum and food, few would show up, and those who did would be the same few who always showed up, so he decided to be creative and spiced it up a bit with: "Vieux Fortians are Lazy: Fact or Myth? *Jan Vieux Fort Feyan: Lavéwité ou Mansonj?"*

Ruben began. "Vieux Fort, good evening. First of all, let us acknowledge Father Pierre and the Vieux Fort Town Board for their courage and foresight in organizing this event."

The audience clapped in recognition not so much of the town board but of Father Pierre.

Ruben continued. "It's not an enviable task to follow such excellent and forceful presentations as given by my fellow panelists, but I welcome the opportunity to partici-pate in anything geared towards the upliftment of Vieux Fort, because I love Vieux Fort. I love the forever angry Atlantic Ocean on its eastern border, the peaceful Caribbean Sea at its front. I like the open, green pastures and the low lying hills of La Tourney, Derriere Morne and Beauséjour that interrupt the plains. I like the unvan-quished Moule-a-Chique, with its towering lighthouse, allowing ships safe passage and guarding the southern boundaries of the island. I like ..."

 "Man, get to the point," shouted a drunk and impatient Popo.

Someone said, "Shut your ass, *wonmier*, and listen to your master."

Popo said, "But the man talking 'bout love. The question eh love, the question is Vieux Fortians are Lazy: Fact or Myth? Fact or Myth, that's the question."

Someone shouted, "If the *wonmier* eh shutting up, put him out."

"Thank you Popo," said Ruben.

"You welcome," said Popo. The audience burst into laughter.

"Ladies and gentlemen, fellow Vieux Fortians, to properly understand the plight of Vieux Fort we have to go back thousands of years to when, after some volcanic activity, a huge mudslide that started at the center of the island flowed across the Vieux Fort area, building up the land, filling up the crevices, and covering all but the tallest hills. Moule-a-Chique was one of the few landmarks that was left to standout."

Popo shouted, "'Fact or Myth?' is because of a mudslide? Man, come on. What kind of child's play is this?" The audience burst into laughter. One of the policemen told Popo if he interrupted one more time they would put him out.

"It is this mudslide that shaped the geography of Vieux Fort, it is this freak of nature that molded Vieux Fort into the largest expanse of flat land on the island. Fellow Vieux Fortians, I am here to tell you that Vieux Fort's problems began with the flattening of its landscape. For indeed Vieux Fort has been a victim of its geography. As the largest expanse of flat and particularly coastal land on the island, Vieux Fort has been the site of choice for a succession of large, externally induced enterprises that have kept its inhabitants landless and dependent on others for their survival. So Vieux Fort's geography has been its greatest blessing and its greatest curse, and has given rise to the great irony that the history of the inhabitants of the part of the island with the most usable land, has been one of landlessness."

"Yeah, yeah," someone shouted.

"Ladies and gentlemen, before the coming of the Americans there was the coming of the Europeans who, once they had completed the messy business of pulling out and crushing the thorn in their sides they called the Caribs, the people they found on the island who called themselves Kalinagos and their island Iouanaloa, settled down to the lucrative business of combining African slave labor with cheaply acquired land to produce sugarcane. But where else but Vieux Fort would they plant the first seed of their greed, a crop requiring easy access to ships and large tracts of flat land that lend themselves to the laying of rail for transporting cane from field to mills, and sugar, rum and molasses from mills to anchored ships? Fellow Vieux Fortians, not only was Vieux Fort the site of the first sugar plantation and the first sugar mill, but for several years it dominated the island's sugar industry. In seventeen-sixty-nine, three years after sugar's inception, there were over sixty-one sugar estates operating in the Vieux Fort area, accounting for over half of the island's sugar acreage. As you all know, later the Vieux Fort Central Sugar Factory, the first in St. Lucia and one of the first of its kind in the Caribbean, replaced the sugar mill."

"Teach, professor, teach."

"Fellow Vieux Fortians, all this was great for the plantation owners but how about the slaves, our forefathers?"

"Tell us, spread the truth."

"Well, the absence of mountains in the Vieux Fort area made it difficult for the slaves to run away to freedom, and since most of the plains of Vieux Fort were suitable for sugar cultivation, there was little of the so called marginal lands for the slaves to grow their own food. Therefore, the slaves in Vieux Fort were more heavily dependent on the plantations for their survival than were slaves in most other parts of the island.

"Ladies and gentlemen, slavery was abolished in eighteen-thirty-eight, but the dependency and landlessness of Vieux Fortians remained because there still wasn't any land, marginal or otherwise, to be had. After all, the plantations, which owned most of the lands, did survive slavery. And even when, in nineteen-thirty-seven, the Vieux Fort sugar factory closed down, rendering seven thousand people jobless and leaving the sugar lands idle, we in Vieux Fort remained landless because we could not afford to purchase the land and we couldn't cultivate it for it still belonged to the owners of the defunct sugar factory.

"Without buyers, the colonial government was left with little choice but to purchase the land from the sugar factory. However, once the land was in government hands, considering the thousands of people the factory had put out of work, I am pretty sure many people were hopeful that the government would parcel out the land to the ex-sugar workers as part of a land settlement scheme.

"But fellow Vieux Fortians, history doesn't always follow logic. The settlement of our forefathers on the land that they had toiled most of their lives and for which their forebears had been enslaved was not to be. Instead, the government of St. Lucia entered into an arrangement with Barbados whereby a Barbados Land Settlement Company would purchase not only the sugar factory but also twenty-five hundred acres of land in the Vieux Fort area. Three-quarters of that land would be set aside for two-thousand land-hungry Bajan settlers, each to receive a lot on which to grow mostly sugarcane and to a lesser extent food crops. These settlers would live in two-room company-built cottages at Beauséjour.

"But what was to become of the seven thousand unemployed Vieux Fortians? They would remain landless, of course, but maybe not idle, for they would obtain employment at the sugar factory and they would work as laborers on the remaining six hundred acres of land the Barbadian Settlement Company had set aside to cultivate its own sugar. By nineteen-forty, the settlement scheme was in full swing. There were already one hundred cottages at Beauséjour, housing six hundred Bajan settlers."

"You see how the government and Castries people been stealing from us! You see! Taking our land and giving it to foreigners,"said someone.

"Yeah, and after they make all their *bòbòl* they turning around and calling us lazy — *chups*," replied another.

"Fellow Vieux Fortians, history makes no promises. In the late nineteen-thirty's Hitler's Germany began invading and conquering its neighbors. Having its own designs on the Pacific Islands, natural resource-poor Japan entered the war on the side of Hitler and drew a reluctant America into the war when it bombed Pearl Harbor. World War II shifted into high gear.

"Vieux Fort's geography once again determined its history. Due to the district's large expanse of flat land lying right next to the coast, in exchange for reconditioned warships the Americans leased from the cash-strapped and war-weary British all of three thousand and thirty-one acres of the plains of Vieux Fort for a military base. The American base subsumed the sugar lands so the Barbadian Settlement Company was dissolved, and the settlement scheme aborted. And any hope of displaced Vieux Fortians owning land grew even more distant because the Americans occupied the plains of Vieux Fort more extensively than the sugar plantations ever did.

"But the good times that some say Vieux Fortians are waiting for the Americans to bring back were short lived. By the fifties the Americans were gone, leaving Vieux Fortians with a wealth of infrastructure, but with a social and economic depression and, according to some, with a deepening dependency on others for their wellbeing.

"Notwithstanding, the story didn't change much. Vieux Fortains remained landless. The Americans' lease was for ninety-nine years, so until the lease expired or (as was the case) the Americans gave it up, the land remained empty and could not be legally touched not even by the government, much less Vieux Fortians. The land has now reverted to the government, not to Vieux Fortians, so we are still landless. Ladies and gentlemen, the truth is plain and simple. Most of us in Vieux Fort are squatters. The land our homes are on belong either to the Roman Catholic Church, the Anglican Church, or the government. We Vieux Fortians have been landless ever since slave catchers snatched our ancestors from their African villages.

"So in other words, what you saying there is, 'man know thyself and do thyself no harm?'" asked Popo.

"Popo, shut your ass, and let the man speak," someone responded.

"But ..."

"Popo, shut up."

"Fellow Vieux Fortians, as Father Pierre explained earlier, this discussion and the others that will follow are part of a government initiative to spearhead social and economic development in Vieux Fort. So what does all this business of citizens owning property, owning homes and the land their homes occupy have to do with social and economic development? To begin with, ladies and gentlemen, people who own house and land can use such property as collateral to obtain loans to send their children to school and to start businesses. Home and land owners have a stake in their community, they have something to lose, something to protect and develop, something to pass on to their children, therefore they feel more settled, they feel more a part of their community, and thus are more likely to work towards the development of their community. Citizens owning homes, land and other fixed assets can be the difference between the development or non-development of a community. Therefore, in all due respect to Mr. Springer, whom I hold in high esteem, we cannot talk about the social and economic development of Vieux Fortians without addressing this issue of our landlessness. I thank you."

As Ruben ended his speech there was a standing ovation and thunderous clapping that lasted for a good minute or two. Some were shouting: "The teacher! The teacher! The teacher!" He had done it again. Their champion, their educator, their scholar, their man of letters, the one who so many times had forced pompous Castries folks to swallow their pride and boastfulness, had done it again. He had climbed the mountain top, surveyed the valley of his enemies and wiped them out. The dark room was now flooded with light. Vieux Fort was about to take off. No matter what Castries and the government did to keep Vieux Fort back, it would soon surpass Castries in importance.

The floor was opened for questions and comments. But the audience knew that they couldn't top what they had just heard. Their questions and comments amounted to praising and agreeing with Ruben and the politician and lambasting the businessman.

Then, when the comments had just about dried up, deeply emotional, Daddy Mano stood up. He praised Ruben for his inspiring speech, and in a trembling voice said: "I have written to both the President of the United States of America and the Prime Minister of England to return to Vieux Fort every blasted cent they stole from us. And they did steal plenty from us. Because when someone comes to your home uninvited, eat all your food, kick you and your sons out, sleep with your wife and daughters, and occupy the whole house and yard, that man has stolen everything of value to you, everything you hold dear. So the Americans have more than stolen from us. They have raped us in more ways than one, and left us dry. After the war they gave Europe plenty of money to rebuild, which they called reconstruction funds. We were damaged just as badly as the Europeans, so where is our share of the reconstuction funds? Well, it's my life's mission to make them pay for every blade of our grass they trampled on. I will continue sending both the President and the Prime Minister letters, even if I have to use up the last breath in me."

There was thunderous applause, and the chorus: "Daddy Mano! Daddy Mano!"

No sooner the chorus died down, for the second time that night Henry reminded the audience that he had written to the Americans. "Daddy Mano," he said, "I wrote to the Americans too." The laughter to this his second intervention on the subject was even louder than to the first.

After Father Pierre's closing remarks, the audience thronged Ruben. Some touching him, wanting a piece of him, wanting to be part of the moment of his greatness. Someone asked, "Man, where did you learn all that history? What books you read? I didn't know St. Lucia had history."

Henry squeezed through the crowd to get to Ruben. He held his hands. He was so proud of Mr. Ruben. So happy that now that Mr. Ruben would be baptized and marry his mother, Mr. Ruben would be his father and he would be able to call him Daddy.

Despite her misgivings about being at what she considered a Roman Catholic function, Eunice too was proud of her man. After tonight she knew for sure that she was marrying a great man, an important man. While glued to her seat, spellbound by Ruben's magic, it had occurred to her that considering the way Ruben was speaking, the way everyone had become so silent that you could hear every squeak of their chairs, imagine what would happen, how many souls he would win, when he became a member of the church and started preaching the word of God to Vieux Fortians.

Even Eugene who didn't give a damn about all this "hoopla" surrounding Vieux Fort came up to Ruben and said, "Eh-eh, I never knew you could speak so well, come by the stall tomorrow I will have some nice mango julies for you."

That night on account of Ruben's speech, except for Popo (who walked away mumbling: "Fact or Myth? Serious matter that, but man talking 'bout child play, talking 'bout mudslide and Romeo and Juliet, eh all he had to say was man know thyself and do thyself no harm,") the audience walked home on clouds.

Big Man, Eugene's father, was born in an era when the land was untamed; when the towns or villages were just a row or two of houses hugging the coastline; when the only mode of transportation was foot, horse, donkey and boat; when the forest was so forbidding and empty of civilization that the only way to tell direction was by the position of the sun and the directional flow of rivers and streams; when living was hard, coarse, meager and frontierish; when men were men and women were women; when both men and women acknowledged and accepted that women were put on earth to serve men; when men had the unquestionable right to beat their women as they saw fit.

In such an era, Big Man had the misfortune of an effeminate older brother. A brother who was the joke of Laborie, who on account of his effeminacy Laborians called *malman-man, makoumè, jamet, boula.* In short 'bugger,' 'homo' 'anti-man.' Whom every child mocked, and every boy who crossed his path felt justified in pushing, slapping, and cuffing. So Big Man lost his identity even before he had one. He was known not by his name but as *fwè malmanman-ah*, the *malmanman's* brother. Thus when most young boys had an older brother to look up to, to help them develop self identity and definition, to imitate and follow around, to initiate or ease their passage into the world of men, to teach them that it was girls and not boys they were supposed to take an interest in, to show them how to recognize and look at pretty women, to teach them aggression, competitiveness and roughness, to teach them how to fight for turf and to protect their manhood, to teach them how to dominate women and to let women know without a shadow of a doubt that men were the bosses, Big Man had an older brother who was his greatest shame, and who was like a millstone around his neck. Every time someone said *fwè malmanman-ah*, in Big Man's mind they were saying that in him lay a *malmanman* that was begging to come out, that anytime now would come out. So not only could Big Man not look towards his older brother for guidance and direction, but to erase any doubt in anyone's mind that he was anything like his brother, to convince himself that there was nothing of his brother in him, he went to great lengths to be the opposite of his brother.

While his brother was quick to cry, from four years old Big Man had steeled himself never to cry; while his brother was expressive, talkative, emotional and behaved as if life was an unending drama, Big Man was reticent, stoic, aloof; while his brother asked and depended on others for help, Big Man was independent, self-reliant, never asked for help and acted as if he needed no one; while his brother wore his fears and idiosyncracies on his sleeves, Big Man went out of his way to hide his fears, to show that he was fearless; while his brother avoided boys and the sports they played and kept the company of girls only, Big Man glorified in doing what boys did and took whatever they did to the extreme.

Starting at five years old, in the middle of the night, Big Man would walk Laborie's Enbakoko Beach alone, forcing Laborians to pronounce him mad. As a teenager he swam further out to sea than any boy his age and to where most grown men dared not venture. He climbed the tallest coconut trees, those out of reach to everyone else in the village. In soccer he played the hardest and the most brutal (in the process breaking a few legs) such that no one wanted to be on the opposing team. In cricket he bowled the fastest and most ferocious, and when most boys were afraid to open the batting and face the opponents' fast bowlers, Big Man was the first to volunteer. No matter how difficult a soccer match, Big Man never admitted to being tired. No matter how badly he was injured, he never admitted to being hurt. Soon Big Man was known as *fwè malmanman-ah ki ka fou-ah*, the *malmanman's* crazy brother; or *nonm fè-ah*, the iron man.

Big Man's heroics didn't stop there. He avoided his brother, he avoided speaking to him, he avoided being seen with him; and Laborie people and beyond soon found out that any reference to *malmanman*, whether pertaining to Big Man or his brother, unleashed an attack so sudden, so violent and so pronounced that the offender was never again to let the word escape his mouth in the presence of Big Man. The age of the culprit didn't matter, nor did his size. It seemed the bigger and stronger the foe, the more Big Man relished the dishing out of the punishment. To Laborians it seemed that Big Man went out of his way to look for fights. Big Man fought so often and so brutally that his fighting stance—flaring, upturned nostrils; angry, menacing scowl; fierce, reddish eyes—was permanently stamped on his face.

By the time Big Man was sixteen, he was the boldest, "baddest," and fiercest man in Laborie, and all but the complete fool had learnt to tiptoe around him, avoid looking him directly in the eye, court him as a friend and leave all the name calling and castigation for when he was nowhere in sight. Even police officers were wary of Big Man. When they were called to a fight involving Big Man, they showed up with great reluctance because, besides beating up his perceived offenders, Big Man was quite willing and capable of beating up five, six policemen at a time, if they dared to interfere.

Long before he turned sixteen, Big Man became a fisherman, an occupation considered by many to be the toughest and most dangerous. Yet this was precisely why Big Man went to sea. Not unlike a gay man joining the military, or the rugby, football or wrestling team to cleanse everyone's mind of any doubt that he was straight. At eighteen Big Man acquired his own canoe. In search of fish he went further and stayed out longer than most fishermen and he became one of the most successful fishermen in Laborie. When he arrived with his catch, no one dared to push a hand in his canoe to select the fish they wanted, at least not before Big Man was good and ready. To do otherwise was to risk a slash of Big Man's cutlass. By then, six feet, two inches tall, muscles bulging, veins sticking out, biceps the size of tree trunks, Big Man was one of the most formidable men on the island, and when talking about him people had long stopped mentioning *malmanman*. Big Man had successfully cultivated his own identity, one separate and different from his brother's. As a fearless fisherman and brutal fighter his name had spread far beyond Laborie.

So successful was Big Man in establishing his name and reputation, that he surprised everybody in Laborie when he married Rufina, a Choiseul woman of Carib, African and European ancestry. No one imagined that a man of Big Man's disposition could co-habit with a woman; or that a woman would subject herself to such a seemingly brutal and unfeeling man. Laborians were so taken aback that, though few had received wedding invitations, at the wedding ceremony the Laborie Roman Catholic Church overflowed with people. A few years after his wedding, partly to put distance between him and his brother and partly to gain a larger market for his fish, Big Man and his wife moved to Vieux Fort.

After five years of consummated marriage, during which Big Man was beginning to doubt his wife's ability to have children, and, though he would die rather than admit it, his own virility, his wife became pregnant. It was a troublesome pregnancy and a difficult and torturous birth. Rufina nearly died in the process.

Having waited so long and so anxiously to have a son, undeniable proof of his manliness, to forever banish any residual doubts he may have harbored deep down of being like his brother, and that all his aggression, fierceness and fearlessness were just a coverup of what lay deep inside him, that no matter in what soil you plant a mango palwi tree it will still bear mango palwi, Big Man had made many plans for him and his son. How they would play and watch ball together; how they would form an awesome fishing duo; and how, after a while, they would buy a second canoe and dominate the fishing scene in Vieux Fort. So engrossed was Big Man in his plans for his son that he never once contemplated that the boy was also his wife's. It was as if Big Man had paid a stranger to have his child and now the child was born it was his and his alone.

So one could well imagine how Big Man felt when he realized that the older his son became, the more he moved in the opposite direction of his expectations; when it dawned upon him that the child of his own loins, whom he had every right to expect to be fashioned in his likeness, was nothing like him. That what he had gone to great lengths and spent a lifetime to get away from, to annihilate, exterminate, eradicate, obliterate, was right there in his house, eating his food, depending on him for its very survival. That an exact replica of the brother who had shamed him and whom he had disowned, denounced, cast off, was staring him in the face every day of the week. That the child whom, as soon as he knew was a boy, he had claimed all for himself showed absolutely no interest in him; in fact cried when he came close to him, but paid rapt attention to his mother in whose presence he came alive. That the boy whom he had expected to ape his every action (the way he talked, walked, snored, sneezed, farted, even), to follow him around like a lost puppy, to hunger after being as manly as his father, was mimicking not his father but his mother, and as far as the child was concerned his father was a menacing presence to stay away from, just as a lamb instinctively knows that a sniffing bulldog meant nothing but harm.

Understandably, Big Man's first reaction was to deny that the boy was his. For it was impossible that he of all persons would father a *makoumè*, a *malmanman*. As the boy grew, Big Man's manhood took a blow. Was it true, after all, that deep inside he who was a man among men was craving to be a woman? If not, how do you explain his son? Still, no one in Vieux Fort, not even the baddest of the Bad Johns, dared to joke Big Man about his son, but in his absence Vieux Fortians took great glee in cutting Big Man down to size, to their size, at the very least. "Big Man of all persons has fathered a *malmanman*! You know he has a brother in Laborie that is a *makoumè*? You see, blood doesn't lie; a fruit doesn't fall far from its tree. An orange tree can't bear grapefruits; now, you can graft a branch of the orange tree to make it bear grapefruit, but all the other branches will continue bearing oranges."

In denial, every morning before Big Man left for sea he held a kerosene lamp over his sleeping son and examined his features, seeking evidence that the boy wasn't his. The boy had his mother's long hair, her reddish complexion, and even her greyish, encircled brownish pupils, but there was no denying that the boy's nose belonged to Big Man. A nose that dominated his face, was the first thing you noticed about him, nostrils perpetually flared up like that of an agitated race horse; nose that, depending on which angle you were looking from, seemed to occupy his whole face; nose that undoubtedly could be found on no one else on the island.

Failing to find physical evidence that would allow him to disown his son, Big Man turned to his wife. He examined her past behavior, her facial expression, how she talked, how she walked, whether there was any night that she had grudgingly given him sex, whether she was spending more time out of the house than usual. But there was nothing to find. His wife appeared to go nowhere except to the produce market and the grocery store. While everybody in Vieux Fort knew the notorious Big Man, his wife was hardly in the consciousness of the town. She rarely spoke to anyone, not even her neighbors. No one ever saw her going to church. To her neighbors she was a foreign recluse. They referred to her not as Rufina, or as Ma Big Man, but as *Madame Choiseul-la*, the Choiseul woman.

It appeared that Rufina had found a more than big enough world in Big Man, and once in that world she had no reason, no desire, no inclination, no compulsion to step out of it, and as a show of appreciation, devotion, reverence, she had dedicated her life to serving Big Man, to catering to his every whim and desire. She woke half an hour before Big Man to make sure that his breakfast was ready before he left for sea at 4:30 in the morning. Not a speck of dust could be found in the house. Big Man's dirty clothes never piled up. No sooner he finished wearing a set of clothes, she washed and ironed them. No matter how late Big Man stayed out and how drunk he returned, she never uttered a word in protest, not even when occasionally he slept out and returned in the morning with clear signs of having been with another woman.

It was as if Big Man was so powerful, hardheaded and strong willed that he could have only cohabited with someone his complete opposite. As if he took up so much space that for the relationship to work the woman had to be as small as he was big, as meek as he was fierce, as submissive as he was willful. It was as if Big Man had searched the whole island and found the only woman who would never, could not, had no desire to, and didn't have it in her nature to challenge, question, or doubt his manhood or compete with him for dominance. With such a woman, even Big Man knew he was searching for the impossible: that this Choiseul woman, this mixture of Carib, African and European ancestry, was cheating on him, *kònéing* him, as St. Lucians would say.

Unable to deny the boy his parentage, Big Man settled for exiling the girl out of his son. He did his best to force Eugene against his natural inclinations and towards the world of men. On some mornings, he would wake his six-year old son and force him to carry some of his gear to the fish depot. He banned the boy from playing with dolls and playing house or rounders with neighborhood girls. He made sure the boy took a haircut every three weeks. He gave the boy a swift beating every time he caught him powdering his face, or plaiting his hair, or trying on his mother's clothes. He forced the boy to go out on the field to mix with boys and to play cricket, football, marbles, *kabouwé*, tops, flying kites. He compelled the boy to do pushups and sit-ups every day.

However, Big Man might as well have let Eugene be, for he made matters worse for both him and his son. The way Eugene carried home the fish his father forced upon him, and the way he played football and cricket sent people into squeals of laughter. Children taunted him: "Eugene wants to be a girl. Eugene wants to be a girl." When he tried to obey his father and go play ball with the boys, none of them wanted him. "I don't want this *malmanman* on my team." "*Jamet*, go play netball with the girls." "*Makoumè*, you see any girls here?" Most times Eugene ended up where the boys were playing ball, but his eyes were glued on the girls playing netball some distance away, saying in effect you can't force a *pomme sitè* tree (golden apple tree) to bear *siwet* (gooseberry).

Unrelenting, Big Man took matters into his own hands when he tried teaching his son to play ball, but the boy's girlish movements, the womanish way he held the bat, or kicked the ball so disgusted Big Man that he knew if he were to continue teaching the boy he would kill him. So he quickly abandoned playing coach. The last thing he tried with Eugene was teaching him to swim. And it was the way Eugene flapped about in the water that finally made Big Man realize that he was fighting a hopeless battle, that once a soursop tree always a soursop tree; so instead he took to ridiculing and castigating the sore in his eyes, the thorn in his side. "Who is this *jamet* sitting down there?" "You mean to tell me, I of all persons have fathered a *jamet*." "Boy, walk properly, stop swinging your ass like a *malmanman*." "You see you, one of these days I will take you to the jetty and drown your ass, *salòp*."

In the midst of this onslaught, Rufina, while not opposing her husband, tried her best to soothe her son's wounds. "Eugene, your father can't help himself, he just wants what's best for you. Stop looking at yourself so much in the mirror, boys don't pay so much attention to how they look. Forget about the dolls, that's for girls. If you were a girl you would be too old to be still playing with dolls anyway. Listen to your father. Stop playing so much with girls, try playing more with the boys. About your father drowning you. Don't worry, he will never do that, he just wants you to learn to swim and be as strong as he is. And don't worry about the boys calling you name, is jealous they jealous of you."

Rufina's plaster on her son's wounds was largely ineffective. Big Man continued making Eugene's life a hell and made him wish he were never born. So when Big Man went to sea one morning and never returned, his son shed not a tear. But what he hadn't imagined or bargained for was that his mother would conclude that her son wasn't enough reason for her to stay in this world. Nonetheless, after her suicide, when Eugene's aunt introduced him to stall keeping, he never looked back. In stall keeping Eugene had found his calling. He was so eager and so successful at selling that he surprised even his aunt. As a stall keeper selling street side morning and evening at the cinema, at dances, at football games, on the dock, Eugene was in his element. He was in the thick of the town's gossip and was well situated to know the business of the streets — who was sleeping with whom, which woman was *kònéing* , cuckolding, her husband, who had caught the *clap* or *mòpyon* or syphilis, or which woman was offering favors to the sailors.

As a man in a woman's world and a woman in a man's body, Eugene was well suited for his business. He brought a shrewdness, a toughness, a dedication, a combative spirit to his job. His coarseness, his vulgarity, somehow didn't keep customers away. Maybe he intrigued them just as much as he did Henry. Maybe he amused them, or just maybe his prices and the quality of his goods were competitive. Whatever it was, Eugene prospered. He moved from selling out of one tray to two trays to three trays to four trays. Soon he had to pay people to carry his trays to wherever he was selling. By the time Henry started taking an interest in Eugene, he was the largest and most successful stall keeper in town. His trays were everywhere: on the dock on banana day, at the Royal Cinema, on Clarke Street, at bazaars, at dances, at football and cricket games. Eugene sitting behind his large trays heaped with fruits, drinks, and condiments, amid a group of women stall keepers, cursing off the very same customers he was serving, or leading the women in gossip, in their women-talk, was one of Vieux Fort's most colorful fixtures.

It was a glorious morning. The sun shone beautifully upon the land. The usually calm Caribbean Sea was even calmer as it glistened under the spell of the sun. A gentle breeze blowing across town was keeping the heat at bay. The trees trembled under the combined charm of sea and sun. The birds raised their voices in celebration of the magical morning, but they were not alone. Gathered on the cotton-white sands of New Dock Beach in Saturday-best garments the fifteen-member strong Seventh Day Adventist congregation were raising their voices in hymnal bliss. Between the Caribbean Sea and the congregation stood in angelic white the church's three newest converts awaiting rebirth. Among them Ruben Ishmael, the pride and joy of Vieux Fort.

For years the Adventists had been holding crusades and house to house soul-winning drives, but they had as much luck winning Vieux Fort souls as Lot had had in finding righteous people in Sodom and Gomorrah. The few converts they had managed to win came not from Vieux Fort town but from the surrounding hamlets of Augier, La Ressource, Derriere Morne, and Piero. Even so, half of these new converts backslided within a year. So it wasn't difficult to fathom the joy in the voices that rose on this Sunday morning to the tree tops that danced under the sway of the gentle breeze. At last a soul was won in Vieux Fort, and this soul wasn't just any old soul. He was a sports hero, a people's champion, a leader of men, Vieux Fort's unofficial intellectual laureate, and, more importantly, a staunch Roman Catholic nurtured by the priest himself. They had ventured into the inmost cave of the enemy and came out victorious. If they were able to convert this soul of all souls, imagine the number of Vieux Fort souls that would follow. This may well be the hammer that would crack open the Vieux Fort nut, or the rupture in the dam through which once water started to flow nothing could hold it back.

The church to the last member pictured Brother Ishmael leading the young people's meeting, becoming church elder, using his eloquent, educated voice at crusades to woo people into the church. Just by mere example, drawing in Vieux Fort people. As sure as the brightness of this enchanted morning and as sure as the sand on which they stood was white, they saw the church growing by leaps and bounds. They counted the growth in their tithes, offerings and ingathering collections. In their minds' eyes they saw over and over again the plan of the new church that these monies would make possible. It would not be long before they said good-bye to the two-by-four rented shack that passed as a church and where toads entered through holes in the flooring, making a mockery of God's House, giving Henry and the other children a holiday chasing toads around, and giving Eunice a near heart attack.

Ah, praise the Lord. Praise ye His name. Let us raise a joyful sound. For what was lost is found. Brother Ishmael. Let ye be a shining witness to the Lord. A knight in shining armor. A city on a hill.

It was a special morning for Eunice. When she, her son and her soon-to-be husband walked from her home to New Dock Beach, it seemed that the world had come to a standstill; that every blade of grass, every bird in the sky, every tree on the hilltop was praising and worshiping God. The breeze was blowing more calmly, the trees were swaying more gently, the birds were singing more sweetly, the animals in the pasture were grazing more peacefully. When her husband-to-be had charged into her yard during the part of the morning when night wasn't sure of whether to end and day of whether to begin, with the announcement, pronouncement rather, that he would be baptized as soon as the church could baptize him, today even, and they should get married immediately afterwards because he loved her, and he had wasted enough time, and how could he have been so foolish taking so long to be baptized, her heart and mind had turned to mush, a tremor that had nothing to do with the morning chill came over her, and the best she could do, the most she could do was mumble his name and fall into his arms.

Five years had passed since the day she received the news that her husband and his swimming partner were found awash on Enbakoko Beach. It had been five years of loneliness, five years with only her son and the memory of her husband to keep her company. But in the past year things had begun to change. For despite her best efforts to keep her heart shielded and buried in Christ, Ruben had begun to occupy her mind as much and on some days even more than her husband. Day by day she was falling deeper and deeper for him. Before he started taking an interest in her, she had already resigned herself to what fate had dealt her. All the men in her church of marriageable age were married. So where would she find a husband? In the midst of this famine she had decided to devote her life to raising her son and serving her God. Then Ruben came along, and despite the jungle and the multiple walls she put up, this man, refusing to back down, had entered her life, providing a glimmer of hope that her loneliness might not be for much longer. But she couldn't allow herself too much hope, for he was a staunch Roman Catholic and she would not be unequally yoked.

Now, standing in the middle of the baptismal congregation, on this saintly morning, on this reverent beach, at the foot of Moule-a-Chique, raising her voice in blissful celebration, she knew her loneliness would be no more, and she would have the rest of her life to admire, enjoy, feast on Ruben's broad athletic shoulders, his muscle-rippled body, his deep probing intellect, and above all his walk that created the impression that he was forever walking on springs and that conjured images of a black panther set to take off. The very man she had ached for at nights and who had filled her days, giving her life color, flavor and form, would soon be hers, all hers.

Praise the Lord, she has won one for Christ. Praise the Lord, she has found a husband. Praise the Lord, she will be lonely no more. Praise the Lord, her son has found a father. Praise the Lord, hallowed be His name.

Even Henry, not much given to singing at church services, preferring instead to watch or gawk, as his mother would say, at women breast feeding babies, young children raising a racket from hunger, heat exhaustion and inactivity, and the animated face of the preacher and those hanging onto his every word, was raising his voice in celebration and thanksgiving. Today, this morning, in the next few minutes, Ruben would be baptized. Two months from this morning Ruben would marry his mother and she would be equally yoked. He would have a father and his mother would have a husband. But the good news would-n't stop there. It would not be long before he had a little brother and maybe a little sister too. Yes, he would be a big brother. Imagine that! As proof of all this, ever since the morning that before the roosters had finished their morn-ing crows, him still trying desperately to hang on to sleep and wondering why in the first place God had created early mornings, Ruben had come in bursting with talk of baptism and weddings, as if baptism and weddings were about to run out of stock, he had started calling Ruben daddy again and his mother had offered no rebuke.

Thank you Jesus. Holy be thy name. Thank you for answering my prayers. Thank you for not forsaking me and my mother. Thank you for sending us Mr. Ishmael. Blessed are those who wait, for they shall inherit the earth.

The spectators gathered. Some on the dock, some on the hill overlooking the beach, a few on the beach to the right of the baptismal congregation.

Many came just for entertainment. It was an event of high drama. They were fascinated by the notion that rather than following the Roman Catholic humane and civilized approach to baptism, which essentially entailed pouring a cup of water over the head of the victim, and doing it at an age when the victim would not even know much less remember what poured down his head and over his face, the barbaric Adventists actually ducked the people whole suit, whole body, under water as if intent on inflicting death by water. That one such as Ruben Ishmael would be counted among the sacrificial lambs, lifted the drama to Shakespearean heights.

The Stall Keeper

It was a rare event. An event not to be missed. In this place lawsuits for personal injuries were unheard of and, in any case, stupidity counted against the victims in court. As if aware of this Vieux Fortians were never in too big a hurry to tempt fate, so the Adventists were almost never able to find among Vieux Fortians candidates for their human sacrifice. Therefore, who knows when there would be another *Semdays* baptism, another ceremony of death by water. Especially where one such as Ruben Ishmael would be counted among the victims.

To some others, those closer to Ruben like the core team of parishioners (of whom Ruben was a key member) who had become an extension of Father Pierre in carrying out his many cultural and social programs, or his sport team-mates to whom the Adventists' gain was their loss, this was no laughing matter. Just the other day they had witnessed Ruben in his full glory. In front of the whole of Vieux Fort he had explained why Vieux Fort was the way it was, and that Vieux Fortians were not to blame for their backwardness. That Vieux Fort was a victim of its geography, and that it was this geography that had kept Vieux Fortians landless and thus backward. He had pointed out that the only way for Vieux Fort to develop socially and economically was for its people to own the land their homes were on. He had made them so proud to be Vieux Fortians. He had made them believe in themselves and in their future, believe that their town would soon take off, believe wholeheartedly that Vieux Fort would soon surpass Castries. Yet there he was joining the *Semdays*, abandoning them as if all what he had said had been a lie, a farce, something he cooked up just to sound good and appear intelligent but in which he held no belief.

Staunch Roman Catholics who couldn't bring themselves to believe their ears, couldn't bring themselves to believe this betrayal, this aberration, came to see for themselves. So too were those to whom he wasn't just a fellow church goer, someone they shared a pew with, but their image of perfection, one in whom they reveled and in whose glory and achievements they shared; the son whom they worshipped, the big brother whom they looked up to for self-definition, the younger brother through whom they lived their ideal lives.

His fellow cricketers and footballers came hoping that the unimaginable would not happen. That a man who breathed and drank sports, who was the first to round up his team to start hitting ball when the cricket season came around, and the first to start jogging to get in shape for the football competition, who was their sports library, their hope and inspiration, their coach, their captain, the one whose leadership and heroics on the field guaranteed that win or lose Vieux Fort would always give Castries a run for their money, would not let them down, would not let Vieux Fort down, would not join this *Semdays one week* business for the sake of a woman who already had a child and who could be his mother.

At first, some of the spectators to whom what was happening on the beach was serious business had joked about Ruben's passion for the *Semdays* woman, convinced that this was a passing thing and he would soon come to his senses. Some could recall that he had been just as intense about the last woman he was with, the one who after an eighteen-month relationship apparently gave him up as too good to be true. So when after several months of unsuccessfully pursuing Eunice, Ruben had returned to his old self and started sleeping with other women, his friends smugly amused themselves with the thought that they had been right all along and their hero was finally cured of the *Semdays* woman. Not that they particularly approved of these other women. They were always a bit perplexed about why a man who could have any woman he wanted kept going after older women and women who were way beneath him. Some even wondered whether despite all his gifts and achievements Ruben suffered from low self esteem. But to each his own, and thank God these women were all Catholics or at least they didn't profess any other religion.

Of course what Ruben's friends didn't know was that his liaisons with these other women brought him little joy. While on top of them he imagined they were Eunice. This made him feel dirty and guilty of defying the spirit of the woman he wished so much to get close to. In fact he got more satisfaction simply brushing against Eunice than sex with these women. So, understandably, he rushed the sex and didn't linger in the company of the women after it was over. So the sex was even less fun for the women than it was for him. Finally, about a year before the morning of his momentous decision, he said, "Enough is enough," and he entered a period of celibacy. By then he couldn't stop talking about Eunice: how wonderful and special she was, and that his search was over; he has found the woman who would become his wife and the mother of his children, even if that meant joining the *Semdays* church.

The people around Ruben were alarmed. They knew what this meant. Father Pierre and the presbytery would lose its main organizer of events, his sports club would lose their captain and their best footballer and cricketer. Some of the most important matches took place on Saturdays, and the Adventists didn't play sports on their Sabbath.

They were baffled. Why would Ruben give up so much for a woman who didn't look anything like fun. Why would such an intelligent and gifted man let this country bookie woman trap him; trap him so badly that he couldn't even think straight? They didn't get it. Maybe they would have got it if Ruben was getting sex from the woman. Then they could have said, "This must be some fantastic piece of ass." But by Ruben's own admission—and not without a sprinkling of pride—no sex was involved and that this was a pure and sanctified relationship. So what was it then?

Devoid of a satisfactory explanation, some of Ruben's associates did what the people of the island always did when they could find no rational explanation for events such as a nasty sore suddenly appearing on one's leg and refusing to go away; a fat, healthy cow dying of no apparent cause; or a once successful business suddenly going under. They turned to the supernatural. Someone has put obeah on Ruben. Of this they were sure. For why else would a man who wasn't a priest deliberately impose celibacy on himself? When even the priests themselves were having trouble keeping their vows as the many married women who could boast of holy sex can attest to; or worse, the young boys whose services to the priests went beyond their roles as acolytes. No, this wasn't natural. This went contrary to the nature of men. Everyone knew it was a man's nature to have more than one woman. That's the way God made them. And who could change the will of God? A man's nature was a man's nature. A cat can't bark, and a dog can't meow. And no amount of talking, no amount of vexation, or of wishing it wasn't so could change that. So it was the *jamets*, the loose women, who were to blame for men sleeping around. These *jamets* just refuse to leave people's husbands alone. Yet here was Ruben enjoying the pleasures of not three or two or one woman but no woman at all, and as far as one could tell he was proud and happy about it all. Something definitely wasn't right. Something fishy was going on. They smelt a rat that had been dead for days.

Still, given what was at stake, in their heart of hearts Ruben's friends were hoping that he would pull through. For if there was one person who could overcome an obeah spell it would have to be Ruben. They knew that once the obeah has started taking effect it was almost impossible not to succumb, but they were hoping that Ruben's superior intellect and physical prowess would neutralize it. That he would pull through in much the same way that in the past he had come up with a piece of football or cricket magic to beat Castries in a close game. But then they heard about the baptism and knew all was lost. But they wanted to see it with their own eyes. To see whether the impossible would happen. So here they were, on the hilltop, on the dock, on the beach, bearing witness to the powers of obeah and wondering whether this was the beginning of Ruben's downfall.

Nonetheless, unmindful of both the spectators who were there for amusement and those who where there out of misgivings, the Seventh Day Adventist congregation raised their voices to the heavens, "Shall we gather at the river . . . In the sweet by and by . . . Showers of blessings."

A pair of ground doves flew overhead, casting their moving shadow on the gathering. Somewhere in the bush a dog barked three times. The Pastor prayed, thanking God for the souls won, and asking God to protect them from the snares of the Devil. He then opened his Bible to Matthew 2:10-11. He preached of the Baptism of John the Baptist, leaving out the part where he was beheaded by Herod as a present to his wife. The Pastor turned to Mark 4:5-8, and talked about having to forsake even your mother and father to serve the Lord. As soon as the Pastor finished his baptismal sermon, the Church burst into song. As they sang the Pastor walked into the sea to waist-height. The moment of sacrifice, the moment of rebirth had arrived.

The first victim, the first sacrificial lamb, a tall, slim woman in her fifties, supported on each side by a Brother, was led into the water to meet the pastor. Holding one hand at her waist, the pastor lifted up his right hand, which held a rag, to the heavens (at this point the singing stopped) and said, "I baptize you in the name of the Father, the name of the Son, and the name of the Holy Ghost." Then, still holding unto the woman at her waist with his left hand, he placed his right hand over the woman's face and ducked her under the sea. As her head hit water the spectators chorused: "*Hee. Hee. Hee salòp!*"

Following the sacrifice, as if invigorated by the salt-laden sea breeze, the church burst into song. The second victim was the woman's thirteen year old daughter. She looked frail and disoriented. But the hecklers took no pity on her. As the pastor ducked her they shouted: "*Hee. Hee. Hee salòp!*"

Finally, it was Ruben's turn. The singing was turned up a notch. He was led and supported into the water. The spectators fell silent. To many they had never seen Ruben look so helpless, so resigned. The indomitable Ruben who, no matter what, once he was on a football or cricket team no one dared bet against that team; Ruben the infinite source of knowledge, the go-to guy when questions arose for which no one else had the answers, the one who wrote and read letters for those who couldn't read and write, now needed the support of not one but two men to get to where any six year old could venture alone. No. The spectators watched in disbelief. The parishioners and some of Ruben's close friends saw further evidence of obeah at work. Even the hecklers were moved. Their "*Hee. Hee. Hee salòp*" was late in coming, arriving several seconds after the pastor had already ducked Ruben. As the pastor raised Ruben from his watery grave, the dog again barked three times, a flock of ground doves took off from a treetop, the voice of the baptismal congregation rose to the heavens.

VIEUX FORT WAS CHASING A TOTAL OF 148 RUNS. It was the second innings of the match that would decide the winner of the trophy. The second wicket had just fallen, it was his turn at the crease. His nervous teammates were looking everywhere for him, the anxious crowd was shouting, "Where is Ruben? Where is Ruben?" His shirt was halfway unbuttoned and not tucked in his pants, one pad was on while the other was in his hand, one of his gloves was missing. He was on New Dock Road, heading to the cricket field to take his place at the crease, but a mighty gust from the Atlantic was pushing him in the opposite direction. He could hear the crowd shouting, "Ruben! Ruben! Ruben!" But fight as he might he couldn't move forward, he was hopelessly stuck. Eunice, Henry and the rest of the Adventist bunch were all laughing at him, their faces mean and distorted. Finally the Atlantic gust let up a bit and he was able to push forward but only to arrive at a game that was over. Without him Castries had won by 52 runs, with three wickets in hand. The crowd booed and pelted him with stones, bottles, cans and whatever else they could find. His students and sport protégés spat on him. His teammates called him traitor, Judas, sellout. One long *chups* escaped the mouth of Eunice. Henry looked at him straight in the eye and said, "That man eh my father."

His head bent from the weight of shame, hopelessness and helplessness. He cringed, his body shrank. The shame was too much to bear. In his anguish he yelled, "Noooo!" Then he woke up, looked at his clock. It was only 5:30AM. His relief and happiness that it was just a dream was indescribable. As he gained further consciousness, he muttered, "What am I thinking, today is only the first match of the season, and it's no Castries-Vieux Fort match. It's just Islanders we playing." Then he said, "Oh shucks!" And a dark cloud blanketed his moment-ago relief and happiness. For he just remembered that today was Saturday, the first Saturday since his baptism. At 8:00AM he was to meet Eunice and Henry and walk to Church with them.

He was now a Seventh Day Adventist and the time between sunset Friday and sunset Saturday belonged strictly to the Lord. For it is written: *Remember the Sabbath day, to keep it holy. Six days shall thou labour, and do all thy work: But the seventh day is the Sabbath of the Lord thy God: In it thou shall not do any work, thou, nor thy son, nor thy daughter,* . . . As a Seventh Day Adventist he must take this Sabbath business seriously, for it was the keeping of the Saturday Sabbath, more than anything else, that separated the Seventh Day Adventist from the rest of the world. Beginning with the setting sun, he must do no cooking, no washing of dishes, no sweeping of the yard, no reading of newspapers, novels, schoolbooks; no listening to the radio, no playing of soccer, cricket, nor any other sport; no thinking of the past week's worldly activities, no planning of next week's activities. It was a special day, a holy day. A day in which his mind, body and soul must completely rest from worldly activities. A day of spiritual rejuvenation. A day in which his mind, body, and soul would be revitalized. A day of worship. A day in which all his thoughts and deeds must be geared toward honoring and praising God. It was a day set aside to acknowledge and appreciate God's handiwork in its full majesty — God's creation of the world. It was a day of remembrance. A day in which every silhouette, every blade of grass, every gust of wind must remind him that it was God who created the heavens and the earth. Every Friday evening should signal to him the completion of a freshly created world. The Sabbath was a renewal of the covenant between God and man, between the Creator and the created, the Master and the servants, the Worshipped and the worshippers, the Holy and the unholy. The Sabbath was to bring him closer to the likeness of God. As an Adventist every Sabbath day he must turn the clock back to the creation, when *there was the word, and the word was with God, and the word was God*. When God first breathed into the nostrils of molded clay and gave rise to man, before Adam and Eve partook of the forbidden fruit, when man was still perfect, when man was the image of God, when man was God.

How could he have forgotten? Midweek he had held a meeting with his sports club during which he told them that he could remain a team selector and the president of the club, but since the cricket matches were played on Saturdays (and Sundays), his Sabbath Day, he would not be able to play, therefore he had to give up the captaincy.

Some of his teammates shook their heads. They were expecting it, yet they had refused to believe it would actually happen. True, they had watched the Adventist pastor duck him whole suit under water, and they had been embarrassed for him, the way he of all persons had to be supported in the water like a lost and helpless child. And true, some of them had toyed with the notion that obeah was involved. But to them the whole scene had looked like child's play, unreal, make-believe, comical, even. So, not fully believing what their eyes had told them, and lacking a proper appreciation of the significance of the Saturday Sabbath to Adventism, they had hoped that at the last minute he would change his mind. Without him how could they defend their title? What would prevent Castries, Micoud, Laborie, and even Gros Islet from walking all over Vieux Fort? Besides being by far their best cricketer: their best batsman, their best bowler, he was the strategist, the brain of the team. When they won the toss he was the one who examined the condition of the pitch to determine whether it was to their advantage to bat first. He was the one who studied the batsmen and bowlers of the opposing team to instruct his bowlers how best to bowl to each bats-man and his batsmen what to expect from the opposing bowlers. But here he was, saying he had to give up the cap-taincy for he would not be able to play the matches, as if he were replaceable, as if playing without him was as easy and as inconsequential as a child skipping to J.Q., Green, Katie or Miss Innes to buy a half pound of sugar. Understandably, the meeting went into uproar.

"Skip, you joking or what? You our best player, you the best player in Vieux Fort, and you going to quit on us just like that?"

"What you talking about? The Skip eh just the best cricketer in Vieux Fort, the man is the best player on the island."

"Is for that old woman he joined the *Semdays*, you know; is for that old woman."

"Guys, have some respect," said Ruben, "have some respect. This is the woman I 'm going to marry. This is the woman who will be the mother of my children. This is the woman I will spend the rest of my life with. So have some respect. Or else I will have no choice but to walk out on this meeting."

"The man right. Have some respect."

"But, Skip, how you expect us to beat Islanders; as it is they already stronger than us? How you expect us to win the cup this year? And how about when we playing Castries? Skip, you cannot be serious."

"Skip, even if you join the *Semdays*, you can still play; it's not like we have a match every Saturday. When we not playing, you could go to your church. And besides, the *Semdays* does have church Wednesday and Sunday nights. So there plenty of opportunities for you to go to church."

"You all don't understand," said Ruben. "Adventists do not work or play on the Sabbath. Period."

"Skip, that's nonsense. Everyone knows it's Sunday that's the Sabbath. And everyone who worships on Sundays does work and play on Sundays."

"Yes, Skip, the man right. The *Semdays* does read their Bible upside down, and they a bunch of hypocrites. Don't let them fool you?"

"No, you all fellas have it all wrong. Exodus talks about remember the Sabbath Day to keep it holy, and that the seventh day is the Lord's Sabbath, and in it people should not do any work."

"But skip, that's the Old Testament. You yourself have heard Father Pierre say that with the coming of Christ, the Old Testament became, how he does put it, less relevant, and many of the practices were no longer necessary because Christ's blood on the cross made up for that."

"Yeah," said Ruben, "but even the New Testament talks about the Sabbath. For example, Hebrews says, 'there remaineth a rest for the people of God,' and in the Greek language, the original language of the Bible, rest means Sabbath."

"Fellas, we wasting time with that man. See how he turn preacher. If the man wants to go, let him go. No one is indispensable. Not even him. And fellas, I tell you, it eh no Sabbath the man wants to keep. Is for that old woman he joining *Semdays*."

"Give the Skip some respect! But serious, Skip, this is a big mistake. Don't go through with it. After all, you our skipper. Don't leave us dry like this. Don't just give up everything, just like that. Something you been doing all your life. Maybe this year is the year it will all pay off for you. Maybe this year is the year you go make the national team, not as an extra but as a bona fide player. And who knows, from there you may make the Combined Islands team, and then the West Indies team will be well within your grasp. Why throw all this away? I just don't understand you."

"Fellas, I tell you all, you all wasting you all time. It's this *Semdays* woman. She has tied him up. She has put obeah on him. So you all wasting you all time."

"Skip, you mean to tell me you doing all that for a piece of ass, when there is ass for next to nothing all over the place?"

"Who say he getting pussy? He doing all that in the hope of getting some! You think these *Semdays* women easy?"

Ruben could take it no longer. He half shouted, half screamed, "I gone!" and walked out of the room.

Lying there in bed, this last meeting replaying in his head, Ruben was miserable with himself. He was a man faced with an unpleasant task that he wished would pass away without him having to make a decision. Like a man summoning up courage to break up with his girlfriend of many years. What will it be? Church or cricket? Either way he would lose. This wasn't the Roman Catholic Church where you simply had to profess to be one and you were one, where a simple trip to confession would absolve you from all your sins, where no matter how much bacchanal you were in, you could still claim membership. If he were to break the Sabbath, the church would be compelled to disfellowship him. That he wouldn't mind one bit, but surely if he were no longer a member of the Church, Eunice, the love of his life, would without a doubt break off their engagement. There were only seven weeks left for her to be all his, every day in the week, every week in the month, every month in the year, every year in his life. He couldn't throw away his one and only opportunity to be happy. So he would have to give up the cricket. With these thoughts he fell asleep. He woke up at 6:30 excited that today was the opening of the cricket season. But as he was about to get up he remembered that it was his Sabbath, he had to go to church. His excitement was replaced with unpleasantness; his day was going to be miserable and joy-less. He remained in bed and soon dozed off again.

At seven he got up and started coffee, then remembered that as an Adventist he mustn't drink coffee. Irritated, he mumbled, "Who will stop me?" He drank the coffee, black, without sugar. That's the way he always drank coffee. He liked to taste the natural harshness of it. He would put sugar in his bush or cocoa tea and in his juice, but not in his coffee. To add sugar or cream would be to take away from the harsh taste. Besides, if it were syrup or milk he wanted to drink, he would have done so. Coffee aroma filled the room. He could never decide which he liked best—the smell or the taste of coffee? As a child when he visited his father on mornings to beg money for his mother, coffee, black and without sugar, was one of the things he saw his father drinking. Then, in his eyes, his father was as big as a mountain and as powerful as an ox. From that time on he would associate black coffee with strength, courage and manliness. Later on his notion of coffee as a symbol of masculinity would be further enhanced by the Western novels he read — cowboys and gunslingers around the camp-fire drinking black coffee and trading stories of their adventures. Between swigs of coffee, Ruben "*chuppsed*" as he realized that as a Seventh Day Adventist this was yet another of his pleasures he would have to give up. Not that he wasn't aware or hadn't given thought to all the restrictions that came along with joining the church, but in his excitement and anticipation of finally marrying the woman of his dreams, he had pushed them towards the back of his mind. But as he was now realizing, it was one thing to munch on something in the abstract but a whole different kettle of fish to confront them in practice.

Done with his cup of coffee, and momentarily forgetting himself, Ruben did what he did the morning of every cricket match. He hung a sock with a cricket ball on a tamarind tree in his yard and started practicing his strokes. Seven-forty-five he was still there hitting the ball, building up a sweat. At 8:15, the sock burst. He made some more coffee and ate bread and cheese for breakfast. He replaced the sock and resumed his practice. Next thing he knew it was 8:45, past the time he was supposed to meet Eunice and Henry. He said to himself, "No matter, I will meet them in church." At nine he took a shower and got dressed. But when he looked at himself in the mirror he was surprised that instead of being dressed for church, he had on his white cricket uniform. He sat down and thought about it for awhile. Then he said, "Oh hell, it's already on me. It's only for this Saturday, next Saturday I will go to church for sure." Relieved he had found a compromise that seemed to work, he picked up his pads, gloves, bat, and groin cup, and walked to the field.

The match started at 10:00, but as always he was the first player to arrive. He looked up at the sun and clouds. They smiled down at him telling him it was going to be a beautiful day for cricket. The scent of the newly mowed field mixed with animal dung from the surrounding pastures, which he would forever associate with cricket and football, filled his nostrils. Intermittent gusts from the Atlantic Ocean whipped up grass particles into a dance. He examined the cricket pitch to make sure that it was properly rolled, that no roughs were showing. He also walked around the field to make certain that the boundaries were properly marked.

When his teammates arrived to find him dressed and waiting impatiently for the action to start, they were in heaven.

"The Skipper is back. The Skipper is back"

"I knew I could count on Skip. I knew no woman, or religion, or obeah could keep him from his cricket, especially the first match of the season."

"Skip, I meant no disrespect last meeting, you know. I was just blowing off steam. That's all I was doing. Blowing steam."

"Skip, I've a good feeling this morning. I've a good feeling we go beat Islanders hands down."

"Skip, the guys voted me captain, but I know is only one Skipper we have and that's you. Skip, what you think? If we win the toss, we should bat first?"

WHEN RUBEN DIDN'T SHOW UP, Eunice was extremely disturbed. How could he miss the first Sabbath service after his baptism? She knew today was the opening of the cricket season. She just hoped that his reason for missing church was that he had overslept or he wasn't feeling too well, and not because he went and play cricket on the Sabbath of the Lord. Throughout the service, expecting Ruben to enter any minute, she kept looking at the door. Nonetheless, the deeper they got into the Sabbath program, the more she began to question his sincerity. Was he really interested in serving God? Had he truly repented of all his sins? Had he joined simply to obtain her hand in marriage? Is it all a big lie? Is he planning to go back to the world as soon as they get married? She sensed that the church members were holding her responsible for Ruben, for keeping him on the straight and narrow path. She couldn't blame them. She was the one who had brought him in, who, through endless Bible discussions, had made him see the light. The whole church had been so excited about Ruben. All of them were saying that with Ruben in their midst they could now make some headway in Vieux Fort. They had praised her for helping to win such a valuable soul for the Lord. She could not let them down, she could not let her Lord Jesus down. She just hoped that Ruben wasn't on the field breaking the Lord's Sabbath. How could he make her look so bad in the eyes of her brothers and sisters?

At one o'clock, after church, Eunice and her son headed home along New Dock Road. They could see a cricket match in progress. Her son said, "Mama, look at Mr. Ruben bowling." Although she wasn't supposed to watch or listen to any sport on the Sabbath, she couldn't help but watch him. He started his runup a good many yards from the stumps. He ran, picked up speed, jumped, delivered. The batsman left it alone. He walked back to his runup mark. He turned around to catch the ball thrown to him by a teammate. He sprinted, jumped, delivered. The batsman played forward but missed the ball completely, it struck his pads, causing Ruben and his teammates to raise their hands and shout, "Umpire!" The umpire shook his head, "Not out." Ruben picked up the ball off the pitch, he walked back, turned, ran, jumped, delivered. The ball flew the off stump and carried it several feet behind the wicket. There was no need to hear from the umpire. The batsman walked off the field. Ruben's teammates thronged him in celebration. A loud "*chups*" escaped the mouth of Eunice. Henry said, "Mama! Mr. Ruben really fast."

To that Eunice said, "Shut up boy, remember today is Sabbath." Still, she couldn't help but notice how beautiful and majestic he was just before he delivered the ball, when he was airborne and his arm outstretched towards the heavens. He reminded her of an airplane about to land, an eagle swooping down on its prey, a whale or dolphin shooting up from under water. He was magnificent.

That Saturday night Eunice hardly closed her eyes. Over and over again Ruben's magnificent bowling action played in her head. Yet she couldn't believe that barely a week since he got baptized, since he pledged to give the Lord his heart, pledged to leave the things of the world behind, he was there playing cricket on the Sabbath. He who had come to her so early in the morning (that she thought something terrible had happened) to beg her hand in marriage, and to beg for baptism as if it was in short supply, for he had seen the light, Seventh Day Adventist was the true church, he would repent of all his sins and give God his heart, was out there in front of the whole world making a mockery of her, of her entire church and more seriously, of God. So in the morning, Sunday, no sooner had she prepared breakfast for her son, she paid Ruben a visit. When she arrived he was there drinking coffee. He tried to hide that fact from her, but who could hide the aroma of coffee? He lived in a one bedroom house where there were no separations between the kitchen, dining and living room.

Books and newspapers were scattered all over the place. His surprise at her visit he made no attempt to hide. Nonetheless, she didn't have to open her mouth for him to know her purpose.

She went straight to the point. "Ruben, you just baptize, but there you are breaking the Sabbath. Why you mocking God? Why you get baptize knowing full well you will not keep the Sabbath holy? And Ruben, don't you know Adventist doesn't drink coffee?"

In a pleading, self-defacing voice, Ruben said, "Darling, I'm sorry. I had completely forgotten that it was the Sabbath. But that wasn't deliberate. It's habit. It was just a slip. It will not happen again. Darling, I promise. God strike me dead, if I'm not speaking the truth."

"Ruben, you mustn't tempt God," said Eunice, and she took the opportunity to give her husband-to-be a lecture on keeping the Sabbath, and the rewards of forsaking the things of the world and serving God wholeheartedly. She told him about the Jews, how it was because they kept the Sabbath that they were so rich. Then she said, "Let's kneel down and pray."

"Heavenly Father," she prayed, "we humbly beseech Thee to take Ruben Ishmael into Thy hands. He is a new convert. He is a lamb in a den of lions. I pray Thee guide and protect him. Give him the strength and courage to resist the Devil and his temptations. Open his mind's eyes so he can see that it will profit him nothing if he were to gain the whole world and suffer the loss of his soul. Amen."

Eunice left convinced that her visit would bear fruit, and her husband-to-be had seen the errors of his ways, and from now on he would keep the Sabbath holy. And it seemed that indeed Ruben had truly repented. He visited her every afternoon. They continued adding final touches to their wedding plans and their life as a married couple. Sunday and Wednesday night, hand in hand, like a family, they (Ruben, Henry and Eunice) walked to church.

But Saturday, when Ruben got up he wasn't sure whether he would go to church or go play his cricket. It was only after he had put on his white, long-sleeve shirt, his washed but cricket-ball-stained white pants, his white Bata (canvas shoes) and his white cricket cap that he knew for sure it would be cricket and not Sabbath. This time his team was playing against Micoud in Micoud.

The church was deeply concerned. Ruben was too precious a soul to allow to backslide. Too much was riding on his back. He was the key to unlocking the deadbolts of Vieux Fortians' heathen hearts. They couldn't leave the task at hand to Eunice alone. So in the evening the whole church, Eunice and Henry included, visited Ruben and held an impromptu prayer meeting at his home. The battle for his soul had gone up a notch. Ruben was so deeply moved that a tear-drop rolled down his face. This was proof enough of his sincerity, so the church went home pleased with their night's work, totally convinced that they had defeated the Devil.

All during the week Ruben beat upon himself. When will he learn? Why did he have to go play cricket on the Sabbath again? Hadn't he done enough damage the first Saturday? How could he be so stupid, throwing so much away for a silly, little game? What's wrong with him? He has found the woman of his dreams, his one and only hope of marrying, of genuine love, yet he was discarding it as if it came a dime a dozen, as if around every corner there was an even better love waiting for him, as if all he needed to do was snap his fingers and love would come running his way, so why bother much about this one love? Wasn't it him who, since he was a toddler still wetting his bedding, had promised himself of not repeating his father's foolishness, of not becoming the ridicule of Vieux Fort, of not having children with different women, of not knowing, feeding and raising his children? So then why was he there throwing his life away, putting himself on a path crowded with his father's foot prints, all in the name of a senseless game in which there was no future? Throughout that week, several times a day, Ruben fell on his knees to ask God forgiveness, to ask the Most High to give him strength to overcome his love of cricket, to overcome the Devil's ploy of preventing him from realizing true and lasting happiness. And indeed it seemed that God had answered Ruben's prayers, and like Christ in the wilderness he had been able to tell the Devil, "Get thee behind me, Satan." Because that week he went to the Sunday night and Wednesday night prayer meetings and joined fervently in the praying and singing, and nightly he teamed up with Eunice in Bible studies. Yes, he has found the right woman. Yes, he would keep his promises. Yes, he would live in marital bliss. Such was Ruben's turn around that neither Eunice nor the church felt any further need to chastise him. But come Saturday Ruben's resolve melted away like butter in a frying pan, so it was the cricket uniform, not the church clothes, that he found on his person.

The church needed souls. Eunice needed a husband. Henry needed a father. So the congregation asked the pastor to have a chat with Ruben. The pastor went and fellowshiped with Ruben. He admonished him, he prayed for him. Ruben showed plenty of remorse. He asked God for forgiveness and pledged to keep the Sabbath. Satisfied that he had succeeded where Eunice and his Vieux Fort flock had failed, providing him with evidence of the need and value of pastors, that the money spent on pastor salaries and on generous housing and traveling allowances was money well spent, and that the generosity of his various congregations in the form of free lunches and prodigious supplies of ground provisions were well deserved, the pastor drove home to Soufriere with a song in his heart. Again, during the week no one had anything to complain about a remorseful and committed Ruben. No one could have been as hard on him as he was on himself. But Saturday nothing changed. Ruben's church clothes remained hanging on its nail, gathering dust, and his cricket pants accumulated more red, cricket-ball stains.

IT WASN'T BECAUSE OF A LACK OF WILLINGNESS or a lack of trying that Ruben continued to break the Sabbath. After all, he loved Eunice wholeheartedly and no one knew better than him that she would not marry him if he continued breaking the Sabbath, if he wasn't a Seventh Day Adventist. But willing as he was, and no matter how much he beat upon himself, he couldn't deliver. Cricket meant too much to him. It was part of his self definition. It was his art, his poetry, his music, his muse, his way of seeing and organizing the world, his life. What could replace the elation of running up to the wicket, jumping, delivering and watching the batsman's off stump fly; or the god-like feeling of driving the ball magnificently and effortlessly through the covers such that no sooner than the ball left the bat, spectators, commentators and fieldsmen alike knew without a doubt that this was four more runs, and realizing the futility of giving chase, not one fieldsman would move; or the adrenaline rush of chasing a ball and catching up with it just inside the boundary, turning around to discover that the batsmen had decided to go for a third run, throwing the ball with all your might and watching it crack the wickets before the batsman arrived safely home; or the excruciating excitement of facing the last ball of the match and knowing that no matter how the ball came you had to hit it for four or six, because your team needed no less than four runs to win; or the nearly unbearable tension of bowling the last over of the match to a team that needed just six runs to win, and the only thing standing between them and victory was the accuracy and cleverness of your bowling.

He was a brilliant footballer too, so much so that they called him "The Brazilian." And few would disagree that football came with its own thrills, and many a football fan would maintain that football was a much more exciting and tantalizing sport than cricket. Indeed, if cricket was his first love, football was a close second. For who could doubt the pleasure of an exquisite through-pass to a teammate that resulted in a goal; the child-like delight of beating a defender flat on his backside, waiting for him to get up and then giving him the same treatment all over again; the unconscious, in-the-zone sensation of hitting a volley to the top corner of the goalpost and watching the goal keeper's hopeless outstretched effort at saving the goal; the honey-sweetened ecstasy of dribbling past three defenders and then the goal keeper and then walking the ball into the goal as if taking a cool, late afternoon stroll under Enbakoko Gui. Clearly, there were just as many thrills to be had in football as there were in cricket, and football too was well up to the task of satisfying his need to be creative and artistic. For what was more artistic or creative than bending a ball away from a goal keeper into the net, or running at full speed with the ball glued to one's forehead?

Still there was something cricket did for him that made it beat out football any day, any time. To him cricket was more of an intellectual game, more of a thinking man's game. Cricket was a game with more nuances, a game with a larger dose of psychology, a game that required more strategic thinking. To excel a batsman had to study a bowler, know his full arsenal. He had to anticipate — by the placement of the field, the bowler's body language, his arm action, the angle of his approach to the wicket, his previous deliveries — what ball the bowler would bowl, and yet the batsman still had to be prepared for the unexpected. He had to study the nature and condition of the pitch and determine whether it was fast or slow, whether it lent itself to bounce, whether it was totally unpredictable. At all times the batsman had to be aware of his surroundings, the placement of the field, because where the fieldsmen were would determine whether a ball hit in the air was a wonderful stroke or an act of stupidity that would cost him his wicket; whether a magnificently struck ball would rush away to the boundary for four or travel straight to a fieldsman for no runs or for just a single.

The bowler's task was no less tricky. He had to know the batsman, know his favorite shots, know the shots the batsman played that usually got him out. He had to be aware of the batsman's state of mind: was he in an impatient mood? Was he unsettled, nervous, shaky, lacking confidence? The bowler had to vary his deliveries. Occasionally he needed to bowl the unexpected — the slower one, the faster one, the yorker, or the bouncer to put the batsman on the defensive and make him think more about his safety than about playing the ball, or the just short of a good length ball to entice a batsman into hooking and thus get him to give an easy catch. Clearly, it was a mind game, a chess game, a mental duel.

The captain had to be a master strategist. If he won the toss he had to study the weather and the cricket pitch to determine how well the pitch would hold up after a day or two of play, and whether it favored the bowler or the batsman? Was it a pitch that was fast or slow? Flat or bouncy? All this the captain would need to consider in deciding whether or not to bat first. If he decided to let the opposition bat first, as the innings progressed he had to decide the mix of bowlers to use, which bowlers should bowl to which batsmen, which of his bowlers were most hungry for wickets. Based on the batsman at the wicket and the bowler in action, the captain had to decide how best to set the field to cut down on runs yet give his bowler the best chance of bowling out the batsman. When it was his team at the wicket, the captain still had to remain alert. If his team was on to a large total, he had to decide when to declare to put the most psychological pressure on the opposition, yet not giving the match away. If, on the other hand, his team had lost wickets in quick succession without many runs on the board, he might need to reconsider the order of his remaining batsmen to best meet the challenge of this unexpected turn of events.

It was this intellectual, chess-like nature of cricket that in Ruben's book gave it the edge over football or any other sporting, artistic or creative activity. No matter how much Ruben loved football, he could have given it up, and no matter that the Roman Catholic Church had helped to give his early life shape and form, he could have given that up too (along with its catechism, saints, pageantry, symbolisms, and the drama and cultural activities that it sponsored). Yes, he could have given up coffee, or the occasional beer, or the occasional shot of Mount Gay rum; or pork, *shadon, souse, bouden* and all the other flesh that, according to the Adventist's interpretation of Deuteronomy 14:3-21, were unclean and therefore forbidden to eat. He could have even kept the Sabbath holy. But he couldn't have given up cricket and since cricket matches fell on Saturdays, he couldn't have kept the Sabbath. He tried, he really tried to keep the Sabbath. But he needed cricket too much. The game sat too well with everything inside of him.

In one shot, the sport satisfied his artistic and creative needs; his intellectual cravings that, deprived of higher education, had been left unmet; his drama and theatrical calling; his need for acceptance, fellowship, camaraderie, popularity. His need to be somebody, to be famous, to be bigger than life.

He loved Eunice with all his might, so of course he wanted desperately to keep the Sabbath and left to his conscious mind he would have succeeded. But an unseen force, an unseen spirit, an unseen being who seemingly knew what was best for him, took control of him every Saturday morning, so instead of putting on the church clothes gathering dust on the nail, he found himself dressed in his cricket attire and once they were on it made good sense to him to follow the program. If he had understood what was going on, or could anticipate what would happen, instead of being baptized at the beginning of the cricket season, he would have been baptized and married to the love of his life during the football season when there were no hidden forces lurking. So when the cricket season came around, he would have been married, and once married there was no way Eunice would have divorced him because while it was true the Good Book said *"Be ye not unequally yoked,"* it also said *"What God has put together let no man put asunder."*

Sadly, he didn't know, and in his ignorance the church arrived at the conclusion that he was a hopeless case. He couldn't be helped. The spirit of God had already left him, and according to the Bible when the spirit of God left someone, he was a lost, unredeemable soul; one destined for the heap of hell fire. Besides, they couldn't wait any longer. He was making a mockery of the Church, breaking the Sabbath for all to see. The soul they had put such great stock on in helping them break the deadbolt lock the Devil had on Vieux Fort was by his very actions helping the Devil to more strongly secure the lock. No, they couldn't have that. The Devil's work, if there ever was one.

Now, maybe if it were a different sin, like taking a shot of rum under the cover of his roof, or partaking of a piece of swine every now and again, or, once the woman didn't get pregnant, fornicating on the sly under the cover of darkness, or even going to dance in some rural hamlet where people didn't know he was an Adventist, the church would have had more patience with him, kept him around but not give him any high ranking post. After all, it wasn't like pastors haven't been caught fornicating with members of their churches, some of whom were the very ones they were supposed to be counselling. But what was next to impossible was to find a pastor who openly broke the Sabbath. The Sabbath was the Adventist claim to fame, their mark of identity; the birthmark on their foreheads that distinguished them from all other faiths, that said loud and clear "I'm a Seventh Day Adventist in the tradition of the prophetess, Ellen G. White." And on top of that, keeping the Sabbath had important undertones for the Church's financial survival. Tithes and offerings were collected during the Sabbath service. If one didn't keep the Sabbath, didn't attend the service, how would the church collect the tithes and offerings that belonged to the Lord in the first place and which were so necessary for advancing His work? So the church was willing to tolerate a great number of sins, especially undercover ones, but not the breaking of the Sabbath. Uh-uh. No way.

All but Brother McIntosh agreed that Brother Ishmael would have to be disfellowshiped. All but him agreed that it was too late; that the spirit of God had completely left Brother Ishmael. Brother McIntosh pleaded with the church to give Brother Ishmael some more time. That God was longsuffering, and as his followers the church needed to exercise some patience. He said, "Brothers and Sisters, Brother Ishmael is too valuable a soul to simply discard by the wayside. He can turn out to be a great warrior for the Lord. When I think of Brother Ishmael, no less a Bible personage than Paul of Damascus comes to mind. Give the young man some time. We mustn't be too hasty. We mustn't do something we all may regret."

The church members heard out Brother McIntosh, but as usual they didn't put much weight on what he had to say. They considered Brother McIntosh as barely an Adventist. He was often in disagreement with well established church principles. And it seemed his interpretation of scriptures was always at odds with everyone else's. For example, the church took as gospel that the earth was six thousand years old. Its preachers would often explain that from Adam to Noah was 2000 years, from Noah to Christ was another 2000 years and from Christ to the present was nearly 2000 years. Brother McIntosh could never accept this time-line because his readings of the National Geographic magazine and other such publications all suggested that the world was millions of years old. Another major point of contention that Brother McIntosh had with the church had to do with its prophetess, Ellen G. White. He would often ask that if Ellen G. White, an American who lived from 1827 to 1915, was such a great prophetess, worthy of being a pillar of Adventism, why was it that she never spoke against slavery? Was it because she herself was racist? To church members Brother McIntosh's doubts about the prophetess were nothing short of blasphemy. It was these and other such radical points of departure that made many in the church wonder why Brother McIntosh had bothered to join the church when he seemed to disagree with most of its precepts, and it had crossed the minds of a few members that Brother McIntosh should be disfellowshiped. But then he kept the Sabbath, so despite his shortcomings disfellowshiping him was out of the question.

Putting aside Brother McIntosh's voice of dissent, on the sixth Saturday following the baptism that had made history in Vieux Fort, the Church cast votes to disfellowhip Brother Ishmael. Brother McIntosh abstained. The rest of the church voted in favor of the disfellowship. Ruben was out. He would no longer be Brother Ishmael. From now on, 'backslider,' the most dreaded word in Adventist vocabulary would apply to him.

For her part, Eunice could not be unequally yoked, so she had no choice but to carry out her own brand of "disfellowshiping." With only two weeks left before the day she should have gotten married, she broke off the engagement. When she gave Ruben back his ring, he refused to take it and he begged, pleaded with her to give him time, give him a second chance, he would be "rebaptized" and reconsecrate his heart to God. He loved her with all his heart, he couldn't live without her.

She listened with longsuffering ears, but it was no use; the Spirit of God had already left him. He couldn't change. He was doomed. Their relationship was doomed. She was no longer mad at him. Pity, yes; but not rage. After all, the blame was hers. All hers. She had put her loneliness and her need to satisfy the pleasures of the flesh before her God. She had been so intoxicated with the wine of his promised pleasure that she had not made certain that he was real, that he had wanted to be baptized for the right reasons, not just to marry her but because he truly accepted God as his Savior. She had been so full of herself, so focused on her own, long unmet needs that she would have married the man even if she had known that his baptism was all a farce. When, even before the cocks had finished crowing, he had come bursting into her yard to ask for her hand in marriage, did she first ask God for guidance? Oh no. So great was her lust that she just fell into his arms. She had put him before God. He had become her god. The work of Satan for sure. God had given her Raphael in a dream, but where was the dream that signaled that God had meant Ruben for her? The only dreams she had were of devilish toads and rotten tomatoes. Dreams that had nothing to say about Ruben or marriage. The Devil had used this man to lead her astray. Thank God he showed his true colors before it was too late. She had asked God forgiveness. Now she would forever put herself in God's arms. She would devote her life to serving her God. If He wanted her to spend the rest of her life alone, without a husband, then let His will be done. There would be no need for the wedding dress she had already taken measurement for; she would have to see if she could return the cloth to get back her money. The extension on her house to accommodate Ruben who would have given up the house he was renting would no longer be needed. The brother or sister she wanted for Henry so he wouldn't feel so pressed to befriend Vieux Fort's disrespectful and unmannerly children would have to remain unborn. She would not make the same mistake twice, to do so would be to tempt God beyond measure, beyond reason. After all, the Good Book itself says, *Man know thyself and do thyself no harm.* Even Popo, the wonmier, knew that much.

Nevertheless, Bible or no Bible, she did plenty of harm to Ruben who didn't give up easily. He came to her every day begging for her forgiveness, begging her to reconsider, swearing his love. To prove his repentance he was the first to appear at Wednesday night and Sunday night prayer meetings. But all this was in vain, because come Saturday he was out there playing cricket, in the eyes of Eunice making a mockery of God and providing her with further proof that the Spirit of God had left him and left him for good and that her decision had come from above. Yet she was never rude to him, never *chuppsed* him, never told him to get lost or get thee behind me Satan. She was beyond that now. When he visited she would greet him politely, asking about his health, his students, and so on. But the tone of her voice, the vacuum in her eyes, the eyes that looked at but didn't see him, the quick turn away to whatever she was doing before his interruption, said it all; said in no uncertain terms that he was a mere acquaintance now, someone who was of no interest to her, someone she greeted only because he so happened to be occupying the same space with her, like a stranger sitting beside her on a bus, or standing next to her in a queue waiting for service, someone she talked to simply to ease the uneasiness, simply to be polite, to not offend. He would be there at her home, trying to make conversation and keep her attention, but she would continue washing clothes, or cooking, or cleaning fish, or whatever she was doing before he came, as if he weren't there at all, as if he didn't exist, as if he had never existed. Such was her apathy, that every time he spoke he startled her. Sometimes in the middle of his trying to make conversation, she would turn to her son and they would talk and carry on as if he weren't there at all. He would meet her on the street, she would reply politely to his greetings, but somehow she would never bring her eyes to meet his, and there would be no change in her pace. He would walk her pace, shift into conversation. She would respond but in a voice that suggested "I've no interest in you nor in what you are saying, it would be best for the both of us if you didn't bother." She said in so many different ways that he didn't matter one bit to her, that he could come, he could go, he could stay all day, all night, he could come to her bed and sleep beside her, roll all over her, lie on top of her, and it wouldn't make a bit of a difference because he was a presence that as far as she was concerned didn't really exist, had never really existed, would never really exist.

Ruben was heartbroken. He couldn't deal with this inattention, this neglect, this indifference, this detachment, this you-are-a-stranger politeness, this you-are-of-no-consequence treatment. No. Not from the person who just a few weeks before used to come to attention at the very sound of his voice, whose gleaming eyes would lock unto his, drinking his every word, memorizing every hair on his eyebrows, every pimpled scar on his face. The woman whose body in close proximity to his would tremble without ever being touched; the woman he had spent a whole night thinking about and when, before day had barely opened its eyes, he had come asking for baptism and marriage in the same breath as if they were one and the same, she had almost fainted in his arms; the woman with whom he had discussed wedding plans: the style of her wedding dress, bridesmaids, the extension on her house, the number of children they would have and the education and professions of those children. The woman whose son, since the morning of his momentous decision, had resumed calling him Daddy with no more objections from her. Yes, Daddy, a name that felt so right because he had long started thinking of the boy as his son. No. He would have been able to deal with the woman slamming doors in his face, *chupsing* him to hell, kicking him, slapping him, spitting on him, cursing him. Anything that would indicate that negative or positive he was still of consequence to her. Anything but this colder-than-spoilt-fish reception.

The Stall Keeper

Unable to carry his cross, Ruben the teacher, the historian, the actor, the footballer, the cricketer, and the coach sought solace in poetry. He wrote:

My heart a teacup shattered into a thousand pieces
I go to bed at nights convinced that I will not see the morrow
Too much pain for one heart to bear
How can I forget you when so much of you remains inside me?
Who else but you could restore the broken pieces of my heart?

But the poem did nothing to assuage his broken heart. Before long, Ruben, the dedicated athlete who rarely drank and then only in the company of friends, was each evening massaging his hurt with rum. At first he mixed the rum with coke, or juice if he didn't have coke, but he soon gave up this ritual and took his rum straight up. Then having fully acquired the taste, at lunch Ruben washed his food down with a shot or two of rum. His alcohol breath made news among students and teachers, not because that was unusual, for a few teachers always had alcohol on their breaths, but because many saw Ruben as above such human frailties. It was only in theater, when he played a drunk, that people associated him with alcohol. Nevertheless, in full swing now, on mornings Ruben laced his coffee with rum. Then abandoning all pretense, he added a rum bottle to the newspaper and transistor radio he always carried around. So alcohol was always on Ruben's breath. Of course, this was no crime. Plenty of men and several women in Vieux Fort always had alcohol on their breath. But then Ruben wasn't just any man. He was Vieux Fort's darling.

SINCE THE DAY OF HENRY'S FIRST ENCOUNTER with Eugene, when the stall keeper had given him the sweetest plum he had ever tasted, every time he passed on Clarke Street where Eugene's stalls were set up, Eugene would shout: "Hey, *Semdays* boy," or "Hey, *Semdays one week*, come here." The boy would approach the stall keeper, his glance sideways. Usually these encounters weren't much fun for Henry because Eugene often poked fun at him and his Seventh Day Adventist religion. But Henry would have it no other way. This was his only avenue of getting close to Eugene. Besides, every so often the stall keeper would give him something or the other — a packet of Shirley biscuits, a coconut tablet, a mango, a plum. Soon, when Henry was on his way to the jetty to buy fish, Eugene would get the boy to buy him two or three pounds of one fish or the other. After a while Henry didn't even wait for Eugene to call him. He would approach the stall keeper. "Mr. Eugene, I going and buy fish."

During each encounter with Eugene, Henry would build up courage to ask follow up questions to the story the older boys at school had related about Eugene. But each time his courage faltered. Each time the stall keeper got the better of him.

"Boy, preach for me, I need to be converted."

"Mr. Eugene, I doesn't preach."

"You mean to tell me you going to church morning, noon and night and you don't know how to preach? Boy, shame on you. O.k., you don't know how to preach, but do you know the Bible?"

"Yes, Mister Eugene, I know the Bible well."

"Then tell me a Bible story."

"Mr. Eugene . . ."

"Go ahead, don't be afraid."

"Mr. Eugene, long time ago there was a man in the Bible called Job. He was the richest man in the world. But he was also a righteous man. Seeing how righteous and rich Job was, the Devil was jealous of Job so he came to God and said to God the only reason Job is righteous is because God was protecting Job. So God say O.K., I will stop protecting Job, do what you want with Job but don't kill him. So the Devil steal all Job riches. He made Job the poorest man in the world. And the Devil kill all Job children and all his servants and his animals, and the Devil cover Job from head to foot with sores. It is in ashes Job had to roll to stop the sores from scratching him. Job wife tell him curse God. Job say no, it is God that giveth and He that taketh. Job was still righteous, Job did not sin. So God gave Job double all the money he had before, and gave him back all his children and all his servants and all his animals. And Job lived longer than everybody in the whole world."

"*Semdays* boy, you sure that's in the Bible?"

"Yes, Mr. Eugene, it's in the book of Job."

"You mean to tell me they even name a book after this Job character?"

"Yes, Mr. Eugene, Job was a man that walked with God."

"Do you walk with God?"

"No, Mr. Eugene, I does lie. It's my mother that does walk with God."

"So your mother righteous like Job?"

"Yes, Mister Eugene."

"So why she eh rich like Job?"

"Mister Eugene, it's you that will get rich like Job."
Eugene laughed until water filled his eyes. He said, "Boy, you ever see a person get rich selling by the street?"

ONE AFTERNOON, after Henry had bought fish for Eugene and Eugene had rewarded him with a turnover, he mustered the courage to ask: "Mr. Eugene, how come you is a stall keeper?"

"Ah, the *Semdays* eh only talking he is asking questions. Tell me why you is a *Semdays* and I will tell you why I sell."

"Because my mother is one."

"You is a *Semdays* because your mother is one. Well, I sell because I like to sell. How about that?"

"But Mr. Eugene, you is a man."

"Tell me, you see I look like a man?"

"Ah ... I don't know."

"Boy, you getting too smart for me. Go on. Go on your business."

EVER ON THE LOOKOUT FOR A *RORO*, Vieux Fortians watched with suspicious eyes the friendship that was unfolding between the stall keeper and the *Semdays* boy with the *bwa kochi*. Soon it attracted gossip the way rubbish attracts flies.

"You know, the *malmanman bouling* the little *Semdays* boy, the one with the *bwa kochi*."

"You mean Ma Auguste boy?"

"Yes, that's who. People say Eugene always giving him something or the other, and he does always go buy fish for Eugene."

"No, not that boy. I notice he a bit strange. His *bwa kochi* and all, and he always staring at people with wide-open eyes, as if seeing them for the first time. But Ma Auguste too strict with the boy. He eh go do something like that. He probably was always staring at Eugene, and knowing Eugene, when he tired of taking, he probably started joking the boy and giving the boy things."

"Stay there. I telling you what everybody knows and you telling me that eh so. Eugene is a *salòp*. He *bouling* the boy."

"*Enben bon*, I would have never believed that out of all the boys in Vieux Fort, it is the *Semdays* boy Eugene would choose to do his *salòpté* with. Ma Auguste don't know that?"

"You know her already. Her nose always twisted one side and her head in the air, as if everything she sees, hears or smells is beneath her, so I eh go be surprise if she is the last to know."

"*Enben*, when she finds out she will die of a heart attack."

NOW, IT DIDN'T MATTER that besides Eugene's effeminate disposition, no one had any proof of his sexual preference or orientation. In fact, the closest information of that kind anyone had would suggest that his sexual appetite was no different than that of any other man. It was known, or rather some people had come to accept, that Eugene had a woman and child in Ti Rocher. Still, few could truthfully say they have seen him in any kind of situation that hinted of sexual intimacy, be it with man or woman. In fact, it was difficult to place Eugene. He seemed very comfortable in the company of women but was highly antagonistic towards men. His quarrelsome nature and bodily movements made him out to be effeminate, but though five-feet-six, he was stockily built. Eugene's sexual preference was anyone's guess, yet the gossip surrounding him and Henry suggested that everyone was as sure of Eugene's sexuality as they were of their own.

The gossip spread from the adults to the children, including Henry's schoolmates, so on top of *Semdays one week, read the Bible upside down* and *bwa kochi*, he acquired a new name — *Semdays boula*.

Henry didn't appreciate this new name at all. In contrast to *Semdays boula*, he had come to accept *Semdays one week* and *bwa kochi* in much the same way he had accepted his birth name. After all, they had been with him since he knew himself. Besides, it was true that he was a *Semdays*, and it was also true that he had a *bwa kochi*, and being called those names gave him a certain uniqueness, a certain specialness. But that new name was something altogether different. It sounded dirty, nasty, evil, abominable; the kind of thing that sent one to hellfire for sure and that his mother was always warning him about. And even though he didn't exactly know what it meant, he knew it wasn't true, it didn't apply to him whatsoever. So he didn't take too kindly to being called *boula*. He took even less kindly to people making Eugene out to be a bad person when, other than teasing him, the stall keeper had been so good to him and was someone he looked forward so much to hanging around. So the *Semdays* boy who, following his mother's instructions, avoided fights even when cursed at, pushed around, or had his things stolen, refused to lay low to this evil his schoolmates were laying on him and his stall keeper friend.

He let loose on the very first boy that came in his face, calling him *boula*. Now, this was the first all-out fight of Henry's life, so it wasn't a well coordinated attack. But his anger and ferocity more than made up for technique and experience. Henry's punches and kicks came from all directions. With each blow he screamed, "Take that," but not so the crowd of children playing spectator to the lopsided fight. With each blow they shouted, "*Hegas.*" "Take that" and "*Hegas*" filled the school ground. The boy fell down crying, begging, "Leave me alone, leave me alone." But his mercy plea fell on deaf ears. Henry's attack continued relentlessly. It was as if in this one fight he was taking revenge for all the heckles and name calling that people had directed at him, revenge for all the freedom his mother was denying him, revenge for having never been to the Royal Cinema or any cinema for that matter to see a matinee movie, revenge for having never been to a Roman Catholic Church bazaar, revenge for not having a father, revenge for Ruben backsliding, revenge for not having a brother and a sister. By the time the teachers came and pulled Henry off his victim, the boy's lips and nose were busted, his eyes were puffed up and his shirt was soiled with blood. This fight didn't stop the boys from calling Henry *boula*, but it wised them up. They took to calling him *Semdays boula* from a distance, and even so they were all set to take off in anticipation of Henry giving chase.

Always on her guard to keep her son on the straight and narrow path and keep Vieux Fort away from her gate, when Henry arrived home with a bruised upper lip, and an overly soiled shirt with a torn pocket, Eunice's alarm system went off. "Henry, what happen to you?"

"Mama, I was fighting."

"You were what?"

"Yes, Mama."

"Henry, look at you. How many times must I tell you we are Christians, and that Christians do not fight."

"Mama, they were troubling me."

"Troubling you, how?"

"They calling me dirty names."

"What names?"

"They calling me *Semdays boula.*"

"Why they calling you that?"

"They say Mr. Eugene *bouling* me."

"Henry?"

"Yes, Mama."

"Have that man ever touched you?"

"No, mama."

"Boy, don't lie to me, because I will cut your behind."

"No, mama, I eh lying."

"Has he brought you to his house?"

"No, mama, I don't even know where Mr. Eugene staying."

"So why they saying that about you?"

"Mama, Mr. Eugene is a good man. Is jealous they jealous. Me and Mr. Eugene is friends and he go be rich like Job one day."

"You and him is friends! Since when? What have I been telling you? How many times have I told you don't speak to strangers, and stop paying attention to Vieux Fort people? You doesn't listen to me. Now you see the abominable thing they saying about you? You see? That's what happens when you just refuse to listen. The Bible says honor thy father and thy mother that thy days be long upon the earth. If you not obeying me you will not live long, you know. You will not live long. And another thing. If every time somebody call you name you fighting, then you go be fighting till kingdom come. Henry, what does the Bible say when someone slap you?"

"Turn the other cheek."

"Yes. So don't let me ever hear you fighting in school. And stop talking to that man. Stay far away from him. You hear?"

"Yes, Mama."

"You sure you hear me?"

"Yes, Mama."

"If I ever see you talking to that man again, it will be you and me. You hear."

"Yes mama."

The next time Henry was passing by and Eugene called, "*Semdays* boy, come buy fish for me." Henry said, "Mr Eugene, my mother say don't talk to you and stay far from you."

"Why-ah?"

"Because people saying bad things about you."

"What bad things?"

"Mr. Eugene?"

"O.k., then you must obey your mother."

Eugene was deeply hurt. He knew Vieux Fort people were spreading rumors about him and the boy, but he was paying them no mind because this wasn't the first time they were spreading falsehood about him, and this would not be the last. Everyone wanted to get into his business: what he doing with all the money he making selling, he who doesn't have man, woman or child? Is he taking man, or is he taking woman, or is he taking both? His reaction to all this was: "Leave them there, let them don't watch their own fucking business. Those who doing jamet; those whose women making money on the side taking sailors; those whose husbands have them there just to hide the fact that is man like themselves they like to take; those who feeding not one, but two, three children that they think is theirs but eh theirs at all. Leave them there. Leave the *salòps* there. Let them don't watch their own stinking business."

He was hurt because the *Semdays* woman actually believed he would hurt her son. Or else why would she tell the boy don't speak to him and stay far from him as if he has leprosy or T-B or typhoid. That really hurt him. Because he would never hurt a child. He could never hurt a child. It just wasn't in him. True, since the days of his father's cruelty, he hated men, all men. So much so, that for a long time he had tried to think of himself not as a man, but as a woman. But not children. He didn't go out of his way to befriend them, but deep down he felt for them. From his own childhood experience he knew how fragile they were, how by simply saying the wrong things to them you could damage their personality, their character, their minds, for life. He felt for them. So he would never hurt a child. He just couldn't. It bothered him a lot that the *Semdays* woman would think he was capable of hurting her son. He understood the boy. Along with everyone in Vieux Fort he knew how the boy used to go around asking, "Mister are you my father?" He understood the loneliness the boy felt being without a father, being without brothers and sisters, being a *Semdays* and all, and having an arm that seemed to have a mind of its own, one independent of the one that controls the rest of his body. He could put himself in the boy's shoes. He even sensed that at some level the boy saw him as someone who was no different than himself. A thought that always cracked him up. Because although on the surface no two persons could be as different as the two of them, when he gave it some thought, he could see that indeed they were very similar, they were both misfits. Which other child in Vieux Fort kept spying on him as much as the boy used to do? Surely the boy must have sensed that they shared some kind of sameness. So the last person in the world he would hurt is the boy. Yet his mother thinks he would stoop as low as lay a finger on her son.

This stayed with Eugene, bothered him, angered him for days, until one afternoon as Eunice was passing by on Clarke Street, he called, "Ma Auguste, a word with you please."

"What does this vulgar man want with me?" said Eunice to herself, as she reluctantly crossed Clarke Street, stepped over the street-side gutter and approached the stall keeper seated behind his two trays overflowing with fruits and condiments.

Speaking over his trays and over the din of traffic on Clarke Street, Eugene said, "Ma Auguste, I know what people been saying about me and your son. But Ma Auguste, I swear on my mother's grave that I have never done anything to hurt your son, and I will never do any thing to hurt him. I know you may not believe me, you being a Christian and all, and I being, well, a person of the streets, but I does look at your boy as if he were my very own son. Your boy is well brought up. You have done a good job with him. Believe me when I tell you I will never do anything to hurt him. He use to peep at me all the time, that's why I started calling him and speaking with him, and most times is the Bible I does ask him to tell me about. Ma Auguste, rest assured that I will never harm the boy, and if I can help it, I will never let anyone harm him. He already don't have a father, I will not add to his troubles."

Eunice was speechless and completely taken aback. She got riled up every time Henry's words, "me and Mister Eugene is friends," rang in her head. What kind of rubbish was interfering with her child? She had tried her best to keep Vieux Fort's filth from her gate, but not only had it entered her yard, it had found its way right into her living room. But as she listened to Eugene, the hurt, sensitivity and emotion in his voice, she had the distinct impression that when he said he would never hurt Henry, it was himself he was talking about. That he would no more hurt Henry than he would hurt himself. That he would rather give up his life than hurt her son. That he understood what it was like for her son to be without a father and without brothers and sisters. He understood what it was like for her to have lost a husband. He understood what it was like to be different, to be singled out for ridicule. He was hurt, really hurt that she would even think that he was capable of harming even a hair on her son's head. And what made his speech so touching to Eunice, touching enough to moisten her eyes, was that it contrasted so very sharply with the vulgar, quarrelsome, uncivilized man she knew. She would never have guessed that such a person was capable of such sensitivity and compassion.

Eunice was so taken by surprise, so awash with tender feelings, that she couldn't find words to respond to Eugene's plea. The emotional shift from loathing the stall keeper to feeling sorry for him, her son and herself, and to feeling shame for thinking that the man would hurt her son was much too sudden. She had insufficient time to adjust. One thing for sure, she believed him. She believed wholeheartedly that this uncouth man would never hurt her son. But the most she managed in terms of speaking her feelings to the stall keeper was to nod several times. Nevertheless, as she walked away, regaining her composure, her thoughts were, "I still don't want Henry associating with that man."

For his part, Henry laid low several weeks. Then one day he came up to Eugene and said, "Mr. Eugene, I going and buy fish."

Eugene looked up, surprised. "Boy, wasn't you yourself who said your mother told you don't talk to me and stay far away from me?"

"Yes, Mister Eugene."

"So what you doing here? Boy, go about your business. I want no trouble with your mother. Next thing I know she reading Psalms on my head. Boy, go; go about your business."

Henry walked away, tears in his eyes. When Eugene saw how hurt he was, he called him back and gave him a coconut tablet.

A week passed, and Henry tried again. "Mr. Eugene, I going and buy fish." This time Eugene looked at the pitiful boy and laughed.

"Mr. Eugene, I serious."

"I know you serious, but your Bible itself say honor thy father and thy mother. Aren't you a *Semdays* anymore?"

"Yes, Mr. Eugene, I still one, but we friends. Mr. Eugene we friends. And what people saying not true. Is jealous they jealous because we friends and one day you'll be as rich as Job. Mr. Eugene, don't worry, God will understand, and God will punish them."

Overpowering the noise of vehicles on Clarke Street, Eugene laughed until tears came to his eyes.

"So God will understand. But what about your mother?"

"Mr. Eugene, she too strict. God eh strict like her. And Mr. Eugene, she eh go know."

Eugene laughed just as loud as before. He said, "Boy, I don't want fish today. Maybe next time. But go on your business before your mother come looking for you. You killing me. You just killing me."

RUBEN'S DRINKING CONTINUED, and as time went by his appearance and hygiene changed. His twice a day showers, one in the morning and the other in the evening, were reduced to a morning shower, and on some days, especially when he didn't play ball, to none at all. The normally proud Ruben who went to school wearing freshly washed clothes that were crisp and well ironed was coming to school with shirts badly in need of washing and clothes that were stained, missing buttons and as rumpled as if they had just come out of a cow's muzzle. And as if to match his clothes, he wore his hair and beard uncut, uncombed and dirty.

Ruben became belligerent and boastful, and overly critical of his teammates, blaming them for every defeat. When given out, he was never willing to walk off the cricket pitch. He argued with and cursed the umpires. His performance on the field became erratic: misfielding, overthrowing, bowling more no balls than he used to, getting out playing careless, ill-advised strokes. Still he was a more valuable player than anyone else on his team and he was the captain, so his teammates weathered the storm believing that he just needed time to get over the *Semdays* woman who in their eyes had done him a big favor because he could now get a younger, more beautiful Catholic woman. At school the once poster-boy teacher would spend more time nagging and insulting his students than teaching them. With his colleagues he would initiate debates and arguments that usually ended with him calling them names like ignoramus, malaprop, illiterate wharf-rat, discombobulated, bombastic jackass; and they wanting to fight him.

This marked the beginning of a change in Ruben's vocabulary and manner of speech. After a few shots of rum he would pick quarrels or arguments that always ended with him browbeating his opposition into silence with big, never-before-heard words (at least not in Vieux Fort). Increasingly, the arguments were over politics, Ruben lambasting the government as if it were the cause of everything that had gone wrong in his life.

Vieux Fortians, including those who at the time of Ruben's baptism had refused to believe that his conversion had anything to do with obeah but everything to do with love, were now totally convinced that someone had done Ruben harm. For how could one explain this sudden change? What can cause a man of such gifts, a man of such stature and standing in his community, a man beloved by all to enter this downward spiral? No. It was one thing for the man to join religion for the sake of a woman, but a whole different matter for him to become unglued like that. True, love is a powerful thing, but in Ruben's case love was being helped along. Someone had done him harm. This everyone was now sure of.

And in their eyes there was plenty of precedence to support their claim of foul play. Take for example Ulric Clifford, the man from Desruisseaux who used to beat his wife so much that it was as if he had married her for that purpose and that purpose alone. According to people, when Ma Clifford tired of taking licks, she consulted a *gadè*. No one was sure what the *gadè* gave her to put in Ulric's food, but whatever it was, it didn't take long to work its mischief. Because soon after that, every time you saw Ulric he was grinning like he was dotish. Yet before his wife went to the *gadè*, Ulric always had a mean face. Now, other than going to work, Ulric would not leave the house; and the same macho man who didn't use to lift a finger at home, could be seen washing dishes, sweeping and even washing clothes, and grinning all the while like a child about to receive a lollipop. Before Ma Clifford opened her mouth, Ulric was beside her at attention. It got to the point where Ma Clifford was complaining that she had a husband who wasn't a man. His only worth was to stick in her feet everywhere she went. And that she didn't understand why, every now and then, he didn't go out for a drink with his friends and give her some fucking space to breathe.

The often told story of Drakes Hilton, the man from Grace who thought he was the greatest rooster in the land, and who was never bashful about boasting of his many exploits, was another case in point. Listening to Drakes you would think he had slept with everything with skirt stretching from Dennery to Choiseul. Such was his reputation that when teenage boys tried to chat girls who weren't particularly impressed with their chat, the girls would ridicule them with, "You think you is Drakes." Apparently, Ma Hilton used to turn a blind eye to her husband's wanderings for it seems he always had enough left over to satisfy her. And besides, what could she do, a man is a man.

Well, people said that all that changed when Ma Hilton found Drakes on top of their fourteen year-old daughter. This, she was sure, wasn't natural. She said, "*Enben bon*, Drakes, I know you does be sleeping around like a dog, but I never thought I would see the day when you fucking your own daughter. *Enben*, I will fix you! I will well fix you!" After she 'fixed' Drakes, no matter how beautiful a woman he was with: how old, how young; how fair, how dark; how slim, how fat; and what these women did to try to arouse him, his member remained as shriveled as the wilted stamen of a hibiscus flower. But no sooner Ma Hilton touched or came near him, his member would rise like a rod. Such was Drakes nonperformance with women, that people renamed him *chandèl mòl*, soft candle.

But the favorite story Vieux Fortians liked to tell as evidence of the workings of obeah was what befell Popovic St. Ville, better known as Popo, a man who came from a long line of carpenters, going back to his great-grandfather who as a slave learned his craft on the Mabouya sugar estate from the French architect and builder, Jean Baptiste Renee. At his peak, Popo was considered the best carpenter on the island. Since his late teens there was hardly a large construction project that he hadn't worked on. He worked with the Americans during the War, and with the Colonial Development Corporation in the rebuilding of Castries after the 1948 fire. The Americans were so impressed with his work, that after most of their war construction in Vieux Fort was completed, he was the first St. Lucian carpenter they selected to send to the Ascension Island in the South Atlantic, off the coast of West Africa, an offer that Popo had turned down because he refused to be separated from his family for any length of time. Rich people would come to Vieux Fort all the way from Castries to get Popo to build their homes, especially if what they wanted were two or three-storey houses. Popo's houses stood out. He was always able to improve on the design of whatever plan he was presented. His great craftsmanship was reflected in every detail of the construction, such that when people saw a certain building they would guess correctly, "This must be a Popo house." And when people spoke about Popo and his work, they would often say, "Popo eh a carpenter, he a artist." Besides the quality of his work, the thing people liked most about Popo was his honesty in giving a solid day's work, and delivering the job on time even if that meant him and his crew working twelve-hour days and seven-day weeks. With such a reputation, Popo was inundated with work and he prospered.

And by all appearances, Popo's family life was just as successful as his professional one. He was married to a beautiful woman from Micoud, and they had three lovely children, all girls. Vieux Fortains often commented on how together they were. Some took real pleasure watching the family, all elegantly dressed, walking to church. As far as people saw it, the only dent in this happy picture was that Popo didn't have a son to carry on his family's rich building tradition.

Popo's success attracted attention. So with great concern and urgency his close friends and a few of his acquaintances would come to warn him. "Popo, don't mind as things are going well with you there, everything can disappear, puff! You know how people does be jealous, and how it pains them to see a *neg* succeed. Now, if you was a *bétché* that would have been different, because to us *negs* the *bétché* is God, so it's o.k. for him to have. But not you the *neg*. Popo, to make a long story short, you need to get a good *gadè*. Not any of those *papicho* men calling themselves *gadès,* but a real *gadè*. Because if you eh careful one of these days everything will go, puff!"

Popo listened, but took no action. Not that he didn't believe in obeah—after all there was proof of it all around him—but he had gained all his success without seeing a *gadè*, so why start now. Besides he was living a clean life, he was one of the few men in the place who didn't cheat on his wife, and he gave everyone he worked for an honest day's work. He had a wonderful wife who was a hundred percent behind him. His daughters were well behaved and the eldest was already attending the prestigious Convent Secondary School in Castries. He was a devout Roman Catholic. He was blessed. He was protected. The Bible itself said, *"Who God has blessed, no one can curse."*

Popo never expressed these thoughts to his unsolicited advisors. If he had they would have said not only was he naive, but he was a fool, and that he had fallen into the trap that a lot of good, honest people like himself got caught in: the belief that their goodness gave them protection, when the opposite was true, because, much like sheep, they never bothered to grow defenses such as claws and flesh-tearing teeth.

Unfortunately for Popo, the advice of his counselors seemed to have had some merit. Because one day, for no discernible reason, his wife of fifteen years left him for a man from Belvue whom she met at the Vieux Fort market where he was selling coals. Vieux Fortians were shocked and baffled. Now, they may have understood what had happened if Ma Popo's new lover was a man of means: plenty of land, two or three houses renting, lots of horses and cows. But the man had nothing. No land, no profession, no trade. He was squatting on someone else's land, and making coals and working under other people's bananas for a living. For no reason people could think of, Ma Popo simply left Popo's nice, big house, equipped with transistor radio, kerosene stove and fridge, and furniture fashioned by Popo's own hands, to join a man in a shack built on land that wasn't his. The woman who, when she was with Popo, only had to take care of the home and never had a need to work outside, was now bending over coal pits and working under bananas alongside her new man. As one could well imagine, the daughters flatly refused to go and live in Belvue in a shack too small for one person much less for their mother and themselves, and with no stove, no fridge, no radio, a few crude pieces of furniture, and where they had to draw their drinking water from the river.

No one could understand that. Popo least of all. He was devastated. There he was, at the peak of his career, the envy of all who came to know him, enjoying a life that came close to perfection, and suddenly when he was least expecting it, his wife, the center of his life, his joy and inspiration, the one for whom he joyfully went to work in the morning and longingly returned home in the afternoon; and for whom (in his mind) he hammered every nail, fashioned every board, crafted every building, and who unawares had motivated him to such heights of perfection that people spoke of him not as a carpenter but as an artist, had left him for no reason he could think of, and there was nothing, nothing he could do about it, except to seek the solace of the bottle and to go around blabbering to everyone who cared to listen, how his wife left him and that what grieved him the most was not that his wife had left him — even though that was bad enough — but that she had left him for a *labouwè*, a laborer. Soon, Popo lost not only his wife but his daughters too, because refusing to let her nieces live all alone with a drunk, even if the drunk was their father, Popo's wife's sister took the girls to live with her in Micoud.

Popo's craftsmanship deteriorated. The man who used to be the best carpenter on the island was now building crooked houses. Soon, prospective home owners stopped requesting his services. So Popo was reduced to making coffins and building hoods for trucks. The last hood job he got was when, a day after putting the hood on the truck, the right side collapsed after the truck entered a deep pothole. And his last coffin job was the one where the corpse could not enter the coffin because it was built too narrow. Popo then had to make do with digging graves and pit toilets for his living.

But the most telling part of the story was that Popo's decline matched almost exactly the rise of Laporte, one of his apprentices. While working under Popo, the best jobs Laporte could get on his own were to build two-by-four shacks for poor people. But no sooner Popo took to the bottle and started falling, Laporte's stock began to rise. Soon it was to Laporte people were flocking to get their fancy homes built. He had a whole crew of men working for him. Gold chains started decorating his neck. He was one of the first persons in Vieux Fort to own a vehicle, one of those Austin vans. Watching Laporte rise as Popo fell, no one needed further explanation to get to the bottom of Popo's predicament. Laporte had put obeah on Popo.

With the benefit of such precedence, Vieux Fortians were doubly sure someone had done Ruben harm. "Someone had 'pulled a Popo' on Ruben." The only question was who could have put obeah on him? Some said that it has to be the *Semdays* woman. "Who could have imagine that this holier-than-thou woman had dirty hands? She couldn't get a man to replace her dead husband so she put something in Ruben's drink to tie him. A potion so strong that she didn't even have to give him sex to keep him around. But somehow the thing had backfired. She was still without a man, and Ruben was there wasting away. You see how hypocritical these *Semdays* are. They say they save, but they worse than the Catholics."

Some said, "No. That *Semdays* woman don't know her head from her tail. Is someone jealous of Ruben who did it. Maybe one of his fellow teachers, or the headmaster. I hear he and Ruben eh seeing eye to eye, and he scared Ruben take his job. Or maybe someone who thinks Ruben is too good in sports. That's how us *negs* are. We can't see a *neg* like us move up."

Some others said, "This looks like the hand of Castries people. They know with Ruben on the team we does give them a run for their money, so they have played dirty tricks on him."

Deeply concerned and lamenting the loss of Ruben, some of the parishioners went and shared their obeah theory with Father Pierre and urged him to take corrective action, but the Father rebuked them and in his heavy Latin accent told them this was utter rubbish. The parishioners concluded that this was beyond religion, beyond Father Pierre, so they went all the way to Dennery to visit Dantes, the most famous *gadè* on the island, a man known to communicate with the dead and have them reveal where they had hidden their money or the deed for their land. Dantes gave them a bottle of blackish liquid for Ruben to rub himself over a one-week period to remove any obeah that has been placed on him and to protect him from further harm. He instructed that Ruben should apply the protection twice a day, as soon as he wakes up in the morning and just before he goes to bed at night, and that during the week of treatment he mustn't bathe. With great urgency the parishioners presented Ruben with the potion and explained to him the *gadè's* instructions. But rather than showing gratitude, Ruben displayed even greater anger than the priest.

The Stall Keeper

He threw the bottle out of his window and into the sea and said, "What the hell is wrong with you all ignominious, abominable, contemptible people? Don't you all have any shame?"

The parishioners were really hurt, seeing they went through all that trouble only to be rewarded with mud-slinging big words. In fact they were more hurt by the big, nasty words than by the throwing away of the bottle of protection for which they had paid a handsome amount of money. This was the last attempt the parishioners made to save Ruben; from then on they waited helplessly to see how far he would fall.

ALTHOUGH FATHER PIERRE HAD REJECTED the theory of his
parishioners, he didn't give up on Ruben as quickly as they
had, nor did he simply wait to see how far his protégé
would fall. Instead he made several trips to Ruben's home
to get him to slow down on the liquor, to encourage him to
start coming to church again and helping with his church
programs. He cajoled Ruben, soothed him, shouted at him,
all in the interest of ungluing him from his malaise. He
spent hours in conversation with Ruben, discussing his
childhood, his fantastic contribution to the church and to
Vieux Fort sports. But always the conversation would end
up with talk of Eunice, more so if Ruben had had a drink
or two.

Father, I really love this woman. This woman is so special.
She is the one that should have been the mother of my children.
Father, she is the only one for me. I will love her unto death.
Father, that woman was all that I had. I love that woman, I love
her with all my heart. I used to look into this woman's eyes and
refuse to believe my luck. Father, it was just too much beauty for

one pair of eyes to behold. Father, thoughts of this woman used to suffocate my sleep and occupy every minute of my day. But Father, she is gone. She is gone. Gone. And my heart feels like a teacup shattered into a million pieces. Father, who but her can pick up the broken pieces of my heart? How can I be whole without her? Father, too much of that woman is left inside me. Father, I can bear it no longer. Please go and speak to her, beg her to forgive me, beg her to come back to me.

Don't despair my son. The Lord takes care of his children. He gives and he taketh away. There are plenty of women right there in the church who would make you a lovely wife and bear you beautiful children. You just have to get up from your stupor, look around and give them a chance. You loved once, you will love again. Just give it time, my son. But you have to get up and stop pitying yourself, stop feeling sorry for yourself. Remember, the Lord is with you always. Have faith, my son. Have faith in the Lord and He will do the rest.

Father, it was God that made me a gift of this woman. Pray to God, ask Him to forgive me, tell Him I beg for his forgiveness. Father, there is none like her, I don't want any other. Father, I love this woman. When I tell you I love this woman, I love this woman. Father, how can I forget her when so much of her remains inside me? Speak to her, beg her to come back. Tell her I'm sorry. Tell her I beg her forgiveness. Father, I cannot live without her. I go to bed each night thinking that my heart will not last the night. Father, believe me when I say, it's too much pain for one heart to bear. Father, pray that I win her back. She is so special. She is one in a million. She is a creature fashioned with God's own hands. Father, how can I give her up when it was God Who made me a gift of her?

Son, I will pray for you. I will pray that God give you strength to overcome your affliction. But son, you must meet Christ halfway. You must get up from your stupor and he will do the rest. You are a child of God, he will not forsake you. But son, you must meet him halfway.

The priest was unable to stop Ruben from falling, but after his many conversations with Ruben and what he knew of his past, and after wrapping his mind around the problem for quite some time he came up with his own theory to explain Ruben's behaviour. He reasoned that the root of Ruben's problems lay in his childhood, and that Ruben's deprived childhood — the necessity of having to beg his father money to keep his mother and siblings alive, the self loathing that came with him having a father who in his mind had rejected him because he wasn't worth the trouble, he wasn't deserving of the attention, he was too unimportant, too inconsequential; the humiliation and shame he suffered from the frequent and varied partners that shared his mother's bed, who literally had to step over him and his siblings to get to his mother's bedroom, because all of them slept on the floor on rags; the days of near starvation, of begging the Americans for money and fighting other children over the leftovers the Americans dumped — had damaged his psyche and caused him to develop an inferiority complex. It was this inferiority complex or personality defect that the priest reckoned was chiefly responsible for Ruben's predicament.

Father Pierre found the first audience for his theory in the person of Daddy Mano when he came visiting at the presbytery on a late Friday morning when the flamboyant trees in the Roman Catholic Church courtyard were in full bloom, suffusing the courtyard with a riot of red and perfume. The great humanitarian wanted Father Pierre's feedback on yet another letter addressed to the president of the United States and the prime minister of Great Britain, seeking redress for American World War II exploitation of his town. Father Pierre was in his study, deep in thought preparing his Sunday Mass sermon. He didn't welcome the interruption, not so much because he was preoccupied, but because he was getting tired of what he considered to be Daddy Mano's folly and futility. Still, being the charitable and longsuffering priest that he was, Father Pierre greeted Daddy Mano as warmly as he would a close friend whom he had not seen in months. Encouraged, Daddy Mano handed Father Pierre his newly revised letter. But before the priest had a chance to read, Daddy Mano lunged into his patented tirade of how the Americans had damaged Vieux Fort and that as long as he had breath of life he would continue seeking restitution. After the tirade, forgetting to ask the priest what he thought of the letter, as if it had been just an excuse to vent about the American atrocities, Daddy Mano said, "You know your boy, Ruben, is getting from bad to worse? It just baffles me how a man of such talent and intelligence could come to such a fate."

Father Pierre seized upon the new opening: it allowed him to sidestep Daddy Mano's tiresome talk of the Americans, and he would get an audience for his theory.

"I know what you mean. I have been giving this a lot of thought, and I have come up with an explanation."

"Really? Everybody saying it's obeah they put on him."

"Daddy Mano, don't tell me you too believe in this obeah nonsense."

"I don't know. If not obeah, then what? It's hard to believe that a man with so much going for him would just fall apart because a woman leaves him. After all, there are women all over the place, and as you know most St. Lucian men have two, three women."

"Well, I think it all has to do with Ruben's childhood."

"His childhood?"

"Yes. What people don't realize is that their personalities are largely formed in the first few years of their lives. Take

Ruben for example. You know better than me the conditions under which he grew up. I think his childhood deprivation and upbringing had damaged his psyche and self worth. Consequently he had developed a low self esteem and a battered self image. So in his mind he didn't measure up to other people, he wasn't worthy of good things. In brief, Ruben had an inferiority complex."

"Father, Ruben ... low self esteem; Ruben ... inferiority complex? Yet he was better than most in so many different arenas. Father, are you sure about this?"

"I know, I know this is hard to believe. But the human mind is great at making adjustments to negate its deficiencies. Here is what I think. As Ruben grew older, to counter this psychological disposition and to make sure no one was aware of it, he dedicated himself to being better than anyone else in everything that he did. So although he had a well above-average intelligence and was a naturally gifted athlete, these didn't fully account for his great accomplishments. More than most people, Ruben pushed himself to excellence. In other words, Ruben had overcompensated for his inferiority complex..."

After his question of disbelief, Daddy Mano listened to the priest with a half smile on his face. It was a smile that seemed to say, "I don't know whether or not to believe what I'm hearing. Karamba! Where did that priest, a foreigner, get all of this? I wonder what kind of psychoanalysis he has done on me. For all you know he must be saying I'm a nut."

Smile or no smile, Father Pierre was glad for the audience. He knew he couldn't talk about this to just any one. People might look at him as if he were crazy. He was comfortable sharing his theory with Daddy Mano because the humanitarian was a frequent visitor and his relentless pursuit of reparation from the Americans and the British couldn't exactly be called a sane undertaking. So unmindful of the smile and intent on taking full advantage of his audience, Father Pierre continued his exposition.

"You see, we can never completely surmount the psychology we formed in our childhood. I think deep down Ruben's childhood fears, insecurities and self loathing lingered. One manifestation of his lingering inferiority complex was that despite the fact that he probably could have gotten just about any woman he wanted, he had kept going after those much below his status in society. In Ruben's mind he wasn't deserving of better. He felt unworthy and was afraid of women of a certain class. So notwithstanding that Eunice was older than Ruben and that she already had a child, in terms of beauty, morality and social standing, she was the most ranking woman he had made a serious effort to get. From that angle you could say that Eunice was the best thing to have happened to Ruben. You see, once he had gained Eunice's friendship, it was as if she had done him a great favor, and he had achieved something great, greater than even his many heroics on the playing field. With Eunice, Ruben had moved up a notch..."

The deeper Father Pierre dug into his theory, the more perplexed Daddy Mano's smile became, the less he concentrated on what the priest was saying, and the more conscious he became of the priest's foreignness (his whiteness, his Latin accent), the perfume of the flamboyant trees, and the din of traffic on neighbouring Commercial Street. Now his smile seemed to be saying, "Eh-eh, the priest is getting carried away, he is taking this theory of his much too far. Since when priests were psychologists?"

"Now, for him to have lost her was to prove that indeed he was inferior, that he was not deserving of women of her standing, that despite all of his achievements he was nothing. Losing out on the woman who had represented his great breakthrough sent his psychology into a tailspin and undid all the repair that his previous accomplishments had done to his damaged psyche and self esteem. It laid bare the psychology of the five-year-old inside him. So everything came crashing down upon him. It was as if by befriending Eunice, Ruben had set himself up for a fall. So maybe the reason Ruben went and played cricket on Saturdays, knowing full well this would jeopardize his upcoming marriage with Eunice, was that deep down at the subconscious level he thought he wasn't deserving of her. I sense that Ruben has a self-defeating personality. He would climb just so far, and then he would have to do something to bring himself down. In Ruben's five-year old psychology, as opposed to his thirty-something one, he didn't deserve to be up there. Contrary to Vieux Fortians' obeah nonsense, he had needed no help to bring about his downfall. It was all self-inflicted. So amazingly, despite Ruben's brilliance, despite his amazing athletic feats, he was to some extent a loser."

"Wow! Father Pierre, this is heavy. Wow! You must have taken a lot of psychology in your study for the priesthood?"

"Yes, we do. Not only psychology, but sociology too. After all, how can we properly administer our flock without a firm understanding of human nature?"

"Father, I 'm a bit baffled. You talked as if Ruben is doomed, as if he can never recover. That's like telling me the Americans and British will never pay for their corruption of Vieux Fort?"

"The American and British situation is altogether a different matter. But no, I didn't mean it like that at all. He may recover, but if he does he will climb just so high and then put himself in another situation that will again bring about his downfall."

"But Father, what about God? Can't he intervene?"

"Of course. With God nothing is impossible. I have been praying daily for Ruben to return to his old self. But who knows the full workings of our Lord?"

"O.k. Father, let's suppose your theory is right. Now, I'm not saying I agree with all of it, but for the sake of argument, let's say you are right, then Father, why Eunice? Why the *Semdays* woman?"

"I don't know," said Father Pierre. "I don't know. I have been asking myself this question ever since, but I have found no answer. The closest I've come to is that if it wasn't Eunice it would have been someone else."

Daddy Mano left the Priest and the presbytery and walked through the flamboyant perfumed churchyard and joined the commotion on Commercial Street. He never did get a response to his newly revised letter of American and British compensation. The talk of Ruben had made him completely forget his original intent. It seemed for once he was occupied with something other than American and British reparation. As he walked up Commercial Street, his unanswered question, why Eunice? kept ringing in his head. But neither he nor the priest needed be too hard on themselves for not having an answer because not even Ruben knew the answer, except that three years before his baptism, on a Wednesday night in August, a force over which he had no control had propelled him forward to chat the *Semdays* woman who, holding on to her son, was rushing to church as if her life depended on it.

Still, it was a good thing that Father Pierre was careful about whom he shared his theory of Ruben with, because if he had presented it to most other Vieux Fortians, out of respect for him they may have smiled and nodded their heads as if in approval, but behind his back they would have laughed at the ugly white priest with the funny accent, and they would have said that this is what happens when people have too much education. They get stupid in a kind of way. Because every fool knows that it is obeah they put on the man, yet the priest is coming up with all kinds of nonsense about when the man was small, and his mother, his father, his mother's lovers, the Americans, psychology, inferiority complex, and that Ruben was a loser. Yet none of that had prevented the man from dominating sports in Vieux Fort and making Castries teams hear and understand.

NO MATTER WHICH THEORY—obeah, a damaged psyche, or some other—was correct in explaining Ruben's predicament, the results were the same. Ruben continued to fall. At school the situation reached a climax when at a staff meeting he said to the headmaster, "You sodom-gomorrahical bugger!" Not too unhappy with this turn of events the headmaster started the process that got Ruben fired.

After his dismissal, Vieux Fortians became even more convinced that someone had done Ruben evil. The common saying was: "*Fanm Semdays-la fè i mal*, the Adventist woman did him evil."

Even Ruben's teammates got tired of his antics. He came to practice and matches drunk, and became increasingly boisterous and obnoxious. So despite his talent, he did more harm than good to his team. They removed him as captain, then they would select him but leave him on the bench, then they left him out of the team altogether. So he started causing trouble at meetings, throwing his arsenal of big words at whomever dared point fingers at him. So they kicked him out of the club. Fired from his team and unable to find another because no other cared to have him, Ruben, to the great delight and entertainment of Vieux Fort sport fans, became an unofficial commentator of matches, an occupation that sat well with his drunkenness and put to good use his stockpile of big words.

Henry, on the other hand, refused to give up on Ruben, nor did he concern himself with theories, be it that of psychology or the supernatural, about Ruben's downfall. All he cared about was for Ruben to give up drinking and walking dirty, repent of his sins and rebaptise so his mother could marry him, and he, Henry, at last would have a father. So on his way to and from school, and to and from church, and when he ran errands for his mother, he kept a close lookout for Ruben. But what he saw did little to strengthen his hope. More often than not it was in a rum shop he would find Ruben drinking and talking loudly. And it wasn't difficult to discern when Ruben was in a rum shop: his loud, quarrelsome voice would be heard far down street. One afternoon, walking home from school, Henry caught wind of Ruben in Leo's rum shop off Clarke Street. He crept close by to listen to Ruben get on and to see if there was any sign of repentance in him. But from what Henry heard it seemed that Ruben was getting worse.

"Man, shut your ass and listen to your master! What kind of imbecility is that? Vieux Fort is backward because Vieux Fortians have it too easy? Man, move your ass from there with your bullshit. You have a government of jackasses, a government of myopic vision populated with people who can see no farther than their bombastic asses. A government that has failed to see that Vieux Fort is the key. That the development of Vieux Fort is the key to the development of the whole fucking island. Instead of seeing this truism and acting on it, they sit in Castries and fart all over themselves and then convince each other that their stinking fart smells like perfume. Yet here you are, an imbecile of gigantic proportions, gibberishing a bunch of poppycock that Vieux Fort is backward because the people have it too easy. So how are they supposed to have it? They're supposed to have it too hard? You see, this is why I must stop drinking with idiots and ignoramuses. My mother always used to say that the worst thing in life was to suffer fools. And she was right. She was damn right."

Ruben paused and just when he was about to further abuse his victim, who was already too drunk to retaliate with his fist as he would have liked to, he saw Henry in his school uniform, blue shirt tucked in khaki short pants, standing in the doorway of the rum shop staring at him with mouth agape.

When their eyes met, Henry quickly took off but Ruben called him back.

"Henry, my boy. Eh-eh, you getting taller by the day. How is your mother?"

"She is fine."

"Come, come. Take a Ju-C, take a Ju-C."

"No thanks, Mr. Ruben."

"Take a Ju-C, boy, take a Ju-C."

"No thanks, Mr. Ruben, my mother say it will spoil my food."

"But how is your mother?"

"She is fine."

"Mr. Ruben, when you coming back to church?"

"Soon, my son, soon," answered Ruben, and he brought a finger to his lips and said, "Don't tell your mother you see me here."

"No, Mr. Ruben, I eh go tell her."

" Good boy, good."

As Henry walked away, it pained him almost to tears to see his hope of a father dashed, to see the man he so admired, the man he looked up to, the man he wished more than any other to be his father carrying on like a *won-myé*, like Popo, *santi caca*. Surely, his mother would marry no *wonmyé*. Still, all was not lost. Ruben sounded so very smart using all these big words, so Henry took a page from the man he wished to be his father. When his schoolmates came troubling him or when he found himself in the middle of a losing argument, he would throw some of Ruben's big words at his opponent, though he was unsure of their meaning. But it was a habit Henry quickly gave up. His big words stang his opponents more severely than his fist ever could, more so because the words, which they couldn't understand, confused and made them feel stupid. So even the most benign arguments quickly turned to fist fights, and it was forbidden for Henry to fight.

The rum shop wasn't the only arena at which Henry would bear witness to Ruben's transformed character. After Ruben was fired from his teaching job he joined the opposition party and requested to be its Vieux Fort candidate in the next general elections. But fearful that given Ruben's fall in stature he would make a poor candidate, the party softly declined his request and instead hired him as a party boy. Ruben made public announcements of political meetings and distributed party pamphlets. Riding on the deposit of goodwill the town had for him, at election time he conducted house to house campaigns. On political platforms he delighted his audiences with the big words he slung at the government. It seemed that everywhere one went Ruben was there in a political argument, putting his arsenal of big words to use.

Henry received a treat one Wednesday night as he and his mother were returning home from prayer meeting. That night a political meeting was in progress. The platform was the balcony of Damascus Guest House. Eunice was hurrying through the crowd, pulling along a reluctant and gawking Henry, when the emcee announced Ruben.

"Ladies and gentlemen, it is with great pleasure that I present to you a son of the soil, the one and only Mr. Ruben Ishmael, a Vieux Fortian if ever there was one, a man of great accomplishments, a man who has done so many great things for Vieux Fort in the area of education, sports, and culture. A gifted man, a man whose talent knows no bounds. Ladies and gentlemen, I know you are anxious and excited to hear the voice of your very own, so without further ado here is Mr. Ishmael."

Henry said, "Mama, wait, they calling Mr. Ruben to speak."

Eunice hesitated. She remembered the debate — *Jan Vieux Fort Feyan: Lavéwité ou Mansonj*? Vieux Fortians are Lazy: Fact or Myth? — at which she had seen Ruben at the heights of his powers. This had been one of the most promising, blissful even, periods of her life. Then everything was in place. Everything was perfect. Ruben would be baptised and eight weeks later they would be married. Ruben would help win souls for the Lord, Henry would have a father and maybe a sister or brother or both. It seemed such a long time ago. So much had happened. How quickly things change? Heading home and still filled with the spiritual high of her prayer meeting, the last thing Eunice wanted was a political rally. She wanted nothing to do with politics. She wanted even less to do with this ungodly, riotous crowd of Vieux Fortians. But her curiosity took the better of her. She was deeply curious about what Ruben had to say; she wanted to see whether with all his drinking he was still as spellbinding as on the night of *Jan Vieux Fort Feyan: Lavéwité ou Mansonj?*

Eunice's hesitation led to a stop. She and her son watched Ruben step from inside the guest house onto the balcony. They watched him stagger a bit. A murmur ran through the crowd, "*I sou*, he is drunk." As the emcee handed Ruben the mic, it fell to the floor and made a loud noise that was accompanied by an even louder "*Esalòp!*" from the crowd. In bending down to pick up the mic, Ruben nearly tipped over. The crowd yelled, "*Esalòp!*" With mic in hand, Ruben straightened up and momentarily surveyed the crowd. He boomed, "Good evening, my people." And even louder, "Vieux Fort, I greet you good evening." Some in the crowd chorused, "Good evening, teacher," and some others, "Good evening, *wonmyé*."

Ruben continued, "Fellow Vieux Fortians, there comes a momentous time in history, a time in a people's life when they have to decide whether they will turn left or right, whether they will march forward or backwards. Vieux Fort, we have arrived at just such a consequential time in our history. This is our moment of truth. We are at a cross-roads, and what direction we take will decide whether our children will attend institutions of higher learning or whether they are doomed to a life of ignorance and serf-dom; whether we are going to be masters of our destiny or the slaves and servants of pompous bastards; whether Vieux Fort will ascend as a great metropolitan city or remain a ghetto where we are fighting with hogs for living space..."

Watching Ruben stagger onto the balcony and then nearly fall, Eunice had felt so very embarrassed for him. It was as if she were the one at whom people were laughing and joking about her drunkenness. Thinking that she could stomach this shame and embarrassment not for one more second, she tugged her son's arm and said, "Not me with this *papicho*, let's go." But no sooner had she said this, Ruben opened his mouth and she was held transfixed. For gone was his tentativeness. Instead his voice flowed

smooth and strong, much like a river relentlessly and melo-
diously making its way to the ocean. Suddenly, Ruben was
transformed from a staggering drunk to a larger-than-life
figure, speaking as if he were a prophet. Now, as he paused
for breath, Eunice said to herself, "This is the Ruben I
know, this is the Ruben of 'Vieux Fortians are Lazy: Fact or
Myth?'" And, she was thinking, maybe there is hope for
him yet.

Unaware of Eunice's presence, much less her thoughts,
in the middle of the crowd's chorus, "Teach! Teach!" Ruben
continued. "Vieux Fort, today you are faced with two
roads, one of the roads, the road you have been on all these
years, has brought you nothing but poverty, landlessness,
and insults that you are lazy and that nothing good can
come out of Vieux Fort. Fellow Vieux Fortians, last night
I laid wide awake. Why, you may ask? I laid wide awake
because I was gripped by a vision, a vision of Vieux Fort, a
vision that refused to depart from me. In this vision I saw
Vieux Fort marching confidently on the other road of
which I speak, the one less travelled, the one, by the grace
of God, we will lead you on."

"Which road, *wonmyé*, the road to the *kabawé*?" someone
shouted.

Raising his voice, Ruben continued. "On this new road
of which I speak, I saw Vieux Fort blossom into a great
metropolitan city. I saw malls and shopping plazas sprout-
ing up like grass in the rainy season. I saw Vieux Fort transformed into a Caribbean center of higher learning,
equipped with a great university and a glorious public
library. Yes, Vieux Fort, in this vision there was a cultural
renaissance. I saw incredible museums, and beautiful
aquariums and public parks. I saw majestic theatres, cine-
mas, and concert halls. I saw cricket, football and track and
field stadiums that would make you proud. My people, the

Vieux Fort I saw had a huge fishery complex, it boasted of industry and commerce that made it the envy of the Caribbean. I saw an endless string of magnificent hotels crowding the beach from the base of Moule-a-Chique to Bois Shadon. I saw Vieux Fort spread out such that Vieux Fort and Laborie became one continuous settlement. I saw Vieux Fort climb the hills of Belvue and Piero and spread out across Aupicon and Savannes Bay to Canelle. My people, I saw Vieux Fort grow to become nothing less than a Caribbean center of culture, entertainment, industry, education and commerce. This was the vision that kept me up all night. This was the vision that refused to depart from me. My people, as I said before, we are at a crossroads and in this election you have to choose which road you will travel. Is it the road of yesteryear that has brought you nothing but misery, poverty, insults and humiliation, or the road of my vision from which Vieux Fort will rise like a phoenix?..."

At this point a crowd of supporters started to chant, "We will rise! We will rise!" But apparently this was too much for some of Ruben's detractors. Fuelled by liquor, a group of young men formed a fence in front of the balcony turned political platform by embracing each other at the shoulders, and as if responding to calypso music, they performed a deafening chant of *"Ruben toujou sou! Ruben toujou sou!"* And it was then that Ruben let loose.

"My people, this is exactly what I am talking about. Are we going to choose the path that will elevate us into a proud, victorious people whom others would wish to emulate, or one that produces ignoramus jackasses of mutilated whoremongers as is being displayed right here in front of me? Vieux Fort, look at these imbeciles, these idiotic sons of disillusioned bitches. Is this how you want your children to turn out? Uneducated, uncultured, uncivilized, barbaric, with their whole mental faculties and self worth posited in the flabby flesh hanging between their legs? These violators of grandmothers and infants in cradles, these scums of the earth. Eh, Vieux Fort? Is this what you want for your children and your children's children? Are you going to continue wallowing in pig shit? Are we going to continue fighting with pigs for places to shit under the bushes?"

This was too much for Eunice. She let go one loud "*chupps*" and, pulling a reluctant Henry, quickly left the scene of the meeting.

The emcee also had had enough. He feared that at the rate Ruben was going, people would soon start stoning the stage, forcing the meeting to end prematurely. Yet the main speaker, the leader of the party, was still to come. He crossed the balcony quickly and took the mic from Ruben.

At that point, pulling against his mother's tugging, Henry turned around to see Ruben staggering back inside the guest house. To Henry his hero seemed suddenly transformed from the bigger than life figure who had just finished mesmerizing the crowd to a deflated, stumbling drunk. It was as if Ruben had been touched by an evil wand.

As Ruben walked back in, his detractors, who a few seconds before had been stunned by the vehemence of his attack, chanted: "*Toujou sou, salope! Salope, toujou sou! Toujou sou, salope! Salope, toujou sou!*"

Standing behind his stall on the sidewalk across the street from the guest house with a   clear view of the political platform, Eugene shook his head at the crowd's ridicule of Ruben and, speaking to no one in particular, said, "Trust Vieux Fortians to turn everything into *bakanal*." Eugene had no sympathy for politics and politicians. According to him they were all liars and *bobolis*. Yet Ruben's vision of Vieux

Fort had carried him away, carried him away into even thinking that in this new Vieux Fort he could graduate from his stalls and open a store. And it occurred to him that if not for Ruben's drinking, he could become Chief Minister of government instead of being the "moose boy" of Castries politicians. So in the middle of the crowd's chant, "*Toujou sou, salope! Salope, toujou sou!*" Eugene decid-ed that he had to have a man-to-man talk with Ruben. He couldn't sit there and let Ruben's great potential go down the drain just because of rum.

So a week or two after the meeting, when Ruben came to buy mango julies, Eugene, looking at the dirty, unkempt, rum-reeking ex-teacher whose clothes looked like he had slept in them for days, concluded that today was as good a day as any to have his man-to-man chat. As he handed Ruben the mangoes, he said, "*En ben bon, Ruben. En ben bon*. What happen to you? You used to dress so nice and clean. Your clothes used to be well ironed, your hair well trimmed. You used to be the envy of Vieux Fort; every-body, even me, used to look up to you. Now look at you. You like a vagabond, your clothes dirty, your hair looking like cockroach sleeping in it, and you always stinking rum. You had your nice teaching job, everybody talking about you being a good teacher and all, and how all the children like you. Some people even used to say that you go be the next headmaster. But you went and cursed the man, and look at you now, going around talking ignorant. I saw you talking at the meeting the other day, and I say to myself, 'You see this Ruben, if not for the rum he could be Chief Minister.' I never thought the day would come when I would see you walking about like a vagabond. Ruben, you better watch yourself, you better stop that rum business and straighten up yourself quick, quick, because right now there isn't much to choose between you and Popo."

Ruben was stunned, and for once he was speechless; for once his arsenal of big words failed him. The only other time Eugene had broached a conversation with him of any length was the day he had told him that people were saying that he was Henry's father, implying that Eunice had been sleeping with him while her husband was alive. Vexed, Ruben had avoided the stall keeper for several weeks. Yet here was Eugene in his face telling him foolishness. Astonished at the boldness and indiscretion of the stall keeper, Ruben reverted to the lowest common denominator.

"*Malmanman*, move your ass in front of me. Who the fuck are you of all persons to tell me what to do? When you stop *bouling*, I will stop drinking. You fucking *boula*." This said, Ruben threw his newly purchased mango julies in the street-side gutter and walked away.

Now it was Eugene's turn to be stunned. Here he was doing the man a big favour, giving him sound advice, but all the man saw to do was insult him. As Ruben walked away, Eugene shouted, "*Wonmyé*, I leave you for dogs to drag your stinking ass across the streets of Vieux Fort!"

AROUND THE TIME Henry turned eleven Eugene left the stall keepers behind and opened a small grocery store. The store stood on top of a small hill within a couple hundred feet from the fish depot and overlooked the very spot at the junction of Walcott Lane and Clarke Street where Eugene had spent so much time selling out of his trays.

Eugene's progress had not escaped Henry. The day he found out that Eugene had a store, he ran all the way home and flung open the gate. "Mama! Mama! Mr. Eugene is getting rich. He has a store."

"Boy, what's wrong with you? Since you small you behind that man. I will never understand what you see in him. The man open a little store and you ready to have a heart attack."

"But ..."

"No but. You better pay more attention to your school work and less to that vulgar man. When I'm gone you will have no one else. You will have to fend for yourself. Remember that."

The Stall Keeper

From then on every time Henry's mother sent him to buy groceries he went to no other place than Eugene's store. When he arrived at the store, he was never in a hurry to make his purchases. He stood aside allowing people who came after him to go ahead. He stood in a corner watching Eugene behind the counter. Watching Eugene, a flurry of activity, weighing half a pound of sugar for this customer, a pound of salt fish for that customer, two pounds of flour for another. His hands and arms spotted with sugar, flour, salt, butter. Talking all the time, gossiping, cursing this and that customer, joking here and there.

Henry saw no change in Eugene's tongue and his womanly ways, but sometimes he detected in Eugene a feeling of unbounded confidence, a feeling of importance, a feeling of invincibility, a feeling of "I have arrived." Standing there watching Eugene, Henry was so proud. It was as if he were the one who had surmounted his miserable childhood and rose from the streets of Vieux Fort to become a store owner, to become rich. Someone of standing, someone of clout, a big man in the community.

Eugene's store was always crowded with customers. Henry was glad that Eugene was giving JQ, M&C, Katie and Green, the largest stores in Vieux Fort, plenty of competition. As if to prove Henry right, a year after Eugene opened shop he extended the store to twice its original size. Whatever had attracted people to buying from Eugene instead of the other stall keepers, was now pulling people away from the other stores to Eugene's store. The way Eugene's business was progressing, Henry was sure that soon Eugene would be the largest store in town. And it wouldn't surprise him if Eugene followed the example of JQ and M&C and opened branches of his store all over the island: Soufriere, Castries, Micoud, Dennery, everywhere.

With these thoughts, an idea began to germinate in Henry's head. Maybe he could work for Mr. Eugene. His school was over at two. He could work for Mr. Eugene from two to four-thirty. "I bet Mr. Eugene will give me a job," he was thinking. But then he remembered his mother. "Is no way she will let me work for someone like Mr. Eugene," he mumbled.

But the idea refused to go away. Instead it grew as a seedling into a forest. Henry saw himself behind the counter, taking stock, weighing flour, sugar, salt fish; wrapping brown paper bags filled with flour, sugar, split peas. Helping Eugene count his hundreds and hundreds of dollars after the store closed for the day. And when Eugene opened his other stores, he, Henry, by then a grown man, would manage one of them for him. In next to no time he would have his own store, and he too would get rich, build a big house for his mother in place of the three room house they lived in, and buy himself a big motor car. The only problem he saw was that when he got his own store, Eugene would be a competitor. But Henry didn't dwell too long on this minor detail.

Twelve going on to thirteen, Henry was no longer looking for a father. Mr. Ruben, his last chance of a father, was well into his decline. The Americans had not responded to his letter, so he had long given up on them. In fact, he didn't even remember ever writing to the Americans. Besides thoughts of getting rich and helping his mother, another thought hit Henry. With all his riches he could help Vieux Fort. In fact he could do more for Vieux Fort than even the Americans had done. As his business expanded he could provide jobs for everyone in Vieux Fort. Soon Vieux Fort would be bigger and better than Castries.

The Stall Keeper

HENRY HAD GOOD REASON to be optimistic. The year was 1970 and the scent of flowers mixed with that of seaweed was in the air. The migratory *pitjwits*, taking a respite from their wintry homes, were flocking the beaches along Vieux Fort's Atlantic coast. Seroc, the Canadian construction company, had changed the course of the Vieux Fort River yet again to lengthen Beanefield Airport into Hewanorra International. The Winera cardboard factory and the Windward & Leeward Heineken Brewery had begun operations. So too had a host of other factories that together (and in keeping with the government's national economic development plan) had pronounced Vieux Fort the industrial capital of St. Lucia. Thanks to the generosity of the Canadian government, three new junior secondary schools (in Vieux Fort, Micoud and Soufriere) had opened their doors, thus doubling the number of secondary schools on the island. Halcyon Days, then the largest hotel on the island, came to Vieux Fort's Atlantic Coast, delighting Vieux Fortians with many firsts, including spectacular New Year celebrations in opulent ballrooms, bean-shaped swimming pools, steelpan on the beach, horse and car races, red double-decker London style buses filled with half naked tourists. Surely, to the older Vieux Fort folks it appeared that the Americans had finally returned.

Long before Henry had written entrance exams, he was so sure that he would be attending the new secondary school that he kept a close watch on its progress, beginning from the time bulldozers leveled off the hill that overlooked the Caribbean Sea to when chalkboards were placed in the classrooms. The school buildings formed a square, enclosing a small playground. This school was different from other schools with which Henry was acquainted. The sides of the buildings were built of galvanized material. Only it wasn't the same type of galvanize sheets that covered the roofs of houses in St. Lucia. Those siding the school buildings came in brown and were thicker and looked more durable. Instead of wood, the chairs and desks were made of metal and some kind of fabricated material not unlike fibreglass. But what caught Henry's fancy were the chalkboards. Unlike the chalkboards he was used to, these were green. After seeing the greenboards, he was sure that they were movie screens. Since his mother didn't allow him to go to the cinema, he was thinking that at last he would be seeing movies. He excitedly shared his movie theory with Ralph who wasn't as thrilled because he went to matinee at the Royal Cinema almost every week-end. But he reckoned if Henry was right and they were going to show movies at the school, that meant less time spent in classrooms doing boring sums and learning inde-cipherable grammar.

One afternoon Henry was passing by the Royal Cinema when a girl his age and the most beautiful girl he had ever laid eyes on emerged from the house adjoining the cinema. Henry fell in love instantly. He didn't utter a word to her. He was too stunned. But he knew the appearance of the girl, whom he would come to know as Cecilia, just as he was passing by was no accident. Though he was seeing her for the first time, he knew without any doubt that their paths would cross again and that would be at the Vieux Fort Junior Secondary School. This was how sure Henry was of attending the new school.

As it turned out, Henry was right about him and Cecilia attending the new school. But the green boards were chalk boards, not movie screens, and Cecilia never became his girlfriend. She probably never knew of his existence. He was never able to muster the courage to make his love known to her.

The Stall Keeper

ONE AFTERNOON HENRY ENTERED EUGENE'S STORE. It was near closing time. The sun had already joined with the horizon, casting fiery red on the blue of the Caribbean. The last customer had just left the store.

"Mr. Eugene, I want a job. I can count, add and subtract. I can weigh."

The stall keeper turned store keeper looked at the breathless boy and started to laugh. He was wearing a pair of gold earrings, and gold and silver bracelets. As he laughed, his earrings danced and his bracelets jingled.

"Boy, work for me! What work you think I can give you? You see any of the stores have little boys working for them? Besides, with what will I pay you?"

"Mr. Eugene, you rich, we poor. Please give me a job."

"Who tell you I rich? Just because I sell a few pounds of sugar, I rich? And what makes you think your mother will let you work for me?"

"Yes, she will. She will. She hasn't got a husband."

"All right, all right," said Eugene. "If your mother says yes, then I'll give you a job."

Henry ran all the way home. And barely catching his breath he began to tell his mother how he could get rich working for Mr. Eugene. When he stopped for breath, his mother cut him short.

"Boy, are you out of your mind? Work for this man? Will you ever stop studying that man? I tired of telling you stop paying that man attention, and study your school work. If you were paying as much attention to your school work as you been paying to that man, you would be getting all A's instead of the B's and C's you making. Go take a book and read. And stop this foolishness."

Henry didn't give up. Six months later, Eunice lost her cooking job at Cloud's Nest Inn. Business had gotten slow and since she didn't work on Saturdays, despite her excellent cooking, she was the first cook they let go. So, taking advantage of the situation, Henry approached his mother on the subject of his path to riches.

"Mama, you don't have to go look for another job. Let me go work for Mr. Eugene. We go get rich."

Eunice looked at the boy who, not too many years ago, was going around asking men if they were his father. She remembered the time when little three and a half year old Henry gave her the fright of her life. Somehow Henry had found out that his father had drowned at Enbakoko Beach. So one Sunday afternoon he escaped the attention of his mother and went searching for his father. By the time he traversed the pasture that led to Enbakoko Gui, he was tired and hungry, but he pushed on determined to find his father once and for all. He got lost in the tangle of coconut palms, sea-ackee, sea-grapes and sea-almond trees that formed Enbakoko Gui. Crying, he sat under a sea-grape tree. When his sobbing quieted down, he became more attuned to the ever present sound of waves splashing on the beach. Squeezing through bush and thicket and getting scraped and tearing his shirt in the process, he emerged on the beach. To him the beach stretched ahead into eternity. But he didn't let the endless stretch of beach nor the vastness of the Atlantic Ocean stop him. Doggedly, sometimes playing catch-me-if-you-can with the waves simmering in the sand, he walked the beach.

Soon he came across a young man on his beach run. The man bypassed Henry, paying no attention to him because he was sure that the little boy was there with his parents. The man only looked back when he heard a whisper that was meant to be a shout. "Mister, have you seen my father?" The man stopped and let Henry catch up with him.

"Boy, who is your father?"

"Mister Auguste."

"Ma Auguste is your mother?

"Yes, the mister."

"Boy, your father is in heaven."

"No, he is not in heaven, they say he drown on the beach."

"Boy, where your mother?"

"She at home."

"Boy, go home. On my way back I don't want to see you on the beach."

"But mister, I looking for my father."

The man continued his running, looking back every so often only to discover that the little boy was still moving forward. The man reckoned that soon the boy would tire and he would go home. But nothing could deter Henry from his mission. He had stayed long enough without a father.

When Henry reached Sandy Beach he was so tired and hungry that the Atlantic breeze was coming close to lifting him off his feet. He sat under a sea-grape tree and, in spite of his determination, fell asleep. On his return the jogger found Henry fast asleep. Night was approaching. He picked up Henry and carried him all the way home to the arms of a tearful, trembling, and ever so grateful Eunice. Henry slept the whole evening and all of the following morning.

Remembering the episode, Eunice shook her head to dispel the helplessness and despondency she had felt that day. She said, "Boy, you may be getting big, but it is me who decide things around here."

"Mama, we need the money. School opening soon. I need new shoes and uniform. Please, Mama. Please."

Eunice looked at the boy again. He was looking more and more like his father. He had his father's cotton-white teeth, and his unbounded optimism. With thoughts of Raphael, her eyes misty, Eunice said, "Boy, you are the spitting image of your father."

"Please, Mama. Please."

The boy's pleading shifted her mind to Eugene. To this day she could remember his emotional plea to her that had conjured images of a wounded animal and that had said, in effect, that he was really hurt that she would think that he was capable of hurting her son. As she had listened to his pain that went deeper than what his words were saying, she knew then that he would never hurt her boy, that he was incapable of hurting him. Yet she wanted Henry to keep away, far away from Eugene. Henry was now twelve going on to thirteen, a man in the making and in the likeness of his father. But she still didn't want him near this uncouth man. She wondered what would Raphael have said. Would he have had a problem with his son working for the stall keeper turned shopkeeper? She wasn't sure what his answer would have been. But her face formed a smile when she remembered how he used to come home from work, apparently phrasing sentences and bringing up topics just to be able to put "shit" in them.

She didn't want her son keeping company with this vulgar man. So she was surprised to hear herself say, "All right. O.K. But get this straight. You eh working on the Sabbath and on Friday afternoons. You go there after school for only two hours. From two-thirty to four-thirty. And this coming term, if you get anything less than a B, you eh working there anymore."

"Thanks, Mama. Soon we go be rich!"

In the evening, lying on her bed waiting for sleep to come, Eunice wondered why she was allowing her son to work for this man of the streets? Why was she allowing Vieux Fort into her house when the last thing she wanted was for Henry to be near the stall keeper turned shop keeper? Was it because she was getting soft and more emotional with age? Sleep came but not the answers to her questions, except that the uncouth but wounded man would hurt not even a hair on her son's head, and that she would never understand what her son saw in him that despite threats of beatings, despite the nasty things Vieux Fortians had accused them of, he flatly refused to leave the man alone.

Later that night Eunice had an annoying dream that took her completely by surprise because it was a long time since she had had one of her bothersome dreams for which she usually had no interpretation. The last dream she could remember had to do with frogs and rotten tomatoes that spoke of disappointment. Eunice had even concluded that she had lost the ability to have these dreams. Yet, here she was, after such a long time, dreaming of making bread in her brick and mortar oven that stood on the hill in the middle of her garden. After placing all the bread in the oven, she barred the door to let the bread do its thing. When she thought the bread was good and ready, anticipating golden-brown crusted loaves, she unbarred the door only to be greeted by loaves reduced to charcoal, and shedding tears, so much tears that the oven was filling up with water. Still in the dream, she was thinking, it was bad enough for all the bread to turn to coals, but crying, filling her oven with tears? What kind of nonsense is this?

ON A WEEKDAY IN MID-AFTERNOON, when Ruben had become as well established a drunk as Popo; when, besides an example of what a woman and obeah can do to a man, he had become an example of what happens to a man damaged by too much education; when to some folks he had become yet another statistic that proved Vieux Fortians to be lazy drunks and prostitutes waiting for the Americans to bring them salvation; when to Eunice he was a reminder of how close she had come to throwing her life away, marrying a man who was soon to became a dirty, worthless drunk; and when to Henry he had become a man who inspired not adulation but pity, he was resting under the balcony of a two-storey building on Commercial Street, not too far from Theodore's Drugstore, taking occasional sips from his rum bottle—his constant companion—and watching Vieux Fort quiet down for the day, when sudenly appeared a boisterous group of four students from the Vieux Fort Secondary School, all boys, all dressed in blue shirt jacs over dark grey trousers. Beads of perspiration on the boys' foreheads and sweat-blotches on the underside of their shirt sleeves spoke of the afternoon heat and their restlessness.

Luxuriating in his blissful drunkenness (interrupted only by a single fly that, no matter how many times he swiped at it, kept coming back, seeking his lips) and watching the boys come down Commercial Street towards him, full of hilarity and furious gestures, Ruben said to himself, "But eh-eh, these fellows behaving as if they have just been released from jail and so they making the most of their newly gained freedom, or that the world belongs to them and them alone and everything in it is there for their distinct pleasure. Eh-eh?" With this thought, Ruben swiped at the persistent fly, took a sip of rum, and shouted and waved happily at Daddy Mano who was about to enter the drugstore. The great philanthropist waved back and disappeared inside.

Ruben's insight wasn't far from the truth. To the boys home and the classroom was a kind of jail and everything in between was freedom. And it was easy to see why they might think that the world belonged to them. The wellspring of youth was gushing out from their every pore, filling their being with impatient vigor, giving them no reason to doubt that the world would meet all their life expectations, and was sure to keep all what they thought of as promises that life has made to them, promises they considered their birthrights and so didn't have to earn.

Unmindful of Ruben's drunken muse, when the boys saw him they quickened their gait. They would have a bit more fun before the final turn of the keys to their jail cell. Ruben was one of the treats that the world had suddenly coughed up for their entertainment. He was a safe source of amusement because they were absolutely sure they would never end up like him, so much so that the thought had never even crossed their minds. And why should it? Were they not soon to be secondary school graduates, a privilege that would guarantee them, all of them, a comfortable office and white shirt and tie job? And were they, without a doubt, not destined to become the elites of their society? Surely their education would provide them safe-proof security against ever becoming a Ruben or a Popo.

As the boys approached, deep into that special happiness that only alcohol can bring him, Ruben smiled as if he appreciated the company just as much as the company appreciated him or that the group of boys were friends he hadn't seen in years. So before the boys could offer a word, Ruben said, "Here come the rookies of higher learning, straight from the halls of academia. Gentlemen, what enlightenment, what edification is pouring from the edifices of today's lyceums?"

"How not to be a *wonmyé*," answered one of the boys, and they all broke into laughter.

"Then I empathize, I commiserate with you. Because in your inculcation they are not indoctrinating you about the vicissitudes of life. And this, gentlemen, is a humongous tragedy, a travesty of epic proportions."

"What's so fantastic about being a *wonmyé*, sleeping in gutters, walking around smelling like shit and flies all in your mouth?" answered a second boy, and again they all laughed.

"Ah, in my great benevolence, I pity you sophomoric students of so called higher learning. Because what you call a drunk, and what I call happy sobriety—yes, happy sobriety—is a distillment of the apotheosis, the epitome of life. For all of life's allegories can be found in the life of one living in happy sobriety. This, my pubescents of ill-fated pedagogics, are not to be found within the walls of academia."

The boys didn't like the sound of what they were hearing at all. They quickly changed the subject.

"My learned comrade, what are your thoughts on the state of affairs in the country? When do you reckon your party will get into power? Is it when cocks have teeth?"

At this last question, the boys playfully pushed each other, and repeated, "Yeah, when cocks have teeth. When cocks have teeth."

"Delighted that you asked, novice of intellectualism. The government, rather those ignominious, bombastic jackasses that pass themselves as government, are there masturbating their gigantic egos and lubricating in self delusion. They know nothing about governance, they care nothing about the impoverished citizens of the nation. Next election we will kick their inflated asses to Timbuktu."

Then Ruben said, "Enough, enough about politics. Let's talk about love. I bet my bottle of sobriety — and mind you, that's betting a lot — that these asylums, these bastions of knowledge aren't educating you on the dangers of love. How love can lacerate your heart and feed it to the hogs. Eh, don't look at me like that. Aren't there nymphets in your lives, providing release from your abounding, adolescent sexual urges? Or am I to comprehend that self-manipulation is the closest you have come to obtaining assuagement from your infantile sexuality?"

Ruben paused as if waiting for the boys to respond, not unlike a poker or chess player waiting for his opponent to make his move, knowing full well what the move would be. In the pause he dug his hand in his back pocket to take a sip of rum, as if to reward himself for the victory that was sure to be his.

As for the boys, at thirteen going on to fourteen, they were all virgins because they were still at the age where they couldn't do much about their newly acquired sexual urges, which thrilled them yet left them in great frustration. An age where they were still unsure whether this thing that was happening to them, dominating their existence, was supposed to be happening, and that some punishment might be in store for their transgressions. And like many boys in their early teens they thought that they were the first and only ones to experience what to them were these fantastic and excruciating sensations. So to them, Ruben's question was tantamount to him eavesdropping on them when they were in toilets, in bushes or on their beds experimenting with, appeasing their newly gained sexuality. It was as if they were caught with their pants down, so naturally they were embarrassed and ashamed, and their self conscious giggles to Ruben's question, accusation, rather, did more to unclothe their shame than to conceal it. Suddenly they felt compelled to make the crazy drunk pay for his indiscretion. They were there to have fun. The drunk was one of the objects that had been given to them for their entertainment. The world belonged to them, remember? So how come it was the dirty drunk having all the fun, making fools of them? In their embarrassment, the boys did to Ruben exactly what they did—teasing and belittling—to girls whom they liked and were trying desperately to impress but didn't quite know how to go about it, their fear and shame of rejection making matters worse.

Just as the rum bottle was about to kiss Ruben's lips, one of the boys grabbed it and, evading Ruben's drunken efforts to regain his property, passed it on to his friend, and thus began a game of catchers with Ruben's elixir. Every time the bottle changed hands some more of Ruben's precious liquid spilled onto the ground. Then calamity struck. The bottle slipped out from the hand of one of the boys, and fell and broke into pieces in the street-side gutter. The boys ran, leaving Ruben stooped over the spot where the bottle broke, lamenting, tears in his eyes, on the hardship he would have to endure for the rest of the afternoon and a good part of the night.

Daddy Mano had stepped out of the drugstore just in time to see the boys playing catchers with Ruben's rum bottle and to witness the bottle's final fate. In recent years Daddy Mano had become an even more important personage in Vieux Fort and St. Lucia. He had become a politician; next elections he would be his party's candidate for the Vieux Fort seat. His visit to the drugstore and his conversation with the druggist, himself an avid political observer, had been all about the notion that as a member of parliament he would finally be in a position to compel the Americans and British to pay for their exploitation of Vieux Fort and its people. "The only reason I enter politics is to put myself in a position of authority to compel the Americans and British to pay back what they stole from us," he had fervently told the druggist.

When the boys saw Daddy Mano, they knew they were in for a scolding from the man whose candies they had relished so much as toddlers. It was too late for them to change course, so they tried to slip pass him. But he stopped them in their tracks.

"Listen, Sonny," he said, "this is a disgraceful thing you all have done today. You all must learn to respect your elders no matter how low in your eyes they have fallen. None of us knows what's in store for us tomorrow. This man you all just finished mocking and making a fool of is an excellent example. Take a good look at him. He was not as lucky as you all to go to secondary school, but still there was a time when he was the brightest man in Vieux Fort. But not only that. He is the best footballer and cricketer Vieux Fort has ever produced. He used to make nonsense of Castries teams. Just ask your parents about him, and they will tell you that, if not for Castries folks, he would have played for the West Indies team."

Chastened and out of respect for Daddy Mano, the boys glanced at Ruben who was still stooped over the drain mumbling to himself. But as they left the presence of the great humanitarian and continued homeward, though much more somber and much less confident of themselves than before they had run into Ruben, they doubted very much that Ruben had been anything but a drunk with a facility for big words.

However, if Daddy Mano could have read their thoughts, he might have told them that it may well be that the only mistake this crazy drunk had made was to have been born ahead of his time, in the wrong town, in the wrong country, and to have fallen in love with the wrong woman.

WHEN VIEUX FORTIANS SAW HENRY working for Eugene, they were both surprised and perplexed. In light of all the rumors, how could the strict, holier-than-thou *Semdays* woman let her son work for the *malmanman*? They were probably just as baffled as was Teresa when Eunice had first announced that she wanted to be a nun, or when Eunice had joined the Seventh Day Adventist Church or when out of the blue she had brought Raphael home to ask for her hand in marriage. The only difference was that unlike Teresa Vieux Fortians weren't privy to the knowledge that Eunice was special. So in the absence of that knowledge they were left to speculate how things must be really hard on the *Semdays* woman, she losing her job and all. With a smirk on their faces, they said to each other, "*Kwapo ka bien fimen pip-li,*" meaning, toads well smoking her pipe.

Henry paid little attention to Vieux Fort's nosiness and smirks. At work he was all business; his fortune was at stake. Eugene weighed the flour, sugar, salt, corn meal and split peas, into half pound, one pound and two pound brown paper bags, and Henry folded the tops of the bags. Henry kept stock of all the canned and boxed goods—corned beef, sardines, condensed milk, evaporated milk, powdered milk, Quaker Oats. At closing, he swept the floor and sometimes helped count the money.

One afternoon, Henry counted a hundred and fifty dollars and forty-three cents. He said, "Mr. Eugene, look at all that money! I tell you, you is rich, but you don't want to believe me. When you open your other stores, I want to be a manager."

"Boy, what other stores you talking about?"

"You know, like J.Q. and M&C."

"Boy, you way over my head. If I were you, I would stop dreaming and concentrate on school."

"But Mr. Eugene, you yourself never liked school. When your aunt took you out of school and make you sell, you was the happiest boy in town."

Eugene laughed until his eyes watered.

"Who told you that?"

"A boy at school."

No one could dispel Henry's dream; not his mother, not Eugene, not Vieux Fort gossipers, and definitely not Lucille, the stall keeper who fought with Eugene several years back. Since that fight Eugene and Lucille's relationship had turned from best of friends to ice cold to tepid. With Eugene's success, their relationship was well on its way back to ice cold.

One afternoon Lucille came to the store with her usual complaints. She said, "Eugene, that corn meal eh no good, it full of worms."

Even before she had said that, Henry knew there would be fireworks. Because the week before, the first thing

Lucille said when she entered the store was: "Eugene, I see you have a helper, make sure that's all he is to you."

Eugene looked at her crossed eye, his eyes turning red. Henry had never seen Eugene so mad; so mad that Eugene of all persons couldn't speak. He just stared at the woman. Henry knew Eugene wasn't one to stay quiet for long, so he had been waiting with great excitement for the next time Lucille would enter the store. Henry wasn't ruling out a repeat of the fight he had seen several years before. The fight that was one of the treats of his childhood. But this time Henry wasn't planning to be just a bystander. He wasn't about to let his boss go it alone.

As Henry expected, this afternoon Eugene hadn't stayed quiet.

"Lucille, *salòp*, if you want to know what's dirty, what have worms swimming every which way, just look between your legs."

"Oh, because you have a stinking shop, you think you high and mighty. You think you is God. Mark my words, you *malmanman*. The higher the monkey climb, the more he exposes his ass. From now on watch it."

"Leave my shop, *ti jamet*. Marsh! Marsh! and never set foot here again."

Lucille took the bag of corn meal and slammed it onto the counter. The bag burst, scattering corn meal in all directions. Eugene opened the door flap that let him out from behind the counter. Henry stiffened his punch, readying himself for battle. The customers in the store held Eugene.

"Let him go, let the *malmanman* go. Let him go for me to make him hear and understand. Today he go finally know if he is man or woman," said Lucille.

With great effort, some customers were able to restrain Eugene, while others blocked Lucille and coaxed her into leaving the store.

After Lucille left, a customer said, "Eugene, don't worry yourself with that Lucille. Is jealous she jealous of you. That's how us *negs* are, we just can't see another *neg* do well. Look at the coolies. See how they stick together. You see one selling at the market, next thing you know they own stores, trucks, restaurants, and is only coolies they have working for them. And don't talk of the Amigos (Syrians). They does come here with just a suit case, passing house to house selling clothes out of that suitcase, everybody giving them jokes, but next time you see them they done have a store, and the next time you see them they done own the whole damn street."

Another said, "Eugene, you know how Dennery people does *gajé*. You must watch yourself with that woman, you know. Just remember what they did to Popo and Ruben."

A third said, "Eugene, that's true. I know you're a person who doesn't take advice. But for once listen to me. As you doing well there, people will be sending all kinds of rubbish after you. You better look for a good *gadè* to protect your business or else everything you working for will come to nought."

"Let them come. Let them come," said Eugene. "It is me that's Eugene. I'm their asses' boss. I don't need no *gadè*. I've gotten to where I am without anyone's help. I eh go start now. If they think I easy, let them come."

The customers left, shaking their heads at Eugene's hardheadedness and downright recklessness. They could remember that this was the same attitude that led to Popo's downfall. They could also remember how Ruben had thrown out the protective potion the parishioners had gone to great lengths to get. And now look at Ruben, they thought, just look at Ruben.

THE MONEY COUNTED and stashed away, Henry began sweeping the floor. After a while he said, "Mr. Eugene, no joke. This afternoon I was waiting for that Miss Lucille. I would have given her one set of punches." As Henry said this, he dropped the broom and fired punches in the air.

Eugene laughed and laughed, and said, "I thought *Semdays* didn't fight. And by the way, don't forget tomorrow is carnival. I closing. Last year I didn't jump up. I wasn't in the mood. But this year I go be queen of carnival."

"Queen, Mr. Eugene?"

"Yes, queen. See me in my solar costume, drinking my rum and whining till I drop."

THE PARADE BANDS met at midday in the Vieux Fort Square for the competition. They formed a dazzling, gyrating circle of color. At an inside corner of the circle the twenty-man steel band was playing away. The air was pregnant with calypso, with jumping up tension, with carnival fever. The carnival feverish mass of spectators, well wishers and revelers swarmed the circle of parade bands. No one was standing still. No one could resist the call of the steel pans, the call of calypso, the call of carnival. Not even Henry. Somehow he had managed to squeeze himself through to the front layer of spectators, and, swept up in the carnival spirit, he was there shaking a leg, negating fourteen years of Seventh Day Adventist doctrine, fourteen years of restrictions, fourteen years of his mother keeping Vieux Fort out of him.

It was a perfect day for carnival. The sun was shining brightly, the sky was clear and wide and blue, an intoxicating salt-scented breeze was blowing across town from the Atlantic.

As Henry shifted and danced to the steelband music, his eyes circled the parade bands. The Green Parrot band was dressed in the manner of the Jako, the St. Lucian parrot and national bird. From the neck to just below the shoulders the costumes were feathery and red. Then sheaths of green protruded from under the red and extended to the waist. From waist down, blue took over and tapered into red tails. On the arms, the costumes became red, green and blue wings.

The Ashanti band had white cloths with front flaps wrapped around their waist. In the manner of war parties, brown-red, white and charcoal-black designs were painted on their faces and all over their bodies. Each member of the band had a short black stick, representing spears but looking more like wands.

At the center of the Solar band was the sun, played by Eugene. He was crowned with a golden, blazing sun, punctuated with sparkling jewels. His costume was flaming red, and his face was sprinkled with gold glitter that flickered in the sunlight. His lips were painted rose-red and he wore large gold earrings. To Henry, flames seemed to leap off Eugene's body, making him think of the fire in his mother's oven. Anyone who came too close to Eugene appeared in danger of catching fire. Eugene was gyrating, whining to the music, and all the while laughing and talking. Smiling, Henry was thinking, "Queen Eugene. Hail to Her Majesty." Besides Eugene, in the Solar band there were the earth and the other planets circling the sun and then there was a moon circling the earth, everyone, in their orbit, whining, gyrating, getting down.

A children's band accompanied each adult band, each a miniature version of their adult counterparts. Henry could pick out many of his classmates in the children's bands. He saw Ralph in the Green Parrot band. When Ralph waved at him, it was as if he was about to take flight. Looking at Ralph the Jako, and getting drunk on the music, the dancing, the costumes, Henry wished that just for once he could freely join a carnival parade. He said, "*chups*," and whispered to himself, "When I grow up I leaving *Semdays*." But just then the thought of the beating that awaited him for sneaking out of the house to go watch carnival, what his mother considered the worst of the worst, surfaced. He quickly forced the fear of the beating out of his consciousness, and allowed the carnival fever to carry him, carry him away.

The Green Parrot band opened the competition. They pranced to the middle of the circle. Whining and twisting, they moved as one toward the steel-band. The steel-band quickened its beat. The dancers entered a frenzy of motion, then they moved back as one to the center of the circle. They moved forward again, waving, spreading out their arms, their wings. Red, green and blue blurred into one. With their wings outstretched, to Henry they looked like a flock of parrots hovering in midair.

The Ashanti band followed. They jumped up and down, holding their spears in their left hands, and waving their right hands wildly. Then they went into a writhing, whining movement, the markings on their bodies creating a dizzying, hypnotic sensation. They embraced each other at the shoulders, forming a line across the ring, and moved as a writhing wall toward the steel-band.

Then the Solar band took center circle. They were a dazzling inferno of motion. With a half-smile on his face, Henry's eyes were glued on Eugene. Eugene was at the center of the band. Flames leapt off his body. He was moving forward, moving backward, moving left, moving right, his arms waving in the air, and all the while the rest of his band orbiting him. He moved close to one of the steel pan players, and he whined and whined as if making love to the steel pan. Eugene danced around the circle, hitting a dance duet with the moon and each of his planets, as if communicating something to each by way of dance, like honey bees communicating the location of nectar.

After the Solar band, the children's bands took turns at center circle. Their small, beautiful, daintily dressed bodies moving, whining perfectly to the beat of the steel pans. Henry saw Ralph breakaway from the group and do a solo dance, bringing the crowd to uproar. Watching Ralph and the other children, Henry felt a deep sense of loss. A sense that he had been left out of all the fun in the world, that he was the only one missing the action, that his mother and the Adventist Church were denying him his culture. A sense that he was a caged parrot with broken wings.

The competition was over. Solar came first and Green Parrot second. It was time for the road march. The steelband headed the procession. Behind the steelband came Green Parrot, then Ashanti, and then Solar. Behind Solar came the crowd. The parade left the Square, danced onto St. Omer Street, and turned right on Belvedere Street. Henry walked on the side of the gyrating mosaic, and level with the Solar band so he could keep an eye on his boss. Eugene was jumping up, waving, drinking from a rum bottle and passing the bottle around. Vieux Fort was filled with the sound of steel pans and the wailing of revelers.

The procession danced all the way to the west end of town, swung around the market and turned left onto Commercial Street that would take it to Clarke Street, a short distance from the jetty. By then the dancing was loose and wild, and rum was flowing freely. Eugene was taking turns holding his band members, and whining, whining on them, all the while moving forward, keeping pace with the procession.

Then a short distance on Commercial Street, the revelers began to smell smoke. One by one, they looked up to see smoke billowing across the sky. Upon seeing the smoke, a few in their drunken, carnival-feverish stupor started singing, "*I cho, i cho, i cho-o-o*; it's hot, it's hot, it's hot." The party continued. The party that the people had spent a whole year planning for; the party at which they were releasing all the previous year's accumulated pain and suffering; the party that allowed them to forget their poverty, their deprivation; to forget about who did them evil, who had placed obeah on them. On this day all was bliss. The Americans had returned. Unmindful of the smoke, Eugene continued to jump up.

Henry saw the smoke, and it occurred to him that it was coming from the direction of the hill upon which Eugene's store stood. But he ignored the smoke. It can't be Eugene's store. Not on carnival day. Not when Eugene was queen. Henry continued watching Eugene and the other revelers. But then an uneasy feeling began playing on his mind. Was this Eugene's store? No, it can't be. Henry moved with the parade. The smell of smoke got stronger, the sky was now thick with smoke. Henry could no longer ignore his unease. He ran ahead of the parade. The closer he got to Clarke Street the faster he ran. He had to make sure it wasn't Eugene's store. It wasn't his future billowing across the sky. At the junction of Commercial and Clarke, Henry looked up the hill. The store was engulfed in fire. A line of people, stretching from the store to the standpipe, were passing buckets of water, like a chain gang, to put out the fire. Henry ran back to the parade, to the Solar band. He grabbed the half drunk, prancing, self-appointed queen of carnival.

"Mr. Eugene, Mr. Eugene, your store is burning! Your store is burning!"

"What?"

"Your store! Your store! It's on fire!"

Eugene let out one scream that startled the other Solar dancers, and he started to run.

"What happen? What happen?" Eugene's comrades were asking.

"The store is on fire! The store is on fire!" shouted Henry as he ran after Eugene. The whole Solar band followed Eugene and Henry.

Eugene, Henry and Solar ran. Past Ashanti, past Green Parrot, past the steelband. Midway up Commercial Street Eugene's sun fell. He didn't pick it up. Henry began to bend down to get it, but he changed his mind. No time to waste, his fortune was billowing across the sky.

At the foot of the hill where his store stood, Eugene let out another scream. He had arrived just in time to see the roof caving in under the vengeance of the fire. Eugene, with Henry and some of the Solar revelers following at his heels, dashed up the hill. As Eugene was about to rush into the crumbling store, his parade comrades held him. As they held him, he passed out. Henry and the rest of the Solar revelers not holding onto Eugene joined the human water chain. Buckets upon buckets of water kept going uphill. But the efforts of the water chain were as futile as trying to empty the Atlantic Ocean with buckets. The fire was too far gone.

Unmindful of the futility of his efforts, the buckets of water couldn't come fast enough for Henry to pass them on. Despite the frenzy of his activities, his tear-filled eyes never left the fire that was devouring a life's work, the lifetime dream of the man who was a woman. A dream Henry had followed and observed from its infancy; a dream he had watched blossom; a dream that had become his dream. The dream of becoming a store manager, of having his own store, of getting rich, of buying his mother that big house, of getting himself a big motor car, of helping Vieux Fort surpass Castries in importance.

The fire brigade stationed at the American built fire station next to the American built airport came. But it was too late. There was nothing left to save. The firemen's efforts were little more than putting out the smoldering charcoals the store had been reduced to.

Just as the fire brigade was leaving, the parade approached Clarke Street. The music slowed down, the parade slowed down, as if paying homage to the burnt store. Many revelers left the parade altogether to witness the tragedy. Everyone's eyes fixed on the charred debris of a man's life, of a boy's dream.

Eugene came out of his blackout, as if it were the music of the passing steel pans that had called him out. As soon as he came to himself, he hurried to the charred remains of his store and searched around. Henry followed him. When Eugene came out, his normally reddish face was drained of all its color. "I'm finished," he said. "I'm finished."

Most of Eugene's money was hidden somewhere in the store. Rumor had it that he liked to have his money handy so whenever he wished he could pick it up, count it, feel it; make sure it was really there, it was really his. To feel a sense of having, a sense of power, a sense that he has arrived, Eugene had to have his money within arms' length.

Henry held Eugene's hand.

"Mr. Eugene," he said in a sobbing voice, "We eh finish, I will help you build the store back. We eh finish. We eh finish."

In a voice that seemed far away, Eugene said, "Boy, there is nothing here for you. Go. Go home. Go away."

Henry looked up into Eugene's eyes as if to make sure that he was still there, to make sure that this was really

Eugene speaking. He was just about to protest that we eh finish yet, that we can build back the store in next to no time, when he saw Eugene's unfocused, vacant eyes that showed him no recognition. Henry swallowed his protest. A new wave of tears rolled down his face. He slowly walked down the hill to Clarke Street. Finished, he was thinking, finished. Henry felt that he was the one who was finished. He was the one whose whole life had just expired. He was the one whose life had suddenly turned to ashes.

A few steps down the hill Henry turned around to look at the now pitiful Eugene. The queen who was no longer wearing her crown. The queen whose once shining, flame-red costume was now covered with ashes and black markings of charred wood. The sun had burnt itself out. Henry felt his whole body sink as if it could no longer support its own weight. Slowly, his face wet with tears, his eyes to the ground, he walked down the hill of Eugene's destruction.

He didn't see Ruben. He didn't see the man he once wished was his father, who was now a dying tree. Ruben was there in a drunken stupor, but, occupied with the fire, no one saw him, no one heard him muttering his favorite line from his favorite poem by his favorite poet. *Why should a man wax tears when his wooden world fails?*

Henry didn't see his mother either. In fact, had Eunice not called out to him, "Henry, oh Henry," he would have walked right past without ever noticing her. Nonetheless, mother and son had become aware of the fire at about the same time. In Eunice's case her hands were deep in dirt, tending her lettuce plants, when she first smelled smoke. But unwilling to divert attention from her garden, she had ignored the scent, but then the odor became overpowering. She tore her eyes from her plants and looked up towards the heavens. The sky was blanketed with a thick, black layer of smoke. She whispered, "Eh-eh, a house burning?"

Noise rising from Walcott Lane shifted her attention to people walking in the direction of Clarke Street with excited urgency. Then Ma Dantes, her next-door neighbor, the one who beat her man each time he came home from a night of debauchery, shouted, "Ma Auguste, you haven't heard the news? Eugene's shop catch fire." Immediately, Eunice's mind switched to Henry. Long before she first smelled the smoke she had realized that her son had sneaked out of the house, and she was sure that he was by carnival. She had said to herself, "Oh, because he is now fourteen, and he has hairs growing in a few new places, and he has a little job he thinks he is big man, he thinks he can do whatever he wants. Well, he will have to think again. When he comes back, I'm cutting his behind." But with news of the fire, she was sure that Henry was at no other place than the scene of Eugene's misfortune. So forgetting all about cutting her son's behind, Eunice was gripped by a different kind of worry. *That boy likes Eugene and likes working at this store too much. The store burning down will kill him for sure.* With this thought, Eunice quickly abandoned her garden, washed her hands, traded her soil-stained dress for a clean one, and hurried in search of her son.

Approaching the scene of the fire, she saw her Henry, crestfallen, head bent, walking downhill from the ruins of Eugene's store, walking as if it didn't matter whether he was dead or alive. Eunice's heart dropped at the sight of her dejected son, and calling to him, "Henry, oh Henry," she ran up the hill and hugged him, hugged him as if her hug would be the difference between him living and him dying.

With his head resting on his mother's bosom, Henry sobbed and sobbed, and in between sobs kept repeating, "Mama, we finish. We finish." Eunice held him tightly to her bosom with her right hand, and with her left she caressed the back of his head, and in response to his, "Mama, we finish. We finish," she said, "Shhhh, shhhh. It will be alright. It will be alright. It will be alright."

When Henry's sobbing began to subside, still holding onto him, Eunice looked over his head and gazed at Eugene. She saw an apparition-like figure of a man dressed in a woman's carnival costume blackened by charcoal and ashes. If not for the tragic circumstances, the comical image in front of her would have surely brought a smile to her lips, or a laugh followed by a "*chups*." But instead, she recalled the time he had accosted and told her how hurt he was that she would think that he would hurt her son, when he would rather die than to hurt a single hair on her son's head. This recollection and the now tragic, pitiful, comical Eugene brought an involuntary tear to her eye. Seeking relief from the hurt and pity she felt for Eugene, she shifted her gaze from him to the crowd of spectators. But this was tantamount to jumping from the pot into the fire, for her eyes fell directly on Ruben whom she could see holding onto a bottle and mumbling to himself.

At that very instance, Ruben, as if aware of Eunice's presence, shifted his head sideways in her direction and his eyes fell in hers. The bottle of rum he was about to bring to his lips remained in midair, and for a few long seconds the would-be lovers remained there staring at each other. Then breaking the spell, or the magic, or the impasse — which, it was hard to tell? — Ruben took a few shaky steps towards Eunice. But it seemed he had a change of heart, for he stopped, made a violent, drunken wave of his arm that seemed to say, "*Chups*, what's the use," and he turned around and staggered away from the crowd, away from the scene of the fire, away from his would-be wife and son, mumbling all the time, *Why should a man wax tears when his wooden world fails?*

For her part, Eunice remained transfixed, gazing in the direction of where her eyes had locked onto those of her would-be husband, and her mind traveled back to the morning that, with sleep still in her eyes, Ruben had come rushing into her yard begging for baptism, for he didn't want to spend not one more day without her, and he would devote the rest of his life to loving, protecting and providing for her, her son and the children they would have, and upon hearing these words, sleep suddenly disappearing from her eyes, she had fallen into his arms, she too wishing to spend not even one more second without him. But no sooner the memory of that magical morning surfaced, it was replaced with that of Raphael, her first and only consummated love, the one given to her by God Himself, white and bloated at the shoreline of the Atlantic, tossing to and fro with the advancing and retreating ocean.

A wave of self-pity, emptiness and desolation washed over Eunice. The tear that had formed in her eyes out of pity for Eugene rolled down her face, and it was followed by another and another. She could bear it no longer. In a voice that neither she nor her son recognized, she held his hand and said, "Henry, let's go home." Hand in hand, mother and son, both in tears, walked home; all along the way the son repeating to himself, "We finish. We finish."

As they walked home, the sound of the receding steelband grew faint. Night was encroaching upon the town. The crowd at the scene of the destruction slowly dispersed. Many shaking their heads dejectedly, and saying "*Pòdjab,* Eugene, *pòdjab.*" They said this as if Eugene had been the last hope for Vieux Fortians to show that they can amount to something; to show that jumping up in carnival wasn't the only thing they were good at; to show that they didn't need the Americans to make something of their lives; to show that, contrary to the general consensus, they weren't lazy, weren't just drunks and prostitutes, weren't unemployable. They said "*Pòdjab* Eugene, *pòdjab*," as if to say it was no use trying, because even when one tried, when one scratched and fought, when one gave it one's all, and when it appeared that one was going to make it, someone or a force beyond one's control would just come and snatch it all away. If it wasn't the French, it was the English; if it wasn't the English, it was slavery; if it wasn't slavery, it was the plantation owners; if it wasn't the plantation owners, it was the Americans; if it wasn't the Americans, it was the government; if it wasn't the government, it was Castries folks; if it wasn't Castries folks, it was someone putting obeah on them; and if it wasn't obeah, it was some fire or some hurricane or some other act of God or of Satan or of both. So why even try?

FROM A STORE EUGENE RETURNED TO ONE TRAY. But this wasn't the same Eugene. His tongue had lost its sharpness, his face had lost its passion, his eyes had lost their fire, his skin had lost its shine and didn't seem as red, his gestures, though still feminine, had lost their vigor. The fire had burnt itself out. Something had died in Eugene. To Henry he seemed a tired, washed-out, old woman. He never recovered from the fire. From a stall to a store and back to a stall. It was as if fate had decreed that a stall keeper was all Eugene was meant to be, and the store had been just a temporary escape from fate.

After the shock the town pondered on how the fire got started. Who had set the fire? They had only one culprit in mind—Lucille. The whole town knew the rivalry and animosity between Eugene and Lucille. Lucille had to be the one who set the fire. Police interrogated Lucille, but they couldn't find anything to connect her to the fire. She was at the Square selling during the parade competition, and from there she went straight home. Witnesses backed up her alibi. The police could do nothing. But everyone knew that one doesn't have to be physically present to do someone harm. Dirty hands, dirty spirits, evil hearts, knew no bounds. After all, one just had to look at the condition of Popo and Ruben, once two of the town's most outstanding citizens, for undeniable proof of what obeah could do. So the town did something. After the fire no one bought from Lucille. Her fruits rotted. Her condiments went bad. Three months after the fire she packed up and left town.

Henry never became a store owner nor a store manager. Instead he became a construction engineer. But no matter how successful he became, occasionally, in the quiet of his office, or on a long flight home, or on a restless night, he would recall the fire that destroyed a man's life and a boy's dream.

The World of Anderson Reynolds

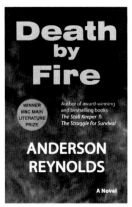

"Death by Fire is an impressive piece of narration … A veritable tapestry of St. Lucian life and culture … Easily one of the most compelling pieces of literature I have laid hands on in recent years."
— **Modeste Downes, author of *Phases***

"The telling of the story is exceptional … A cunningly-woven tale … A journey back into St. Lucian life … (which) paints the dark side of the struggle for survival in a young country." — **The Voice**

"A novel on a grand scale … A broad canvas of St. Lucian life … If one is looking for a key to the feeling and conscience of the age in which we live, this novel is a guide."
—**The Crusader**

"*The Struggle for Survival* is an important road map of St. Lucia in the pre and post independence period."
— **Sir John Compton, Prime Minister of St. Lucia**

"a 206 paged gem … a powerful commentary … A deep sincere analytical look into the state of things in the island today. *The Struggle For Survival* is truly a compendium of St. Lucian life from early times to the modern era … "
—**Modeste Downes, author of *Phases***

"… an invaluable book…a source of much information. Much scholarly research has gone into the writing of this work. In a very definite way, establishes the Saint Lucian personality, the Saint Lucian national and cultural identity."
—**Jacques Compton, Author of *a troubled dream***

The Struggle For Survival, although obviously well researched, is an easy-to-read intriguing story of the social and political development of St. Lucia.   —**Travis Weekes, Author of *Let There Be Jazz***

"Dr. Reynold's mastery as a fierce storyteller is yet again reaffirmed. This memoir calmly and thoroughly takes the reader along the rough terrain of a family's epic struggle for survival..."
— **Peter Lansiquot, CARICOM diplomat and Economist**

"A pulsating ... riveting ... and compellingly readable narrative."
— **Modeste Downes, author of A Lesson on Wings."**

"A love ballad, a joy to read and a privilege to be savoured."
— **Dr. Jolien Harmsen, author of A History of St. Lucia.**

Other Jako Books

The Brown Curtains embroils readers in a steaming love story involving Raj, an Indo Guyanese emigrant to St. Lucia, and Felicity, an Afro-St. Lucian beauty. The only question is whether their love can withstand the racial and religous bigotry of Raj's parents.

"Whether you are Black, Indian, Christian, Hindu or Moslem, *The Brown Curtains* gently goads you in the direction of forgotten trails and alleys of the diaspora. It is a novel for everyone because it shows that adapting to a new life is the same wherever you arrive."
—**Michael Aubertin, Author,** *Neg Maron: Freedom Fighters*

The Brown Curtains is a novel of great humor, and philosophical and intellectual insight."
— **Allan Weekes, Author of** *Talk of the Devil*

"Phases is a collection of over fifty dew-drenched poems that speaks powerfully to a past when living was peaceful and growing up was fun, and a present whose dynamic invokes nostalgia and a craving for a return to the past."
—**Augustus Cadette, author of** *In My Craft.*

"Some of Modeste Downes' poems are acrid, like the taste of the sea-grapes that festoon the beaches of Vieux Fort. Others are nostalgic, insightful, cynical, bold, but all elements of a veritable feast."
—**Michael Aubertin, author of** *Neg Maron: Freedom Fighters.*

"Like the works of Derek Walcott, *Phases* lifts us from the deepest woe to the highest contemplation of what life could be ...Downes is a nationalistic and romantic poet with echoes of William Wordsworth, and Oliver Goldsmith and *Phases* is reminiscent of Derek Walcott's *Another Life."*
— **Jacques Compton, Author of** *a troubled dream*

(A Lesson On Wings) is a compilation of extraordinary poetic work ... an enthralling mixture of poetic genres ... destined to be heralded as one of the all-time great collections of Caribbean poetry ... no home or school library should be without a volume of this work.
— **Victor Marquis, author of Search and The Adventures of Lennie Zandoli**

Modeste Downes is a master of the craft that builds narrative tapestries ... He embraces the entire palette of emotions and finds words to embody them all ... His use of language is impressive ... (and his) easy blend of Kweyol, Latin, 'high' English and profanity works like a dream ... You cannot get more St. Lucia-in-your-face than this. It is a brilliant collection of poems. Buy it. Read it. Share it.

—**Jolien Harmsen, author of A History of St. Lucia, and Rum Justice**

www.jakoproductions.com

Anderson Reynolds was born and raised in Vieux Fort, St. Lucia, where he now resides. He holds a PhD in Food and Resource Economics from the University of Florida. He is the author of two other award-winning and national best-selling books, namely the novel ***Death by Fire*** and the creative nonfiction ***The Struggle For Survival: an historical, political, and socioeconomic perspective of St. Lucia***. Dr. Reynolds' books and newspaper and magazine articles have established him as one of St. Lucia's most prominent and prolific writers and a foremost authority on its socioeconomic history.